TO FIND ONESELF

Book I

DYING IS NOT SO FINAL

Book II

By Dr. David Ivor William Taylor

TO FIND ONESELF

Book I

By Dr. David Ivor William Taylor

(The Retired Major)

To Find Oneself

Paperback: (979-8-950072-16-1)
Hardcover: (979-8-950072-17-8)

Table of Contents

Chapter One
Life So Far

Standing there in his room, with the moon's desolate beauty framed in his window, Gough pondered the ageless problem of the meaning of duty in a world where even tradition bowed to the march of progress. What was in store for him as a Celestial Brigade Marine (CBM) Captain? What would he be called upon to do as a CBM captain? He was prepared to do what he had to, but at what cost to him?

Standing at 180cms tall with square shoulders to match. A shock of blonde hair, properly groomed with a parting on the left side of his head. His hands were in proportion to his body, which meant they were slightly bigger than other people's. When walking, he had a slight swagger, but only slightly. He ran his fingers through his hair and sighed. His flex cap tucked into his belt.

His training had just finished, and his dress uniform hung on its hanger beside the closet. He stared at the captain's pips and looked around the room. What would those pips do to his future, and how would they reflect upon his family traditions? Gough had not wished to be in the military for his whole working life, unlike his relatives. He was here for experience. Had things been different, he might have been preparing for diplomatic negotiations on Kaeluria rather than the captain's pips to his uniform–but duty had led him here, and there was no turning back now.

His room on the moon was, to say the least, quite basic: bare walls and minimalistic furniture. Even in this modern age, military rooms and barracks have not really changed or offered much. A simple officer's billet. One closet for hanging uniforms, a single bed, desk with an attached seat. On one wall, there were shelves for each officer's kit. A shelf came out next to the bed, and on it, he had placed a photograph of his lady,

Simona. Looking intensely at the photograph. Though it had been far too long since he last saw her, the memory of Simona lingered vividly in his mind. She possessed a quiet elegance–her curves neither exaggerated nor understated, just perfectly balanced. The rich cascade of her black hair framed eyes that held their own intensity, a gaze that once captivated him and, even in mere thought, still did. He wondered, *"If time had dimmed the warmth of their last embrace or if, when they finally reunited, it would feel as though no time had passed at all. Was she his or was she ever his?"*

Black hair and brown eyes that followed you everywhere you went. Legs that were the right way on. Gough smiled to himself as military people still referred to legs being on the wrong way around for people with fatter lower legs. They had met whilst he was at university. She was a fresher, and he was a senior. They had hit it off straight away, albeit that he was studying astrophysics, and she was reading sociology.

Gough's thoughts changed as he looked out over the moon's landscape from the small circular window and thought back to the hardships of the past months. Basic training as an officer, following the path of his great grandfather, and father had followed. His father had made colonel in the Corps, and his great-grandfather, the first in the family to make a commission, made major as a paymaster. He was told that his great-grandfather used to say, "I was in the game when they needed them, not just feeding them."

Basic training had not been too tough, lots of running up and down the hill everyone called "cardiac." He remembered his mate Wally stuffing his beret into a younger officer's mouth because he had shouted at Wally to run faster to impress the directing staff. Wally, of course, had been charged with "actions unbecoming an officer." Yet the younger recruit kept a safe distance from Wally afterwards. Wally and he were the oldest people on the course, and it was demanding. He wondered what had become of Wally, as he had not heard from him in over a year.

Next came marine training, as a lieutenant. Here, he opted for land-based operations training and demolition specialism. He exhaled slowly, shoulders slumping as the weight of the weeks pressed down upon him. Glancing around the barren waste of a room with his things packed and the uniform cover needing to be put on his dress blues. Waiting was the one major drawback of being in the military.

He had been taught how to command marines in the field, how to blow things up with the minimum of effort, and how to defuse explosive charges. Something in the past other Corps would do. Gough had also learned how to polish his boots and shoes to get a perfectly clear shine, using black and brown boot polish, water, and cotton wool. Spit and polish, making circles of polish and then rubbing them into the leather.

"Some things in the military don't change," his dad had told him.

This was the modern CBM Corps, not the 21st-century old - fashioned, historical, and antiquated Corps. They still say, "Semper Fi," short for Semper Fidelis. Yet today's training staff were AI based automaton's and virtual reality combat simulations, which changed for each officer. These were based upon the psych profiles and physical performance. However, the togetherness of all being in the same boat, supporting brother officers to achieve the tasks, and leading group formations would never change.

He had graduated and moved on to space training on the moon and, of course, the final pass out parade. Walking in weightless environments was crazy, but you had to learn. Understanding the problems associated with space wear and how your clothing matters when fighting in this environment. All his gear was packed into the small grip he had on the polished floor next to his blues uniform.

Finally, he reflected upon the parade in the training hangar, and his being awarded the Leader's sword and promoted to substantive Captain as the overall top recruit to the CBM. A Brigadier General had taken the salute and presented him with the sword. No one knew that Brigadier General Sutcliffe was a distant relative of his father. However, it was the base commandant, so no conflict of interest or emotional ties there, granted the sword. That had already been sent to the Corps HQ, back on earth. Weapons are forbidden on civvy on transit pads.

Here he was, ready to take the transit pad back to the UK, to his home in London, and see Simona. A spot of vacation on a Mediterranean shore, and then his first operational detachment. Was it going to be "offshore," not on earth. That is all he had heard, and not much else.

He reflected upon the odd comment the Brigadier had made to him when he was presented with the sword. *"How about you catch me some rogues, my boy?"*

A knock came on the door, which raised him from his thoughts and brought him back to now. His female Andie came in the room. Females or males for straights, same sex for prismatic.

He called out, "Hi Gladys, how are you today?"

"As well as an Andie can be expected to be, Sir. Overworked, underpaid, more like no pay, and dreaming of my retirement."

"Well, take it easy for a moment!"

"I cannot vary my workload, Sir. Please clarify your request."

She moved towards his uniform and placed it into the carrying case with such deft skill, Gough could not have done it better. The dexterity of Andies was utterly amazing, and they looked fairly good, too. Glady had no sense of humour and found it difficult to understand Gough when he tried to make a joke. Like the time he had asked her to,

"Cease fire, as the target has already surrendered."

To which she replies, "I am sorry, Sir, but I cannot detect a target that is surrendering. Can you specify coordinates?"

Her face was partially covered with a material that resembled human skin, soft to touch, but very heavy wearing. The same material was on her hands. Dressed in a tailored uniform jacket, without pockets. Her lower half was intriguing, as she had three supports, not legs, which made her a little unpredictable in her movements. She had a self-righting balance capability, which only seemed to work at odd times. All Andies from Andro-Tech, the manufacturer, shared this. It had led them to become quirky companions in the military, as well as for executive helpers, and sometimes even "friends."

"Shall I take your bag, Sir? Or will you bring it yourself with your dress blues?"

"Would you take the bag, and I will bring my blues. I can take it on the transit pad without a glitch fall."

"As you wish, Sir. May I take this opportunity to say gratibyte for your cognisance toward me, Sir? It is rare, even for officers. Thank you."

"It has been my pleasure to work with you and to have you look after me, Gladys. Let's get this over with," and they walked to the transit pad, please. "I actually hate goodbyes, even gratibytes."

The door hissed shut behind them, sealing away his past as the corridor's pulse-like lights pushed them toward the future. No pictures, not even previous commanders, and such like. More bare walls and no light pads, just automatic lights going on and off as someone walked along it, dark behind and light in front.

Chapter Two

Looking forward to some R & R and something Unsuspected

Andie placed his bag on the transit pad and typed in the journey authorisation. She turned and left, no more farewells.

Dressed in slacks, sports jacket, collar, and tie, he looked every bit a Rupert. A Rupert was the troops' affectionate name for officers they liked, well liked a little. It came from the stereotype associated with upper-class British men that aligns with the perception of officers as coming from privileged backgrounds. Yet, Gough hadn't a privileged background, just a military family.

Stepping off the transit pad, he felt hot. He always did, but as an officer, he would not undo his collar and tie. Standards had to be maintained, didn't they? His transit pad had taken him to the terra jumper station at Paddington in London. From here, it would not be long before he could walk the short distance to the family "seat." Gough was odd, funny odd, because he liked to walk places, not use a quantum driver or terra jumper unless it was an exceptionally long way to walk. "Old Habits Die Hard," he thought.

He needed a coffee and was not too worried about arriving home later. He moved to the standard coffee shop that could be found near every transit pad, Bartholomeus. Ada Leighton founded the coffee shop in the 22nd Century, in an era dominated by synthetic food tablets and virtual taste simulations. Ada wanted something real–a place where people could connect over a cup of freshly brewed coffee, not some engineered espresso. Inspired by the rich history of coffee houses dating back to the 17th century, she set out to create a sanctuary for tradition in a rapidly developing world. It had worked, and her dream had continued into the 23rd century.

Entering the wooden structure that had been sourced from reclaimed wood, Gough asked for an espresso two-shot. Using authentic methods–grinding beans harvested from Martian coffee plantations and water sourced from Earth's polar caps. Each cup is a tribute to craftsmanship, and Gough just loved the taste. There were no seats in the shop, just ledges to rest on around the walls. These were warm in the winter and cool in the summer. These ledges were different colours and did not fit the idea of a traditional and an old coffee shop. However, they were comfortable, and he leaned back to drink his hot coffee. Remembering drinking Martian coffee on Mars when they had an away weekend during basic training. His squad had taken a group of one-parent families on a camping trip to Mars for a long weekend. The children were all military brats, and the remaining parents were profoundly grateful. It was fun during the day, with exercises and hangar competitions. The evenings were light-hearted with the parents. Still, he mused about seeing Simona again. It had been many months. His doubt crept back. Were things the same, or had she changed? Had he changed with all the experiences and situation he had gone through?

Finishing his coffee, he put the drink container back on the counter and the server thanked him. Carrying his blues and a small case, he strolled along streets that we different somehow. He hadn't grown up here in London, but after his father's promotion, the family had settled here. It had become the family seat.

The streets were empty of people; everyone was using their Aethers. Energy-efficient transit pods designed for seamless urban and inter-city travel. Trouble was, they all looked the same, travelled in lanes like the old roads and dropped back down to the ground to land.

Gough stopped at the front door of an old-fashioned house amongst the blocks of pulse towers. It looked really out of place, but it was all his. Designed and built to the 21st century standard, it had all the mod cons, plus a few extras from today's pulse towers. Placing his hand over the metallic door panel, the income voice called his name and greeted him.

"So glad you are home safe, Captain Gough. Congratulations on the promotion, it was gazetted two days ago. Please come in." The door swung open, and he walked into a short corridor, wooden panels, and a circular flight of stairs. He dropped the bag and hung the uniform on the coat's hangers inside the door and to the right. The door had opened left. Silently the door had closed behind him and the lights had illuminated, and a smell of fresh brewed coffee was coming from the kitchen area. He changed his outdoor shoes and felt the leather of his slippers.

The house intercom started talking once more.

"What was your journey like, Sir? Can I get you anything? There is fresh coffee in both the lounge and the kitchen. My sensors noticed you walking down the street. You are so funny, walking places." Her tome tumbled out in a stream, like a child excited for the school summer break.

"OK Lesley, allow me to get in through the door, before all the questions, please?"

"Yes, sir, sorry sir, I will shut up, sir." But of course, she did not!

Gough moved into the lounge area, old-fashioned leather chesterfield sofas and a modern body support chair, a body haven which promised total satisfaction or a full refund, he mused. Sitting down, the chair melded into his shape. It felt excellent, as it supported every part of his body. The chair also provided hot or cold and asked if he was comfortable. Voice activating the Chemeralink he called Simona. The screen came to life and there was a beautiful woman, same brown hair, but a little shorter, brown eyes and a plain "Onesie" silk bathrobe in a tone of orange. Simona possessed an effortless elegance, the kind that turned heads not through extravagance, but through the quiet command of presence. When she listened, she had a way of tilting her head ever so slightly–not in curiosity, but in understanding, as if she absorbed not just words, but intentions. It was a gesture that set her apart, a quiet assurance that she saw the world in a way others never could.

"Well, hello stranger!" Her voice carried that unmistakable mix of amusement and detachment, the kind that left him unsure whether he was being welcomed or reprimanded. Simona stood with arms crossed, leaning casually against a doorframe, as though she had all the time in the world to decide whether or not he deserved her attention. "You remember how conversations work, don't you?" she adds, one brow arching slightly. "Or has military protocol stripped you of basic social skills?"

"Hi Simona, how are you? It's been too long, I am afraid, but that's the problem with military training: little free time and fewer communication breaks. How are you, angel?"

"I am good, been keeping busy. A few parties, but nothing too serious. Where are you, please? The Moon, or somewhere on Earth, or, God forbid, in London?" She laughs and flashes him a smile that could melt the strongest metal.

"I have just arrived in London and went to the house to check things and am calling you to offer a few weeks on the shores of the Mediterranean, swimming, sunbathing, if you wish, and generally relaxing. What do you think?"

"When?"

"How about starting tomorrow? I have a reservation at the Chateau Mirage in Fréjus combines historical intrigue with coastal beauty, making it a unique destination for a little R & R? I think you will enjoy it; can you get the time off, and would you like to spend it with me?" That left him open to rejection, which he had not wanted to do, but the words seemed to just come out.

"Simona looked at the small echo cube on her wrist. The personal communications device projected a calendar. She scans it. How long?"

"Up to you, say, two weeks perhaps."

"I can manage ten days. Will that do? What's the weather like?" Standing with her face to the comms screen, he could see her bathrobe pulled tightly across her lush figure. She was beautiful. He thought to himself, "*I am so lucky. She is wonderful.*"

"Meet you at the transit pad in Paddington at, say, 09h30 tomorrow, yes?"

"Yes, Gough, transit pad, Paddington, nine thirty tomorrow. Oh, and buy some good swim wear please, not military issue." With that, the screen faded, and she was gone.

Gough had missed her a great deal, much more than he was prepared to admit. He had lots of thoughts going through his head about the future with Simona and family: Children and a calm life outside of the military. Had he made the right decision to give up academia and go into the forces, like his late father had suggested? That had been an interesting discussion where his father had gone on and on about tradition, and he had talked about geopolitics' impact on his research into Astro physical dealing with space policy and treaty acceptance.

"Lesley, may I have a coffee, please? I feel too good to get up and move just yet."

A hover trolley came into the lounge and Lesley asked,

"Do you require some substance, Sir?"

"I shouldn't, but how about a bacon sandwich, please?"

"Too many fats and not sufficient good ingredients. Well-cooked or lightly, Sir?"

"Grilled to perfection, Lesley, as you always do, please."

Gough rested in the chair and was enjoying doing nothing. His sandwich arrived, and he ate it slowly. I will pack soon but feel like a rest now.

Chapter Three

When Words Aren't Enough

Gough was up early, packing with practiced efficiency. Not quite throwing things–he was too meticulous for that–but each item found its designated place in his grip without hesitation. He slid open a drawer and pulled out a fresh pair of Hydra Flow swimmers. *"Designed for the fluidity of the water."* The advertisement promise rang in his head, earning a scoff. "*What a load of rubbish.*" Still, they were new.

Running a hand over his face, he decided a shave could wait. With that, he strolled downstairs, the scent of breakfast drifting from the kitchen.

Lesley had ensured that breakfast was ready on the kitchen bar, French coffee, and croissants, which were not French!

"Good morning, Sir, how was your stasis? Can I get you a terra jumper to Paddington, sir?"

"Come on Lesley, when do I use those things?"

"Sorry Sir, I just thought, with your case and needing to look fresh when you see Simona, you might not want to walk." Gough laughs at the thought of Lesley thinking, a very human trait.

"Nice idea, but I always walk when I can. It keeps me looking fit and good looking." He finished his breakfast, checked his bank balance and the credit tickets for the transit pad. He looked at his bank balance, 500,000 Quors, and two million in his savings account. Not rich, but definitely not poor.

"I will be away for about 2 weeks, Lesley. Please look after the shop, 'til I get back."

“Sorry sir, have you bought a shop? Where is it, so that I can arrange some guardians?”

“No, sorry Lesley, me being human and trying to be funny. The shop means here.”

“Oh Sir, how operationally efficient. Ha. Ha. Ha.” Her laughter sounded more like a pre-programmed vocal output rather than a genuine expression of amusement–but she was a machine, after all.

Gough was strolling down the road towards Paddington and looked at the weather, clouds, and minor breaks to let the sunshine through, almost like a child’s painting. Touching his breast pocket, he took out a well-worn leather wallet and checked that his travel docs were there, along with his bank card and military ID card. Can’t travel without that, he thought. It was quite quiet. He always did a grounding ritual before any journey. Ahead were the polished chrome edges of the transit pad entrance, catching the morning sunlight.

Entering the transit pad, Gough saw a Chinese lady standing chatting with a slightly older man. He looked hard and saw that she oozed class. In her late twenties, with warm brown eyes that radiate intelligence and kindness. Brown hair that framed her face with effortless elegance, complementing her glowing complexion. She carries herself with an upright yet graceful posture, wearing a soft-knit turtleneck sweater. The ensemble was completed by wide-leg trousers and ankle boots that offered both comfort and timeless style. Her movements were poised and purposeful, exuding confidence and a subtle charm that captivates those around her.

Simona was stunningly beautiful, to die for sexy. However, to his dismay, she was deep in chat with this slightly older man. He was broad shouldered, wearing a linen slacks and a matching jacket, white cotton shirt, open at the neck and a pair of what looked like Italian penny loafers. Gough had little idea who he was and felt a pang of unease because of it.

“Hi Simona, if I may interrupt?”

“Oh Gough, this is my boss. Isn’t it funny? He’s taking a vacation at the same time as us–pure coincidence, of course. Something about a meeting in Fréjus, but he’ll get some relaxation, too. Honestly, it’s quite charming, don’t you think? He works so hard, always carrying the weight of things bigger than any of us. It's refreshing to see him take a moment for himself."

Gough stretched out his hand and the man looked at it but did not reciprocate.

"I have heard something about you, young man from Simona. You are incredibly lucky to have her. But then again... She's never been one for the ordinary. We go back, don't we, Simona?" With that, he turned and moved toward his valet, who was waiting at the front of the transit pad. Gough was a little surprised at the comment but let it pass. Was it the unexpected presence of her boss or the way she laughed him off with an effortless ease, that he did not like? Gough did not appreciate the incident.

"Are you ready, baby?"

"Yeah, let's do this. I need some sun."

They move towards the pad and wait until a voice called,

"Captain Veylan and his guest." They moved forward, tickets checked, and both stand on the transit pad. Gough wondered if Simona wanted to hold hands, but there was no movement by her. They were standing in bright sunshine and the heat hit them like stepping into an open oven. It pressed against their skin, dense and unrelenting, stealing their breath and leaving a haze that blurred the world around them. A voice called to get them to step forward,

"Step forward and move off the pad, please. Please move to your right and follow the path down to ground level."

With Gough carrying both bags, Simona moved effortlessly down the well-trodden path to the street.

"Have you booked a terra jumper, Gough?" Simona asks.

"No."

"It's too hot for me to walk sweety."

Gough hailed an Andie and requested a terra jumper to the Chateau Mirage. The terra arrived, and the doors opened automatically. Simona walked in and Gough put the luggage in the space behind the two seats.

“Been a long time Simona, hasn’t it?” Gough looked at her eyes and face.

“Yes, too long, but if you need to play soldiers,” her voice tailed off to silence as the jumper gained speed.

At the entrance to the hotel, the terra opens its doors and wished them an enjoyable time in the hotel. The polished black marble floor added depth and brilliance to the scene, while the strategic placement of accent lights enhances key architectural features. The huge archway which was the entrance to the reception. Lighting was soft and had integrated lighting fixtures illuminate the curved designs of the ceiling and walls, creating a vibrant interplay of light and shadows. Functionality with ambiance made the space feel both luxurious and futuristic, even for the 23rd century.

An Andie approached them and asking.

“Are you here as guests, or are you here for the conference on Social policy in the greater swan galaxy, please?”

“Guests,” Gough replies, “I made a reservation for a superior double room, please.”

“OH! Captain Veylan, we had hoped to upgrade you to a suite. However, Sir with the conference. Please follow me to room 1711. The up tube is in front of us.”

“I need to make a quick call, Gough darling. You go ahead.”

“Can’t you make it in the room first, honey?”

“Not really, get the Andie to leave me an access token. I won’t be long.”

The up tube would have coped well with three people. Well, two and an Andie. Gough waved farewell as he was effortlessly taken up to the seventeenth floor.

Andie opened the room door and left Gough with two access tokens and said it would give one to Simona later. Gough dropped the bags on the floor, the soft thud that echoed in the empty room. Pouring himself a citron presse, from the minibar–lukewarm, bitter, and far from refreshing. He asks himself, *‘Where was Simona and what was so important that she could not come to the room with him? Did it matter? Was it really that important, as they would have two weeks together?’* He suddenly felt tired. With a sigh, he kicked off his shoes and lay on the bed. It was both a luxurious and contemporary bedroom, designed for comfort and elegance.

At the centre of the room was the spacious, plush bed with multiple pillows and a striking, vertical-panelled headboard. He fell onto it and pushed some pillows on to the floor. The ceiling added a sophisticated touch with recessed, circular lighting and a reflective surface that enhances the room's depth and ambiance. Floor-to-ceiling windows at the far end of the room were draped with sheer curtains, allowing some natural light to filter in while preserving privacy. A small seating area featuring two rounded chairs and a table adorned with floral vases, contributing to a serene and inviting atmosphere. It was not inviting. Was it just him? He had wanted everything to be exactly right, and it wasn't. Gough closed his eyes and let the silence sink in. This was supposed to be perfect, a retreat for them to reconnect. But now, it was just him, alone, wondering how everything had seemed to go so wrong.

Simona came into the room, giggling, which stopped as soon as she saw Gough.

"Oh darling, I am sorry, this was for us to be together and there I was sorting out work issues whilst on vacation. Will you forgive me, please? I promise I will make it up to you, promise. Let's go for a swim, shall we?" She moved over to the bed and kissed him on his cheek.

The sunlight filtered through the sheer curtains, casting soft patterns on the walls as she stood by the edge of the bed. Her movements were deliberate, unhurried, as if she were savouring the moment. She reached for her swimwear, the fabric catching the light in the room. A deep, shimmering blue one piece that mirrored the sky's reflection in the mirror by the windows. With a quiet grace, she slipped out of her travelling clothes, folding each piece with care and setting it aside. Her silhouette was framed by the light and shadow in the room. There was nothing hurried or self-conscious in her actions; instead, there was a quiet confidence, a natural ease that spoke of someone entirely at home in her own skin. As she adjusted the straps of her swimsuit, the fabric hugged her frame like a second skin, its design both functional and elegant.

Gough got up and with simple, unhurried movements, put on his Hydra flow swimmers, engineered for zero-resistance in both terrestrial and aquatic environments. He thought, *"I wonder if I will need these for the mission they are planning?"*

In a corner of the room was a transit pad to the pool, which they used together. Simona still did not reach for his hand, and it felt like she had brushed his hand away as he tried to reach out to her. At the poolside, Simona glanced toward the water, her expression serene yet contemplative, as if the pool held secrets only, she could uncover. The moment was fleeting, yet it lingered, etched into the stillness of the air. She elegantly dived into the water and swam lengths effortlessly. Gough watched her before he dived into the pool and started swimming the butterfly. His favourite stroke. However, he could not clear the air of distance, almost the indifference that appeared to exist between him and Simona. It was not lost on Gough, who was feeling like the third man at a wedding.

They swam a little more and Gough attracted some attention, as he was a powerful swimmer and did extra lengths of butterfly with fluid precision. Simona swam with style and grace she put forth when she was either swimming, on land, or in anything she did, really.

They lay on the sun beds and relaxed. Gough felt a little less anxious and asked if Simona wanted sunscreen on her back? She declined, saying,

"I can't stay out here too long as I burn."

To Gough, it all still felt wrong. He could not understand why she had agreed to a vacation and then appeared to be cold-shouldering him. Had she found someone else? Gough was not sure if he should ask or just wait. Was he being played for a fool and worst still conned?

They returned to the room and got ready for the evening dinner dance in the hotel's premier restaurant. Showered, shaved, and having attended to his DJ and bow tie, self-tied; Gough sat and waited for Simona to dress. Simona walked towards him in a shell pink evening gown, which glimmered in the light. It almost looked as if it had fireflies sewn into the garment. He breathed the words stunning, and she giggled.

They went down to the restaurant and were guided to a table near the dance floor. An Andie in a dinner jacket arrived and offered them the menu or a la carte. Gough chose a la carte and offered Simona to choose what she would like to eat.

"Just order for me, please, darling. I have seen my boss and need a quick chat." As she left the table, she glanced back at Gough, as if to check that he understood. He didn't, but at that moment, she did not care. She wanted to be elsewhere, and separation was a relief for her.

Her words lingered in the air, deceptively light yet heavy with unspoken intent. As Simona walked away, Gough's gaze followed her, watching the subtle grace of her movements. As she walked away, Gough saw that she was fixed on the older man. Who rose to greet her, his posture assured and his hand hovering just above her elbow as if to guide her closer. `Air kisses and then a discussion. She leaned in, her expression softening in a way that felt reserved for him alone. Gough felt the tension knot in his chest. It was a silent pang of doubt that he quickly swallowed but could not shake the feeling.

Turning back to the Andie, he forced a polite smile, letting his instinct for politeness take over. Slipping into French, he ordered,

"Pour entrée, je pense Lobster bisque. Plat principal Confit de Canard avec Salade Niçoise, et pour le désert Tarte Tatin. Un Bordeaux pour le Canard." The familiar cadence of the language steadied him, offering a brief reprieve from the unease that threatened to consume his thoughts.

Afterwards, he looked up and saw Simona dancing with her boss. Who was holding her a little too close for Gough's comfort? This was not going the way he had hoped or intended. Still, she had not told him good night, yet. When he looked up and saw Simona gliding across the dance floor with her boss, the room seemed to shift, tilting slightly as if the centre of gravity had moved toward them. Her laughter soft, as usual, was like the hum of a distant melody that carried across the room. The melody, the dancing partners, cut through Gough more sharply than he cared to admit.

His hands tightened around the edge of the tablecloth, the delicate fabric buckling under his fingers. A myriad of questions welled up in his mind; "*Why did she agree to this trip? Why bring me here just to leave me adrift and go after an older man? Even if he was her boss?*" He glanced down at his untouched glass of Bordeaux, its crimson hue catching the light. For a fleeting moment, he thought about leaving. Yet, his sense of decorum shackled with tradition kept him glued to his chair. He waited. The wine breathing in its glass, and Gough holding his breath, they both waited.

It suddenly occurred to that he was the useful idiot, and he was a *"sprat to catch the mackerel."*

What was it his mother had always says, "Use 'em, abuse 'em and then get rid of them."

Well, he was not about to be got rid of that easily. As the melody changed to a slower tune, Gough drained the last of his Bordeaux, savouring its rich warmth as though drawing strength from it. Watching Simona for a moment longer with her figure pressed close to her dance partner, moving seamlessly with him. Part of him wanted to march over and punch the guy in the nose, but that wasn't his style. He refused to compete for attention where it should have been freely given. Instead, he rose from the table with quiet resolve. The maître d' approached, alarmed.

"Is everything to your satisfaction, sir?"

Gough gave a polite smile, though it didn't quite reach his eyes. He adjusted the cuffs of his dinner jacket with a deliberate precision, as if tethering himself to the moment.

"Perfect," he replies, his voice calm but detached, like glass on the verge of cracking. "But I think I'll stretch my legs a bit."

He rose, his movements measured, almost ceremonial. At the reception desk, he checked out! The click of the pen as he signed his name was sharp against the stillness. The transaction was quick, clinical, as if severing ties. He paid for the room, one night only, as though the brevity had always been planned.

Andie appeared with his belongings. He nodded once in thanks, a man too preoccupied with the weight of his own thoughts to muster warmth.

"Jumper to the transit pad," he instructed, his tone clipped, resolute.

As he stepped into the vast emptiness of the departure area, the tailored lines of his dinner jacket a stark contrast to the sterile lighting, a finality settled over him. The vacation that had never really started was over. She was going to be a memory now, a ghost lingering somewhere in the corners of his mind.

He adjusted his DJ one last time and moved to the pad. It didn't matter anymore. He was going home.

Chapter Four
The Mission Brief

Sitting outside the Colonel's office, Gough studied the decor. The walls shimmered with an unnatural fluidity, as if liquid metal coursed beneath their surface. Yet they weren't metallic–this illusion defied explanation, teasing the edge of his understanding. A faint hum permeated the air. It wasn't music, nor the mechanical buzz of air conditioning, but something else entirely. The sound was faintly disorienting, like a sensation caught between hearing and feeling.

He let his gaze drop to the low table in front of him. A stack of electronic readers displayed animated magazine covers, their glossy projections flickering with restless energy. The devices themselves, though, betrayed their simplicity–cheap casings with a utilitarian design. Everything about the space wore a mask of modernity, yet the underlying frugality was palpable. *"What was his mother's expression? Fur coat and no knickers."* Chairs, moulded from uninspired composite materials, offered little in the way of comfort. The lighting, faintly blue-toned, bathed the room in a cold, clinical glow. Efficiency ruled here; aesthetics were a distant afterthought.

"Captain Gough Veylan of the House of Drasken. Enter!"

Gough rose, crossing the room to the heavy door. He pushed it open with effort, stepping into a spacious office dominated by a single, imposing desk at its centre. Behind it sat a tall, striking woman, her full colonel insignia gleaming on her jacket. Rows of medal ribbons adorned her chest, a testament to her decorated career.

"Ah, Gough," she says, her voice cool yet commanded. "Please, sit. We haven't met before. I am Colonel Tarrin, your commanding officer and the commander of the interstellar force for special operations. You've been assigned to me."

She gestured to the chair opposite, and Gough sank into it, her piercing gaze fixed on him as she continues.

"I need to brief you on a mission we're assigning to you and a selected team of Marines. This briefing will be classified. The hum you're hearing is the Faraday shield, which ensures no one can listen in or record this conversation."

She leaned back slightly, her tone softening just enough to offer a hint of civility. "This will take some time, so settle in. You drink old-fashioned coffee, right?"

"Yes, ma'am," Gough replies. "Black, no sugar, if you're offering."

Colonel Zarek Tarrin looked to be in her early forties, her sharp features softened only by the ease of her movements. Her physical presence exuded authority, the result of years of combat experience in galaxies far from Earth. Accelerated promotions had followed her stellar record, shaping her into the commanding figure now seated before him. He imagined that *"She can't be married, unless to the job."*

An Andie brought him a coffee, which was hot, black, and very drinkable. Nothing for the Colonel, who said nothing but waved her hand for the Andie to leave. She pushed a button on the desk, and a view screen came out of the surface.

"The planet on the screen is Nebulon Seventeen, in the purple quadrant. It is about fifteen light years away. As you can see, one moon, two suns, which support human life.

The moon is called Scar Grimmel. Currently, home to General Otto Harbour or GH. He is raiding various planets in the quadrant and causing the Vilkyries on Nebulon 17 some genuine problems. We have a detachment of marines there, led by Major Growton of the House Varok. We have a problem! You need to fix it, Gough, understand?"

"Sorry ma'am, not, yet. Who is the problem, Major Growton, General Harbour, or the people on Nebulon 17?"

"The Vilkyries are our allies, which is why Growton was stationed there. But he's either ineffective or unwilling to take the lead on anything. Our assessment is that the real threat is GH and his band of Crimson Shards. We have selected you because you are not known to both of them and to Growton. I don't think your house has ever come into contact with GH, either. That is your edge, the only one you have beside your ability as an officer. You will take a Blade Squadron with you. Have you seen Vilkyries before?"

"No, I have not actually been out of the quadrant yet."

"OK, I will try to give you some idea." She pushed a button, and the screen changed to a picture of otherworldly beings, blending beauty with an unmistakable alien essence. Their features possess a striking symmetry that exceeds human norms. The woman in the picture was ethereal, almost unnerving in their perfection. Her skin shimmered with a bioluminescent glow, reflecting shades of Nebula's purples and blues, matching the background in the photograph. She had an aura of cosmic mystique. Eyes like liquid silver seem to pierce into his soul, radiating both intellect and strength. The hair was flowing, energy-like strands that shift and pulsed as their emotions changed. She was wearing armour crafted from materials unique to Nebulon 17, sleek yet functional, adorned with patterns resembling constellations or ancient glyphs. Stunningly attractive, even to a human. Yet utterly alien, a reminder that they belong to a realm far beyond human comprehension. Gough was curious.

"I have given you a full brief here, as some humans find them exceedingly difficult to get on with. They are friendly up to a point and can see through lies easily. They are also incredible warriors. Believe me, for the most part men come second."

Gough was going through all of this in his mind and trying to understand why a newbie like himself had been selected for a tough mission.

"You have the situation, the mission, and the people. Questions, Gough?"

"Well, yes, ma'am. Why me? I am more than pleased to take this on, but why me?"

"Good question. We believe that someone is feeding GH information from the Vilkyries mission control HQ or the Marines barracks. We don't know if it is a Vilkyrie or someone from the detachment of Celestials. Either way you need to find out, and to do that, you need to be a new challenge to everyone. Understand?"

"Yes, Colonel, yes." Gough's voice faded away. He was beginning to understand the risks associated with this first mission.

"You will meet your team and then leave from the military transit pad x 37n6 direct to NB17 Citadel. No visits to girlfriends, parents, or any other diversions, Gough. This is a red-line mission. Go meet your team."

He rose, saluted, and walked to the door. His swagger was still there, but only just. He was worried.

The adjutant guided him down some stairs and into a large, bare briefing room with about twelve Celestial Brigade marines in combat fatigues. The men stood up immediately, and the Blade leader addressed Captain Gough.

"Captain, Sir, your team! Do you wish to inspect them first?"

"No, I want to meet everyone first and talk with them. Then, we can brief the mission and work out who will be doing what. OK?"

"It's a little unusual to meet the team, sir."

"It isn't if you are all going into a situation where you can die." His voice hung in the air. Yet no one looked away or responded. The Blade leader replied.

"System normal, Sir. That is what we do. We lost the last Captain on the last job. We are happy to get to know you a bit, Sir."

There had been no salutes, just the men standing up. Now they sat down, passed drinks around, and chewed Yargar Gum. This was only military-issue, infused with specialised compounds to help with hydration and sustain energy levels. The team formed up for their first "inspection" by Gough. Even in this simple act, Gough could see that they maintained awareness of the room's exits and threats, as they moved with purpose. Five men and four women lined up in a variety of battle fatigues and marine uniforms. All their clothing was clean and well-pressed, but not all the same. Their stance and movements reflected not just confidence and precision but their years of drilled expertise as front-line shock troops. Gough caught himself smiling, just a little, and he forced his facial expression to change into something more appropriate for this first team meeting: sombre, yet relaxed. Each face bore the hardened expression of those who have seen and survived the worst of military situations.

The blade leader commenced the introductions of Gough to each team member.

"Jamie Stent, sir. She is the Titan Commander. Speaks three languages in additional to English, heavy weapons specialist, and an expert in unarmed combat. Three tours in the outlands region of quadruple seven in the orange sector."

Gough spoke briefly, "Good to have you on board, Stent. How long have you been with this team, please?"

A silky voice did not match the physical fitness and muscles that could be seen under the one piece of battle fatigue. She replies,

"Thank you, sir, two sessions and I signed up for this mission, extending my enrolment."

"Arthur Renman, sir. Medical and battlefield trauma specialist. A tour in Saturn moons and a tour in the Embassy on x57 site 123. Good man in a scrap, sir."

Gough acknowledged the man but did not ask questions.

"Carol-Anne, sir. An echo scout with enhanced hearing capability, which places her as the reconnaissance and infiltration expert, skilled in gathering intelligence unnoticed."

"How far?" Gough asks.

"Depends on the terrain, sir, and the conditions." She shut up like a trapdoor falling closed.

"Gus of the House of Bent, sir. One of our four strikers. Forward, please. Eric Freemantel, Jenny Crost, and Rachel La Bombe. That them all, sir."

Gough nodded and walked to the last person in the line.

"Davin Walker, if I remember correctly." The Blade Leader was a little surprised.

"You know this reprobate, sir?"

"Yes, I do, Blade Leader. We grew up a few miles apart on terra. He did not make officer selection, but still a good man."

Gough turned and quietly says, "At ease and listen in team."

The troops all stood easy and waited for the pep-talk that always happened.

However, Gough startled them as he opened his brief with, "Today is not a pep-talk. You have experienced enough of them in your life. We are looking for a traitor and a coward. This is a one-off mission and anyone who does not wish to remain in the team can leave now." He waited as Davin Walker moved and asks to be excused.

"OK, acknowledged. You are out, Walker." Walker left the room and closed the door with some gusto. Gough couldn't be sure if Walker wasn't leaving because of the mission itself or because of something unspoken within the unit, or did he know something that no one else did? Still, it did not matter now. He turned to the remaining team members.

"Please sit and gather round. Leader switch on the anti-listening device and turn up the white noise level. Just in case anyone trying to listen in. Our mission is to break up and destroy a band of renegades on a moon in the purple sector. We believe that there is a mole working on the planet, who could even be a marine, or a local. The only people we can trust will be ourselves. No one else joins or leaves, got it? We will be transit padding to a planet whose natural inhabitants are all female. Vilkyrians, people you might have encountered before. There is a marine camp on the planet, which is commanded by a major. Kit for the duration of the mission, which should be about fourteen weeks. Combats and warm weather clothing, please. Standard armoury out load, plus personal weapons of choice. Questions?"

Someone says, "If there's a mole, how do we stop them from making us the next target?"

Gough used this moment to reinforce trust by replying,

"We stick together. No one moves alone. No surprises. Transit bay fifteen bravo tomorrow morning at 04h00. Kit goes via fifteen golf, so be on time. Transit in civies, nothing too much to attract attention, please. Send messages to your family before you bed down for the night. Do not mention the mission, only that you will be gone for about three months. This is not a general run-of-the-mill mission. The outcomes are important to the Corps and The Astralis Compact. Last chance, questions, comments?"

Nothing, not even a grunt or an ugh.

Chapter Five

Arrival, Renewed Friendships, Perhaps?

The group stood around in the waiting area as another group of marines was being moved through the transit pads first.

"All the kit has been stored and will be sent to the required location, sir."

Blade leader had seen it all he thought, *"brash officers, cautious tacticians, men burdened by their own insecurities or inflated egos. He could read them in minutes, sometimes seconds. Usually, it was the same pattern: a show of authority, a hint of bravado, or the weight of experience shaping their posture. When he first saw Gough, he expected more of the same.*

No combat record? Then likely hesitant, reliant on procedure. Polite? Perhaps the type to overcompensate with rigid decorum. Yet within moments, the assumptions started falling apart. No arrogance, no uncertainty—just a quiet steadiness. Every word measured, every movement deliberate, without the slightest need for performance. He wasn't bluffing his command, nor was he shrinking into it. No Horah Henry. Nor a Rupert. Just Captain Gough."

Gough nodded and continued to drink his coffee, in quiet reflection of what was to come.

"Blade leader, Stent, Renman, and Crost, you will form the first wave to our new location. I will bring the second wave. When you arrive, wait for me. Do not go looking for the kit or anyone else. I will be the last to arrive. Then we will meet the leader of the colony and perhaps the Marine major. Is that clear, everyone?"

Nods of acceptance were the replies. The movement number was called, and Blade leader ushered everyone to the transit pad. Larger than usual, but it was military.

"Buddy, buddy, check, and then step onto the pad in formation. You know the drill."

The marines moved into position. Gough and the others watched as the first wave had "magically" disappeared. Gough ushered the second wave, and they also formed up without a word of command and this group, too, disappeared. A few moments later, as it appeared, they were all standing in a wooded area with various gaps between the trees. Gough scanned the area and called everyone together.

"We are to wait in area seven, that gap in the trees there." He pointed to a cove in the treeline with a symbol on it. It did not look like a seven, but neither did the soft, green sky look quite right. Pale blue clouds of sorts float in the sky. It was different. As they approached the cove, the kit had been stacked neatly in the far righthand corner of the area. The benches seemed to grow out of the ground and were similar to wood, but not really.

Carol-Anne seemed to be having some problems with her uniform.

"What's wrong?" Gough asks.

"Oh, nothing really, just put on a few centimetres, and these uniforms are not forgiving." Someone shouted if she needed a hand to take it off. Everyone laughed, including Gough. Then silence, as some Vilkyries approached the cove.

The lead Vilkyrie was ethereally captivating. Her hair was a shade of blue and shone as if it was rinsed in Lumesilk. She came straight up to Gough as if she knew who he was. Perhaps she had seen an image creator of him. Gough came to attention and called the detachment to do the same. Orvessa hadn't expected the moment to feel like this—like gravity had redefined itself solely for the man standing before her. Gough's presence hit her like a force she hadn't trained for, something woven into the very fabric of the universe itself. Her pulse hammered in her wrists—a drumbeat only her kind knew. The Zyphir's Call, her grandmother had named it: the body's betrayal when fate intervened. The stories had always seemed distant, the stuff of history, until now. Until him. Captain Gough. The name settled like an echo in her bones, something older than logic. He was the one. Not by choice. By something deeper—a drumbeat only her kind knew.

Orvessa exhaled, steadied herself, then stepped forward. She had seen countless human officers before, studied their movements, their postures, the ways they carried command like an armour or a burden. She had prepared for formality, for protocol. Yet what she hadn't prepared for or expected was recognition to strike like this. Her people spoke of it in hushed tones–a pull in the blood, a shift in the air. To most, it was simply a myth. To her, now, it was gravity itself rearranging. Captain Gough. The name echoed in her bones. He is the one for me. Not by choice. By something older. Yet, as her throat tightened and her hands flexed at her sides, she knew she had never been more certain of anything in her life. Gough came to attention. The detachment followed. He saluted and waited.

"That's different. Your major never does that. What is the hand signal, please? Is it friendly or respectful or what?"

"It's the proper sign of respect from a junior to a senior person, ma'am." Gough replied, "It is also a friendly greeting, ma'am."

"You might find our greeting a little different Captain Gough." She leant forward took his hand and placed it gently upon her lips.

"This is called Velmari, in our language and means a ritualistic or tender act. I am sure we will find time for many more of these if you do not find it offensive. Do you?"

Her hand against his lips left a warmth that simply did not fade. His skin was as if he had been touched by someone, something beyond chemistry.

"Not offensive, ma'am. Different, yes–but surprisingly pleasant."

With the formalities out of the way, three Vilkyries moved past Gough and walked up to two of his detachment. One stood in front of the Blade leader and undertook a ritualistic Velmari. The other had stood facing Jamie Stent and did the same. Carol-Anne met the third and they exchanged a real kiss.

"Uh hum," says Gough.

Blade acknowledged Gough questioning. "Sorry, sir, but this one is my wife and Jamie and Electa have been an item for a couple of years. We don't get much of a change to get home to see our families." Blade's Vilkyrie wife smirked as she kissed him. *"Always so shy, even after the Recognition. Humans."* Electra made a sound that was a bit like a giggle, but it was more guttural. "That's Carol-Anne's squeeze!

Gough turned to the Leader.

"I am at a loss ma'am. You know my name, but we have never met formally or informally. May I have the pleasure of knowing your name, title, or what should I call you, please."

"You hold formality with charm, Captain Gough. You may address me as Orvessa. I am the hereditary leader of the Vilkyries from House Zyphrya. You can address me as Prime one in public, unless I tell you otherwise, please."

"Yes, Prime One. Thank you."

"Please sit on the Mimora Platforms and you will be Orrvek'tal, our silent transport system. Something likened to your monorails, but ours are guided by intention, not tracks. It will take you all to your accommodation. For those who don't know our language it means "The guided path." Captain Gough you are with me, please as we will arrange your pod later. We need to Zorlath, sorry you say talk, first."

Chapter Six
Friendships or Intimacy This Early On

Everyone moved off and Gough and Orvessa stood alone, observing personal space, but not quite. Gough barely noticed it at first. Then just a shift in the air, as though the atmosphere had thickened slightly around him nor was it like the humid weight of an Earth summer–it was targeted, almost aware. A presence. The warmth pressed against his skin in a way he couldn't quite explain. The sensation wasn't oppressive, nor was it like the humid weight of an Earth summer. His skin responded before his mind did. The warmth wasn't coming from the sun or the air around him, but from somewhere else. Someone else. He glanced at Orvessa. The realization landed just enough for him to question it–but not enough for him to understand it. Not burning, not stifling–just there, waiting to be acknowledged., so he asked,

The warmth was not harsh, not heavy, but present. Gough didn't flinch. Instead, his posture adjusted, the smallest shift in stance–not defensive, just measured.

Something was happening.

He took a slow breath, controlling the rhythm, keeping everything steady. Observe first. Process. Then react. His training had drilled discipline into his bones; his instinct told him to assess before concluding. It wasn't the heat of the climate. It wasn't the air itself. It was her, Orvessa.

A flicker of awareness sharpened in his mind, but he didn't move. Stay neutral. Stay in control. Yet, beneath the stillness, a realization settled–she was testing him, whether intentionally or not. His fingers flexed briefly at his sides, barely perceptible. A silent reaction. Then gone, replaced by composed stillness once more.

"Is it me, or is it getting hotter, please Ma'am?"

"You don't know much about Vilkyries, do you, Captain?"

Gough's reaction was quiet observation, not discomfort.

"Gough..." She said his name slowly. "When a Vilkyrie likes someone, they emit additional heat–beyond the ambient temperature. And sometimes, their hair changes. What you're feeling is me. My heat. Do you find it uncomfortable?"

"No, not uncomfortable–just... Zarvek. Isn't that the word? I'm just not sure if this is... proper. You're a leader. I'm a soldier." Gough's reaction was quiet observation, with no discomfort.

"No, Gough. I was at your passing-out parade, watching from the shadows where I see things others do not." Orvessa had stood at the edge of the parade ground, her fingers curled tightly around the fabric of her coat. The world around her blurred into insignificance–brass notes of the band, the rhythmic stomp of boots–but Gough was sharp, distinct. As he stepped forward to accept the sword, shoulders squared, his uniform immaculate, something inside her clenched. It wasn't just pride; it was the unbearable weight of knowing how much he had endured to stand here, how much he had sacrificed, without knowing why.

She had watched him train–had seen the exhaustion crease his features, the way he forced himself past breaking points time and time again. The silent determination. The quiet, relentless fire. And now, as his name rang out across the square, she swallowed hard, blinking against the sudden sting in her eyes. He was no longer just a recruit; he was something more, something untouchable.

"The commandant may have trained you, but I had to approve you. Without my word, you would not be standing here. We may not have met face to face so to speak. Yet, I have a feeling about you. We show our feelings here Gough, sit down. We can talk here–no other ears will be listening."

"Why would a Vilkyrian leader need to approve me?" The thought unsettled him, almost confused him, but he held back his questions for now. Orvessa brushed her fingers over the platform's surface, and the world shifted. Walls folded into place where there had been open air. The hum in the space wasn't loud, but Gough recognized its meaning–the

deep, unnatural silence of something designed to keep conversations hidden. The faint hum reminded Gough of the Colonel's office–sealed, silent, secure. Whatever this was, it carried the same weight as any military SKIF.

"This setup is known as a SKIF in security circles. No doors. No records. You have my word. So, we can talk between ourselves. You have my word on that. Let us get to business as they say on earth."

Gough kept his stance steady, but something about the air–about her presence–felt different. The warmth pressing against him wasn't just the climate; it was intentional. Controlled. He wasn't sure if he should lean into it or step away. She was a national leader after all. He did not want to upset things by being interpreted as rude. The instinct for distance was there, but so was the curiosity. But where could he go to step away? He just sat and waited!

No exits, no roof, only words exchanged in a sealed void. A SKIF–but unlike any he had known.

"Orvessa, why is it necessary to speak like this?"

"A total lack of shared information due to the level of secrecy–that is Cosmic Top Secret. In addition, there is a caveat of only need to know at this time. Harbour is seeking to overthrow the Vilkyries. He keeps sending his raiders and causing maximum damage to our defence sites. But we can't catch him, or his team come to that. Your marine major keeps justifying his inaction, claiming it's not his role–which is untrue. He speaks like a man serving two masters." Orvessa lean in towards Gough as if sharing a closely guarded secret,

"I cannot trust anyone except Gough I don't trust the marine team, but I have no proof they are compromised–yet. I am now going to share a Emarald classified information."

"What the hell is Emarald classified? Gough burst out. "Never heard of it!"

"It is above Cosmic, and eyes only. It relates to Vilkyries classification adopted by your Commander on earth. Only fifteen people have this clearance."

"I–what? I'm cleared for this?" or "Emarald? Above Cosmic? I–how? No one told me." Gough was gobsmacked as he did not know what to think.

"Yes, but no one on earth was allowed to share it with you. Not even your Commander was permitted to tell you. That is why I'm telling you now."

Gough pushed his hand through his hair and burst out "Shit!"

"Sorry, what does shit mean, please?"

""It's just an English expletive for being shocked. Kind of like saying 'oh crap.' Not polite." replied Gough.

"So, is it a rude word?"

"Sorry, yes."

"So... would it be correct if I said the Vilkyries are in a great shit?"

"Yes, something like that, Orvessa."

"Harbour and his team are using advanced counter-surveillance tactics to cover their tracks. There could be a Spectral Drift - an intelligence leak within my defence forces that allows him to evade capture. I suspect compromised communication channels, which forces me to rely on this unconventional method of talking to you, Gough."

"We are here to invade the moon and wipe out Harbour and his forces. We can and will do that. What else, please?"

"The marine major's justification for his inaction is paper-thin. His role demands action, yet he refuses to engage. Whether it's fear, allegiance, or sabotage–I don't know. Perhaps he fears repercussions from some higher authority? Or perhaps he is trying to sabotage our defence efforts for reasons I have not yet uncovered? I can't just set him up without directly accusing him. That is why you will have to be discredited as a traitor, and your team with you. You will be allowed to escape to the hills outside of the citadel. You can plan the attack on the moon unobserved, except for me."

Orvessa was not sure that trusting Gough is a totally good idea. Yet, she was keeping her own counsel. She had feelings for him. The Zyphir's call, fate! The Seylira was rare–a bond written into Vilkyrian blood. She had doubted it existed. Until now. Gough pondered sensitive to her apparent paranoia and his own uncertainty. *'High-level clearances are only useful when you understand them. Gough did not—and that terrified him more than he cared to admit.'*

Suddenly, Gough realised that the temperature had increased once more.

"Orvessa. Are you all, right?" he asks.

"Sort of," she replies. Her pulse became subtly visible, a sign Gough recognises but did not fully understand. The air itself seemed to shift–charged, heavier–forcing Gough to think and react differently. Fate was not a variable in his training manuals. However, her touch was electric. Orvessa had unconsciously moved closer. She was testing the boundaries of trust not just in words but in proximity. Gough was not sure what he should do, as he was alien to her. His training screamed distance, whilst his body said something completely different. Her heat had intensified, and droplets were running down her face. Some fell onto Gough's hand. The droplets landing on his hand were warm like tears but heavier–soft, refusing to disperse as a normal tear would. Gough sat completely, unaware of whatever came next. It was beyond his understanding–but not beyond hers. He did not understand the Vilkyries' culture, and she was not just any Valkyrie–she was their ruler. He was not sure how anyone could be that aroused, that quickly. Then he realised that he was aroused as well, and it showed.

Orvessa was physically aroused. Her hair shimmered in the low light, an unearthly glow that Gough couldn't place. Her gaze held him–liquid, unreadable, charged with something beyond simple emotion. The surrounding air shifted, thickening with an energy neither had acknowledged outright. Gough couldn't turn away, nor was he sure he should. Orvessa suddenly gave him a ritualistic Velmari. Yet, much more deeply than before, and with a hint of sexuality. Gough felt a subtle hesitation–an instinct to evaluate. He had to let his understanding catch up with what was happening. The Velmari had always been a formal exchange–but this was different. More deliberate. More... intimate. The charged air thickened, pressing against his senses as Orvessa held the ritual longer than before.

Her lips barely parted, the motion not just ceremonial but purposeful, leaving him questioning its meaning. Was this an extension of trust? A test? Or something far deeper than political manoeuvring?

Her proximity unsettled him–not in fear, but in unfamiliarity. He was still an outsider in this world, still learning its rules. Yet Orvessa had just pulled him deeper into them. He wasn't sure if he should keep still or lean in. She was stunningly gorgeous. A vision of pure beauty. A symphony of starlight, woven from the fabric of the cosmos itself.

"You feel it too, don't you? The Seylira. My people don't choose it. It chooses us. Your scientists would call it pheromones. We call it truth."

The decision was taken from him as Orvessa stood up, her temperature cooling slightly. "Another time, Gough. Later, I will have time to understand the way your people do things on Earth, please. We will get to know each other better. You know what I mean, Gough. I like you."

"It will happen, Gough—I promise you. If that is what you wish."

The grove returned. The SKIF dissolved like mist, and yet something had formed between them that could not be undone.

Chapter Seven
In the Name of Doubt

Gough felt lost, which was unusual, very unusual. He did not know whom to trust. He had still not found the major to report to, as protocol required. He sat on his rack and let his thoughts float through his mind. *"Life could be a real sh1t."*

Gough leaned forward, elbows on his knees, weighing the silence between them. It wasn't just protocol–it was instinct–that told him to seek out the major. He *should* trust his command structure. He *should* assume that the chain of command was intact and reliable. That's what experience dictated. That's what every training scenario reinforced.

Yet, deep down, there was something gnawing at him. If he let himself admit it, the *want* to trust came from familiarity, from faces he had fought alongside, from voices he had learned to rely on in the chaos of battle. But familiarity could be a double-edged blade–it made betrayal all the more personal. He wanted to believe the Blade leader was as frustrated as he was, genuinely seeking answers, genuinely concerned. But the *want* to trust didn't change the facts. And facts were brutal.

He let out a slow breath. Wanting to trust was dangerous. He should trust only what he could verify. And right now, verification was near impossible. Roused from his thoughts, there was a knock on his entry port.

"Who is it, please?"

"Blade leader, Sir. Do you have a minute, please?"

"Yes, enter. What's up?"

"I think we have a problem, Sir."

"Please sit down; we need to discuss the operation. Grab a stool."

The blade leader pulled up a plastic stool, which was not comfortable but functional.

"Shall I go first, Sir?"

"Yes, of course. Fire away!"

"Well, Sir, it is really odd. We have only been here a few hours, but no one at the barracks will accept my call. Normally, I can get the local blade leader to return my call within a few minutes. But this time, nothing! Not a peep, which is really odd. Almost like there is not one there."

"Yes, I can't raise the major, either. So?"

"I want to take a couple of the lads down to the barracks and see what is happening and understand why they are not returning our hails. May I?

"Yes, but not until you and I have had this chat. OK?" The blade leader nodded and took out a small notebook and a pencil.

"No, sorry, it's above TS, so no notes. We have a real Up the creek without a paddle, so listen carefully. You can't share this with the men, either! You have to invade a stronghold on the September moon and capture General Harbour. That, in itself, should be easy enough. Yet there are some problems that will make it more difficult. There is a traitor either here in the Vilkyries, or the Marines. We have to catch the traitor, mole, if you will. However, if we don't, we will be taken out in the firefight on the moon. We will need to set up a trap, and we are the fall guys for that. Then, when we have been able to take out the traitor, we can invade the moon, and life can return to normal here. So don't allow the men to unpack and get ready for a very quick bug-out. Even so, it will be messy! You cannot tell the men any of this, do you understand? They will think the traitor is me, and that is what we need to happen. How this will be achieved is I will brief, the two people we believe are in the frame for collaborators. If the General Harbour gets to know, we will know who has grassed us up as the story will be slightly different for each person. Questions?"

"Yes, Sir, a few. Who do you think is the mole in our setup? Have you been given any lead as to a mole in Vilkyries? Where will we bugout to? How can I control them men if they think you are not to be trusted? I've followed orders through thick and thin,

Sir, but this one feels...uncharacteristically reckless. Are we sure this isn't some grand manipulation?"

OK the first question is easy. You go the barracks and speak with your opposite number. You say that I am too inexperienced and should be replaced and you could lead the attack on the moon in three days unless we are attacked first. I will find the major and tell him that I think we will plan the attack for five days unless we are attacked and need to push it back. If this doesn't go exactly as planned, suspicion could collapse in on itself before we find the mole. We have one shot at this. The Vilkyries is more difficult, that is where you lady comes in. You tell her that we will be planning an attack, but she is to tell no one. I expect her to tell Orvessa. Who will accuse me of spreading rumours and banish me and the troop out of the city. We have already planned this. As for the real mole in Vilkyries their leader will pass on the following tale. I have gone rogue, and they think I am the real traitor and am already in league with General Harbour, who might try and contact me in the next few days.

Gough took a slow breath, feeling the weight of his own deception settle into his chest. He had orchestrated schemes before, but this was different. This time, he wasn't just playing with tactics; he was playing with trust. His own men, the ones he had never fought alongside, would soon suspect him. Some might whisper in dark corners, questioning his loyalty, while others might silently weigh whether they should act against him.

It was a necessary illusion. The trap had to be perfectly, airtight. Yet, for a brief, bitter moment, the thought gnawed at him, *"What if it worked too well? What if suspicion hardened into certainty before he could spring the final act? His reputation, his command, his very place in the unit—none of it was immune to collateral damage. He wasn't just risking lives; he was risking the foundation of everything he had built."*

He clenched his jaw, shaking off the doubt. This wasn't about pride or comfort. It was about getting the traitor. If he had to walk the edge of the knife to do it, that is what he would do.

"What do you think, please?"

Blade leader listened carefully, but his expression barely shifted–except for the faintest flicker of a smirk at the corner of his lips. He leaned back slightly, arms crossed, exuding the measured confidence of someone who understood the weight of command but didn't necessarily respect where it came from.

"So, let me get this straight, Sir," Blade says, voice even but edged with sharpness. "I walk into the barracks, tell my counterpart you're unfit to lead, and then–what? Expect them to just nod along and hand me control?" He tilted his head slightly, assessing Gough.

"The problem with handing someone power is that they have to deserve it, Sir." He let that sit, the silence stretching for a fraction longer than necessary to allow for the point to sink in.

"And then there's Vilkyries. You expect me to rely on my woman to spread the bait, but she won't move unless she respects the one giving the order. Which means I either trust your word, or I step in myself." He tapped his fingers against his knee thoughtfully, calculating. "So, here's the real question, sir–not whether the enemy will see you as the mole, but whether your own men will still believe you have the spine to carry this through."

A pause. Then, deliberate, coolly:

"I don't follow weak leaders. And I don't carry their burdens for them."

"OK, let's break your thoughts down. As for leadership, you run the troop, not me. That is as obvious as the nose on your face. We both know that! The troop will follow your lead. As for how the guys will accept that I am the weak link. You will tell them that, in our conversation, I let things slip that worry you greatly. Under section 57 of the Code, you can and will do what is necessary. Gough held Blade's stare for a long moment, letting the challenge settle between them. He had expected pushback, but something about Blade's tone–the measured calculation, the quiet insinuation–felt more like a test than simple scepticism.

A leader had to earn their place. He knew that. He had built his career on it. But now, he wasn't asking for loyalty; he was asking for doubt. That was the hardest pill to swallow. He wasn't just directing strategy; he was turning himself into the very thing men feared–a weak link, an unreliable cog in a machine that depended on precision and trust.

"If Blade hesitated; it meant the plan had cracks. But there was no room for hesitation."

Gough exhaled slowly, leaning forward, his voice low but unwavering.

"You think this is reckless? Maybe it is. Maybe it'll be the worst decision I ever make. But here's the truth–you don't catch a mole without setting a trap. And right now, there's no one else in this damn unit who can play that role and walk away."

He let his words settle, measured. Then, deliberately:

"I'm not asking for your approval. I'm telling you, this is how we find the traitor. If I burn for it, so be it."

There was steel in his voice now, something unshakeable–not arrogance, not even stubbornness, but sheer resolve.

"When we bug-out we will all be going to the caves just outside of the city in transport that Orvessa will have pre-positioned for us. When we get to the cave, you and I will share the actual plan with the team. We need to do that together to reconstitute the loyalty and confidence we need for the mission. Orvessa will contact us and let us know what feedback she gets, if any, from the Major of Marines and from her agent on September moon. Are you in? Or do I waste time finding someone who won't hesitate?"

"I'm in, Sir. You've thought this through, and I see the strategy taking shape. I'll head to the barracks with two of the team–that should start planting seeds of distrust early. If you arrive about twenty minutes after me, it'll give things time to settle. And if the timing's off, cutting my conversation short when you walk in will only reinforce the doubts I've put in their heads. After that, I'll leave quickly, get the troop prepped for bug-out, and make sure we're ready to move the moment things shift. I'll talk to my lady first–before I take the men to the barracks. That way, everything is in motion before suspicion spreads too far. That sound right to you, Sir?"

"I like it but give me enough time to get to Orvessa and brief her first."

Blade swiftly left the room, having saluted Gough before leaving. Gough took that as a good sign, not just a perfunctory acknowledgment of rank. Gough got himself ready with anything he might need to brief Orvessa. He was ready and stood at the doorway when there was a harsh knock. Opening the door, he saw Orvessa's primary guardian. Who nodded and moved to one side to allow Orvessa to enter the room. She moved with such precision that Gough barely had time to step aside. A shadow of movement, a whisper of presence–and she was in.

"I was just about to come and visit you. This is a surprise!"

Orvessa put a small cube on the shelf, and it glowed a sickly green.

"That will make sure our conversation is private. I need to know what your plans are and how we can support you. Has anything changed? Because things have started to unravel at my end, which is also why I am here."

Gough recounted the plan that h had shared and agrees with Blade. Orvessa nodded at various points but said nothing until he had finished his explanation.

"My head of security was kidnapped, and no, I had shared no details with her. It seems that Harbour is trying to find pawns to make me bargain with him. I have no idea what he wants except for me to give up the planet and my role, which I would not do even for my bestie friend. Something's unpicking our social framework, Gough. Faster than I expected. Tell me–how much worse is this going to get?"

"It's going to unravel, as I think the Harbour situation is almost a sideshow. The traitor is trying to get people to side with the Crimson Shards without mentioning Harbour. If that happens the situation gets a lot worse, and I am not sure about the local marines detachment and how supportive they will be Orvessa. That is why I want to work faster than the opposition expects. I am off to see the detachment major in a few moments. In fact, as soon as Blade sends me a message. You need to go back to your apartments and keep a solid number of guards around the area."

Orvessa passed him, what looked like chunky ring.

"With this you can contact me at any time, just rub your thumb over the surface and it will activate a mini view screen, and I will answer, no matter what the hour." Then unexpectedly she leaned into him and kissed him on the lips saying,

"I was foretold of a human who would come into my life and change me, I know it is you." As quickly and silently as she had arrived, Orvessa was gone. Gough was in total surprise. She was an alien, and she had kissed him like no one had ever kissed him. Her lips were softer than the purest silk, and her hair, well it was something else, the ways it glinted.

His comms link to the blade buzzed, on my way, better start now was the message.

Chapter Eight

The Judas Principle

Gough was dressed in barracks uniform and a beret, waiting outside of the major's office. Blade slid out of the complex, flashing three fingers downward–quick, deliberate, through his peripheral vision. Was that a quick warning sign from Blade as he hit three fingers down. "*Fallen Banner. A leader compromised. Betrayed. Removed. But who?*"

The scene was set for what could be a shown down or establishing an endorsement for action. Gough felt open to either, he simply did not have enough information to decide what would be the outcome of this meeting.

The adjutant opened the door and clearly asked him to enter the major's office.

Gough entered and saluted the major, who remained sitting behind his wooden desk. *"A wooden desk here on an alien planet. He must have contacts in supply," Gough thought.*

"Captain Gough of the House of Drasken, Sir. Here are my detachment orders." Gough took out a thin piece of plastic and placed it before the major on the edge of his desk. Still, the man did not look up or acknowledge Gough. Gough waited at attention, not moving save for his eyes scanning the room.

"Why are you here, Gough?" The major asked and slowly looked up at Gough through steel-blue eyes.

"All covered in the orders, Sir."

"To hell with your orders, Captain. I demand an answer, or are you trying to piss me off the moment we meet?"

Gough ignored the comment and said, "I expected to see you at the arrival area, Sir. I must assume you're busy with the issues of General Harbour and his Crimson Shard, which is why I am here, Sir." The tome of his voice was classic dry authority, and it hit its mark!

"Major Growton of the House Varok, Captain Gough." The major had stood up, but did not offer a hand or a salute. "You come from a military family, yes, Gough?"

Gough looked at him up and down. Pressed uniform, beret in his waist belt, toe caps were polished on boots. A Scythe Mark II rested in a holster beneath his arm–positioned like an agent's sidearm. Growton had a Graff Diamonds Hallucination on his wrist. At the last take, which was over 55million Quors. Gough hesitated. *"That watch—on a major's salary? And the Mark II? Not in general circulation, yet. Either he had serious contacts, shady ones, or very deep pockets."*

"So, you're the man to solve the Harbour problem, and command thinks that I am not. Tell me your plan, mister Gough, so that I can understand your brilliance and why command sent a stripling straight out of training for a Storm binding." The sarcasm dripped from the major like oil from a leaking engine–slow, slick, and bound to leave a stain.

"A direct assault upon Scar Grimmel is suicide and will mean more dead bodies and probably more raids by the Crimson Shards on the planet here. Are you aware of the difficulty the head of the planet is facing in terms of an uprising, Gough? Was that mentioned in you briefing?" Growton was building himself up for a climatic upload. He was striding around the office, like a man possessed, or on drugs.

"Hold on, Sir, I am here under orders, not by choice. What are you driving at? That's why I am here, Sir. Initially, to present my orders and secondly to discuss with you and seek your local knowledge before I take the men into an assault on Scar Grimmel, Sir. My orders are to capture General Harbour and return him for treason, Sir."

"Oh, please excuse my attempt at laughter, you fuckwit. What do you and command think I have been trying to do?

"Hold on, Sir, I am here under orders, not by choice. What are you driving at?" Gough wasn't just playing into the major's hands; he is directing the entire narrative. Forcing

Growton to overreact, he makes himself the scapegoat, turning his own imprisonment into a calculated move.

"I don't care if you're here to play footsie with my adjutant, share you plan with me now, or I will have you locked up for failure to address a direct command."

"My plan, Sir is to attack the base in five days' time."

"Do you know that your earth weapons will not function on Scar Grimmel? How do you plan to get to the moon arsehole?"

"Orvessa will provide transport for us. That has been agreed. What do you mean our weapons will not work on Scar Grimmel? And as a matter of fact, please cut out the derogatory comments. I am not here to be lambasted by you. I am here on orders and to do my job, which you seem to have failed spectacularly." Gough waited to see if that hit home.

Silence between both men was palatable and the intensity of the moment was not lost on any of them.

"You stand there with your posh watch and a firearm not available to the Corps yet. Perhaps you are on the take, Major. Perhaps I should have you arrested for dereliction of duty, failure to follow orders, and possession of contraband. Unless, of course, you'd like to explain how your house has suddenly acquired deep pockets?"

Growton fell silent, his face a warzone of fury and tightening worry lines. Gough wondered, *"Have I done enough, will he react?"* To be absolutely sure, Gough pushed once more.

"I know your dirty little secrets, you scumbag. You're not fit to hold any rank in the Corps. Toss pot; you are a fraud!"

Growton straightened, fury surging beneath his composure. He was on the verge of erupting. He didn't speak, merely stared–his jaw tightening, breath measured but sharp. The room felt heavier, as if the air itself had thickened between them. Then, with deliberate precision, he turned to the adjutant, his voice clipped and cold. "Arrest this officer and place him in detention block 7. Then send for his Blade leader and tell him to bring the troop to the barracks for immediate detention. Do it now!"

With that, he lowered himself back into his chair, eyes scanning the papers before him, but not seeing them. His fingers drummed once–just once–against the polished wood. The adjutant shoved Gough toward the door, barking for marine troopers to assist. Gough maintained his cool and smartly walked away from the major's office.

Chapter Nine

The Games afoot

Gough was smiling to himself when the Adjutant said,

"What are you smiling at, tart? You've messed with the wrong major, you silly boy. You're in for it now. He has contacts in the highest places, I know. Your career is gone effing, finished. You didn't even make it to Scar Grimmel. What a wanker."

Gough said nothing, he just took in the route to the detention block and memorised the turns. He was pushed into a cell without being frisked for comms units or anything. *Pretty poor setup, this barracks,"* he thought. As soon as the door had closed and he had heard the steps walking away, Gough sent an immediate message to Blade leader to,

"Get the guys out of the Vilkyries accommodation and into the transport at the east gateway, follow the map inside the traveller and use the caves as a new base. Do it immediately, and do not respond to the request to come to the marine barracks. No questions. Move now."

With his time running out, he pushed the comms link to Orvessa.

She answers immediately, "What is it?"

"I've been arrested by the major, as we planned. I'll need help to get out and reaching the safe cave where the troops are headed. Can you assist?

"Yes, wait out."

Now that his head was clearing, Gough could truly take in his surroundings–the stark walls, the reinforced door, the metallic toilet, and cot. Cold. Functional. A holding pen, nothing more.

He exhaled slowly, grounding himself.

The guards would be back soon to take his comms unit. He needed to be ready.

Whilst Gough was preparing himself for a possible beating or unpleasantness, things were happening with Blade and Orvessa.

Blade had called all the team together and made them pack as soon as he had returned to the accommodation complex. He told Stent to go and get the transport, which would be parked outside of the barracks complex, and power up the transport.

The entire team where kitted and on the transport within fifteen minutes. They left out of the rear entrance just as the Marine Corps detachment commander arrived, arguing to get into the site from the main entrance. Orvessa arranged for her vehicle and a detachment of guards to be made ready. She had briefed for another jumper to be placed in the underground park and the power switch to be activated by anyone.

Next, she turned to her guardian and spoke in a low tone, "We have to break Captain Gough out of the Marine Corps barracks and get him to the jumper. I will be out on official business, and you will have to lead the team for the evacuation. No deaths, stun everyone, and I mean everyone. Captain Gough is not to be injured in any way. Questions?"

"I will use the Neuromist, ma'am. That will give us plenty of time to find him and get him out." With that, she and her team were gone.

Gough was bleeding from his mouth, cuts, and bruises on his knuckles, and bruising in various places on his body. He thought to himself, *"Well, at least you can see the damage on the other guys."* Two guards lay sprawled out on the floor, whilst two equally severely damaged Marines held him firm as the fifth man punched his stomach again and again. Gough threw a kick with his right leg and caught the assailant in the gonads. He crumpled, and the two either side tried to punch and hold at the same time, but to no avail. Gough pulled one towards him and produced a brilliant "Glasgow kiss." Just about to start on the last guard when the adjutant came in and hit him with an electric "Shadow shock." Gough collapsed on the floor, bleeding and injured.

"Leave him on the bed and get the rest of you idiots outside, quickly," shouts the adjutant. As the motley crew dragged themselves out of the cell.

"That'll hold you quietly for an hour, Major mistake, mister asshole."

Chapter Ten

Under Their Very Noses

Orvessa's guard commander was as stunning as her leader. Slightly more muscular, but no fat on any part of her frame. She called the chosen guards to her briefing and explained the mission. Orvessa had left with the remaining guards and was on her way to a speech she had to make in the grand hall.

The guard commander's name was Syphera Dragun. No one knew her age or her background. She had suddenly appeared at the guards' meeting and was introduced by Orvessa. That was enough of a recommendation for anyone on Nebulon 17. She had quickly risen through the ranks and very few could recall a time before she stood at Orvessa's side. Questions about her past remained unanswered, yet no one dared to ask.

Commander Syphera Dragun moved through the ranks with measured precision, every step carrying the weight of unquestionable authority. Her hair–marked by the distinct genetic heritage of her world–shifted in luminous strands, responding subtly to her moods, a living testament to both her battle-hardened discipline and the vibrant spirit within.

Her armour bore the scars of countless conflicts, each mark a silent chronicle of victories won and sacrifices made. She spoke with a voice that could steady an army, sharp as tempered steel, yet in its quieter tones. It carried the warmth of a leader who saw beyond strategy. Someone who understood the people she fought to protect.

In battle, her movements were a masterclass in efficiency and force, weaving power with precision. Yet off the field, there was a grace to her presence–an unwavering composure that held space for both command and compassion.

However, now, the mission demanded her full focus. She turned to the chosen guards, her voice sharp with authority.

The guards listened intently.

"What the Marine barracks do not understand is that We built their barracks. We built their escape routes. What they don't know is that those tunnels belong to us. We move in–fast, silent, precise. No mistakes. No unnecessary force. So, we go in quietly, quickly, lift Gough and get out without any fuss. We will be armed, but stun not shadow them. Sound off and I will give your specific duties. If Gough is compromised, the balance shifted and Nebulon 17 couldn't afford that."

They affirmed their positions one by one, until the team were ready for their special briefs.

"One to three cover story and protection. Eight and nine medical, I expect they will have given him a going over. Five and six with me, and three and four provide the defence for the vehicle. Do you all understand your tasks?" The team acknowledged Syphera and moved towards their transport, a Shadowveil.

Shadowveil wasn't just a troop transport. It was a ghost on the battlefield, engineered for precision infiltration and swift extraction. Its adaptive plating bent light and radar waves, allowing it to vanish into urban landscapes, dense terrain, or even open space. A quantum-dampening field ensured soundless movement, muffling both engine output and onboard noise to eliminate detection.

Its kinetic shielding absorbed shockwaves from projectile fire, dispersing impact force rather than deflecting it, ensuring a smooth ride even under heavy enemy fire. Integrated AI-driven threat analysis scanned the battlefield in real-time, predicting enemy movements and recommending optimal entry and escape paths before anyone's boots hit the ground.

Shadowveil's thrusters allowed it to hover without detection, with zero-point energy core enabled near-instantaneous directional shifts. The internal command module provided holographic tactical briefings and direct uplinks to reconnaissance drones, ensuring ground teams had constant intel on enemy positioning.

The transport's emergency phase-shift cloaking could temporarily distort its visibility, bending surrounding light for brief periods to ensure near-invisibility, which was perfect for bypassing enemy scanners or launching surprise incursions.

Built for quick deployment, Shadowveil carried specialised insertion pods that could drop operatives directly into hostile territory with minimal risk. It wasn't just a machine; it was an unseen force, a silent promise of dominance, arriving without warning and leaving nothing unchanged.

Fully loaded with troops, medical supplies, and armaments, the vehicle started its mission, moving over the terrain in silent mode.

The Shadowveil slipped through the atmosphere like a phantom, its emergency phase-shift cloaking flickering across its surface, bending surrounding light until it was nothing more than a distortion in the air—a shadow even the keenest scanners wouldn't catch. A war machine without a signature. A threat without a trace.

Inside, the specialised insertion pods hummed in, waiting, cradling operatives like shells ready to crack open in hostile territory. This wasn't just transit—it was a calculated descent into danger. No alarms. No warnings. Just boots hitting the ground where no one expected them.

Tarka broke the heavy silence, her voice barely above the low hum of the Shadowveil's thrusters.

"No one knows where she came from. You ever wonder why?"

The guardian next to her didn't shift, eyes locked ahead.

"Does it matter? She's got us this far."

A pause. A breath. Then, "It matters if she's playing a bigger game."

Silence. Thick, weighty. The kind that wasn't just an absence of sound—it was the unspoken certainty of a mission that wouldn't leave them unchanged.

The Shadowveil halted with surgical precision beside the emerald-toned outer wall of the Marine complex. No cameras. No sensors. Just an expanse of non-scalable barriers designed to keep intruders out—and yet, Syphera was already moving.

The team egressed in practiced formation–no wasted movement, no hesitation. They ghosted from the transport in seconds, their exit so seamless it barely disturbed the air. A gentle touch, a small, imperceptible panel pressed, and the wall before them shifted, no longer a barrier but an opening.

They were inside. The mission had begun. They deployed, as the brief had explained. Syphera had taken a passage to her left and walked some fifteen paces. Placing her hand upon another panel, which looked like a picture of the Nebulon 17 sun rise. She saw Gough in a heap on the floor, blood oozing from his forehead and shoulders.

"Medical team, action. Then get him out of here!"

Swiftly but quietly, she moved to the cell door and pushed a view tube through the locking device. The view panel burst into life and showed no one was outside guarding the corridor. She withdrew and watched as the guards took Gough out of the cell on a gravlift, fitted with a PulseArc that offered integrated bio-monitoring.

The panel closed behind them, and they carried Gough back to the Shadowveil. The collapse of the guarding was like clockwork, with no commands, just a pure and simple practised extraction. The bio-monitoring was busy pushing needles into his arms and checking his body for broken bones and contusions, and Gough could be seen responding to the pain of the injections.

Syphera says, "Well done, team, well done. Quieter than a fart in a thunderstorm."

Gough coughed and tried to speak, but Tarka, touched his shoulder and gave him a shot to allow him to sleep.

Chapter Eleven

Under Everyone's Noses

The Luminar Council chamber looked wonderful, the lights shone on the rows of VoidNests offering a high-tech cradle for weightless support. Whilst the eiders raised stellar mantle placed the most senior members of the nation above the stage with its VeloxThrone.

Orvessa would speak from the VeloxThrone to address the eiders and the Eclipsars. The collective noun for all the Vilkyries. She needed to brief everyone on the new foreigners and the justification for their coming to Nebulon 17. Orvessa was a little concerned as this would be the very first time, she had spoken without her security chief or her guardian.

"Still, it had to be done," she said to no one. Orvessa waited for the Celestara Mantle to be placed upon her shoulders. It is more than mere attire–it is a statement of sovereignty and wisdom. The fabric flowed like liquid starlight; a seamless cascade of shimmering threads infused with refractive nanofibers that capture and scatter ambient light. At each step it was as if the wearer is cloaked in the very essence of a nebula.

The high collar, sculpted with precision, rises up the wearer's neck like an imperial crest, its structured form both commanding and regal. Embedded within its lining are micro-crystalline prisms that amplify its luminous glow, signifying rank, and influence.

The Celestara Mantle whispered against the solstice trail, each shift a silent declaration of power. Each pulse a reflection of the wearer's presence and emotion. With each measured step, the solstice trail pulsed, a living current, bending in silent tribute as Orvessa approached the VeloxThrone. At the VeloxThrone's crest, Orvessa turned, deliberate and measured, as though the very air held its breath. Above, the sky stretched unbroken, a canvas of deep indigo flecked with the first embers of night. This section of the chamber was open to the elements. As the temperature seldom changes it made the evening session more dynamic as the darkened opening was met by the internal bright lights from the body of the chamber. A single shaft of light shone on to her as she bid welcome to one and all.

As Orvessa had turned, the murmurs among the Eiders faded into a hush. Some inclined their heads in reverence, whilst others studied her in silence, unreadable. The chamber did not merely hold voices–it held judgment, unspoken but present, hovering in the electrically charged atmosphere. Orvessa started her inceptum,

"Gathered Eclipsars, fellow eiders, my friends. We are gathered here to consider the state of new foreigners entering into our space and the impact that will have upon the harmony of our commune. I will explain the details of why they are here and then seeking to justify the calling of these people to our shores. Please listen to my words before we break into chatter groups for feedback, my friends and Nebulon Sons and Daughters."

Orvessa paused for effect and impact, the chamber waiting–yet the true impact did not stem from her inceptum. It came from above. Silhouettes dropped through the open vault at the chamber's edge, flight packs droning as they spiralled downward. Their formation was precise, their movements coordinated. A tightening perimeter. There was no offering of any route to escape.

Orvessa drew a Quantum Prism to defend herself but was hit with a steady stream of Nebulium Core 350 cosmic rays that harnesses deep-space radiation for limitless energy. She collapsed, all strength drained in an instant, leaving behind only the echo of her last breath.

The humanoids gathered her up and placed her on a hover chamber, which was dispatched into the night sky. Only then did the guards and people start to react. Crying, shouting, weapons being drawn and fired, all to no avail as it had happened and was over before anyone could do anything. Orvessa was gone!

Chapter Twelve

The Pieces are Moving, but Do I Know the Game?

Shapes wavered before him; Gough was not sure what he was seeing. Blade, maybe, someone with Orvessa's stance, and another figure moving toward him. She moved toward him–not hurriedly, not hesitantly, but with a calculated ease, the shifting camouflage across her jacket making her seem less solid, less fixed. A presence, not a person. Gough tried to focus, but the blur remained. Colours flickering across her uniform like rippling water. His vision swam, struggling to pin down details. A voice cut through the haze,

"How are you feeling, Captain?"

Gough could not understand where he was, or what was happening. He ached and found that his chest hurt when he breathed.

"Two cracked ribs, a concussion and bruised knuckles and hands. Plus, skin under your nails and one broken finger on your left hand. What did the other guy look like?"

Gough was slowly starting to realise his surroundings. He was lying on a hard table and looking at bright lights in the ceiling of what looked like a cave. Blade came forward and touched his chest.

"It's OK boss, you're safe. We all are safe!"

"Who exactly is 'we'?" asks Gough.

"It's all long story, Captain, but Blade is correct."

The voice sounded familiar, but Gough could not place it. He tried to sit up and could not, as the pain in his chest hurt when he moved. His head was still swimming, as if he had been knocked out. Yet he could not remember that happening. Just some gorgeous Vilkyries bringing him out of the cell. He tried once more to raise his head, but it was too much.

"OK, guys, he needs rest. Leave him now please and we will see after a few hours what else can be done." The doctor ordered them all out of the room. They left in dribs and drabs, reluctant to leave Gough until they were sure he'd be all right. The doctor remained and only then did a curtain move a little and an unexpected visitor entered the medical facility.

"Was he drugged, or could they have implanted a Phageborer?"

"They are unpleasant bugs, boring into the skin to live and secreting an acid compound which causes disorientation," comments the doctor. "I gave him *a* physical. But I could not find a bore hole."

"But just a beating should not have caused this level of concussion, or would it?"

"Let me try some Lucidex. I call you if things improve." The unexpected visitor left as secretly as she had entered.

"Fifteen cc of Lucidex, please nurse." The doctor injected the clear liquid into his hip and Gough seemed to relax a little. As the doctor was checking the dials and monitoring equipment, she saw a blip as Gough rolled over and vomited. As the doctor moved forward, she saw a bronze Lipid crawl out of his one nostril. She froze as the bug lifted its head, looking for another host. The nurse further away grabs a phase probe and used it to shoot at the Lipid. As the ray hit the creature, the doctor grabbed a metal kidney dish and chopped it in half with the disk edge. The nurse gave it another burst for good measure. The Lipid died without moving from the vomit on the bed besides Gough.

After they had cleaned him up and made him comfortable, Gough spoke,

"What has been happening, please? I feel better but have no idea what was going on." The doctor explained to Gough that a Lipid had infected him, and it was out now, and he should start to feel much better, no brain fog, no major aches anymore.

This time Gough was able to raise himself up onto his elbow. A sour, acrid scent clung to him—his own sweat, blood, and something chemical. He grimaced at the smell.

"Can I shower, please?"

"Not yet, in a while. But not yet! We need to observe you a little longer. Lie back down and rest, please."

"I need to talk to Blade. What's going on, Doc?"

"OK, but for a short while," the doctor called blade into the room. Blade entered and could smell the stench.

"It's ripe in here, Doc. What–"

Blade froze mid-sentence as his eyes met Gough's. The sarcasm drained from his face.

"Boss... you're awake. How do you feel?"

"Back among the living. Bring me up to date, Blade."

Blade went through his report in a semi formal manner,

"We evacuated the base camp and transferred to the caves, which is where we are now. The troop is equipped but baffled–who would call you a traitor? We just got here. That can be fixed later. Syphera and her team got you out only after you had taken a severe thrashing. You are back in the caves with your team, me, Syphera and her team. The next bit is not so good."

"Go on."

"You know that the head of security has gone missing. Orvessa was mid-inceptum when humanoids grabbed her. No one knows where she is. The central command of the Vilkyries are organising search parties all over the place. Yet no leads at present. Finally, we are picking up comms between here and the various moons. We can't work out which moons or where they are being transmitted from."

"What the... Orvessa is missing? Ask Syphera to join us, please."

"No!" The doctor stopped Blade and Gough. "You can deal with that situation when you are back on your feet in a few hours." Gough grumbled and felt the nano fusion shot into his deltoid muscle. He was gone. Out like a light.

"Thanks, Blade. Stay close. Check in in three or four hours and let the team know he's alive–and fine." The doctor turned away from Blade and looked at various machines that Gough was still linked up to.

Chapter Thirteen

Let's Piece Things Together

The room within the cave was large, with subdued lighting and benches alongside tables. A hatch from which the kitchen issued food. Gough sat in a chair with arms at the end of the table. He gripped them for support. A terrible tasting cup of coffee was in his hand, and he sipped it slowly. *"Still, it was coffee—after a fashion."* Blade sat on his right and Syphera on his left. The troop, intermingled with Syphera's guards, stood on the far side of the cave, looking concerned and confused.

"OK, let's get down to brass tacks, please."

"What are brass tacks, please?" Syphera asks.

"Sorry, an English old-fashioned expression meaning getting to the essential facts or core details of a situation."

"An essential factor has to be, are you better now, Captain?"

"Yes, my bad. I should have thanked you for my rescue."

"But you said you were better. So, what is bad now, please?" Syphera was having trouble with Gough's English.

"My bad is a twenty-first century term for getting something wrong. It has stuck within the military. Shall we carry on? How long have you been in the caves, Syphera?"

"Two nights and just over one day. Why?"

"Will the base camp be missing you?"

"No, I can say we heard the messages about the leader and went straightway to look for her."

"I need you to return with your guardians and gather intel on the marine base's status. Will you do that?"

"Of course. When do you want me to go and how shall I report to you, please?"

"Blade, set Syphera up with a comms device on our frequency and show her the ropes."

"If you get the device and leave now, you can be back at base camp before dark. Please let me know you have arrived safely and thank you once more, Syphera." Gough took a swig of his coffee.

He had not told anyone about his ability to contact Orvessa, but dare he use it now? He was worried about her and how this would affect the task. He thought of his training and the three Venn circles, "task, individual and group."

Blade returned in what seemed like a noticeably short time. He saluted and asked to sit down. Gough rose slowly and returned the salute.

"You had me worried sir, I can't say less than that. When will you brief the team, please they are as anxious as I was?"

Bring me up to date with the message listening first. Then, I'll brief the team, and we can start from there.

"I want you and the team to start planning the attack on Harbours camp and brief me in the morning, please. Not before eight hours of sleep. Is that OK with you, Blade?" Gough's voice was tired and slow, laboured almost. Gough's words dragged, his voice thick with fatigue. He took a slow swig of coffee, the bitter taste grounding him."

"My job, sir, you get some well-earned rest. I am on top of it."

Gough walked back into the medical room and asks the nurse to leave him to speak with the doctor.

"Doc, can I trust you?"

"Depends on what," she answers.

"I can contact Orvessa, but I can't do it in the main cave area. I need somewhere with a lot fewer people."

"Go behind that curtain over there. Use your right-hand index finger on the keypad. She is in there, more worried about you than I have ever seen her."

The door opened and Orvessa jumped up and ran towards Gough. She wrapped her arms around him–solid, real. The shock stole his balance, and he started to falter, but she held firm, keeping him upright.

Chapter Fourteen
Feelings

"You hold your breath when you think too much." Orvessa's voice was quiet, measured. "I see it–your jaw goes tight, like you're fighting something you don't want to say." She exhaled, watching him, letting the silence fill the space between them."

"Since I came around, you're all I've thought about."

"Why, you've been distant. Is it me–or my rank?" She cared for him – more than she expected in so little time I feel things with you–intense, unfamiliar things. Passion. Joy, and I want more. How are you feeling, please, Gough?" They were touching–without realizing it, at first. Neither pulled away. Neither of them moved away her hair shifted wildly, colors flickering in chaotic waves, and Gough could see the colour and variations moving so quickly. Something stirred deep inside him–a dull ache, a sharp awareness.

"You know... as well as can be expected. Trauma's part of the job." He glanced away. "It's nothing." Gough shifted, fingers flexing against his leg like he needed something to hold on to.

"Nothing doesn't leave bruises and broken ribs." Orvessa tilted her head, lips curving slightly. "I meant how you feel about me, Captain. And don't think about dodging."

Gough exhaled slowly, letting the silence settle between them. The space where they'd brushed against each other felt charged, like something had shifted–not just in the room, but inside him. He looked at Orvessa, really looked, as if seeing her for the first time.

"You–" His voice was rougher than he intended. He cleared his throat, trying again. "You're not just in my thoughts, Orvessa. You're under my skin. And I don't want that to stop."

He let the words hang, watching her reaction, feeling the weight of them. There was no dodging now. No brushing it off as just circumstance or necessity. Something worth holding onto. And for the first time, he wasn't afraid to want it.

Orvessa was silent for a brief moment. She shifted her weight, as her fingers brushing against his sleeve—not an overt gesture, just something light, barely there. Yet a gesture of meaning.

"You don't have to hold your breath anymore, Gough," she says, voice softer now, more certain of their relationship and their feelings towards each other.

"Under your skin, huh? That sounds suspiciously like the start of an addiction, Captain." A small grin plays at her lips.

"This is so quick, is it real, do you mean it, Orvessa? Or is it a pure flirtation because I am something new?"

She didn't respond right away. Instead, she let his words settle, sinking into her, shifting something inside her that she wasn't sure how to call it. Slowly, she inhaled, steadying herself. Then, her fingers curled slightly against his shoulder —not clenching, but anchoring herself, as if making sure this moment was real.

"I don't know if it's real," she admitted finally. "But I know I want it to be."

Then, she looked at him—fully—daring him to hear the depth in her words. Then, without thinking—without questioning it—she took a small step forward. Just enough to close the space, to make sure he felt the warmth of her presence. Their lips as close as they could be without touching and she breathed,

"It scares me."

He doesn't hesitate. He doesn't second-guess. When Orvessa's words land—'It scares me'—he doesn't second-guess. He just knows. Without a word, his hand moves, rough fingertips tracing lightly against her forearm—grounding her, grounding himself. Steady. Certain.

"It doesn't scare me," he says, voice low but sure. "Not anymore, Orvessa."

Then, without asking, without thinking he closed the tiny space between them and kisses her gently on the lips. Not a conquest. No hesitation. Just a choice between two lovers. She met his gaze, unguarded for the first time, surrendering to the quiet intensity between them. No strategy, no defenses–just the raw, undeniable pull.

She barely registered the warmth of his lips before instinct took over–before thought slipped away, replaced by something deeper, undeniable. The hesitation, the fear–it all shattered beneath the weight of it. A sharp breath escaped her as she pressed forward, her hands sliding up to anchor herself against him, fingers curling into the fabric at his shoulders. Not to pull him closer–he was already there–but to make sure this was real.

Her hair danced in the heat between them, wild and untamed. She let it flow, unfettered, refusing to pull away.

"I want this," she murmurs against his lips, breathless, certain. "I want you." She'd expected fear–but all she found was fire. Not anymore, not now and she knew not ever.

Without any hesitation, Gough presses forward, deepening their kiss–not out of desperation, but certainty. His grip shifts, strong but not forceful, anchoring them in this moment before they realize what they've just stepped into. The warmth between them burns incandescently. Orvessa can't pull away–she meets him, as an equal, her choice, a full surrender to something neither of them expected. Then, as instinct gives way to realization, they break apart–just enough for the truth to hit them.

Alien and human.

Two worlds colliding in a way that should have been impossible, but it wasn't.

Orvessa's breath is unsteady. Not from fear–never fear–but from the weight of it. She lifts her gaze to his, searching–not for doubt, but for confirmation that this wasn't a mistake. All Gough does is hold her there, unwavering.

"This is real," he murmurs, voice like steel wrapped in warmth. "You feel it too."

"Yes," she whispers, warm breath against his ear, her head sinking into the solid certainty of his shoulder. Hair a mess and all over him. Gough didn't care–this was everything. For once, he didn't want to resist it. They didn't speak. There were no words big enough for this.

Gough shifted, easing them both onto an old-fashioned sofa, the creak of old fabric barely registering between them. Orvessa rested her head in his lap–not in surrender, not in fragility, but in absolute trust. His hand found its place, fingers moving absently through her wild hair, feeling the warmth of her against him. Too much to go back now. Too much to ignore.

"I can't lose this," Orvessa murmurs, voice barely audible.

Gough exhaled, steady, centring them both in the moment.

"Then don't."

No hesitation. No doubt. Just the certainty of knowing what they had was real, and neither of them would ever let it slip away. Orvessa rests against him, her warmth seeping into him, her hair wild over his chest. The weight of what just happened presses into Gough, and he doesn't question it. He just knows. He strokes her face, gently and feels the softness of her skin.

"Real," he murmurs—not as reassurance, not as a question. As a fact.

Orvessa shifts, breathing steadily and melting in the moment. She had never experienced the feelings that were coursing through her frame. The tension, the joy, the fact that he cared for her and would show it. In that moment, solitude faded–replaced by the steady presence beside her. The certainty of it settled deep, undeniable. No hesitation. No doubt. Only the certainty that they had already crossed a threshold they could never step back from.

It was no longer two worlds colliding–just a new one, forged between them, neither fully human nor alien, but something wholly their own.

Chapter Fifteen

Poor Planning means Poor Performance

There was a gentle knock at the door, and the doctor's voice called out to Gough.

"Captain, you are needed, please, at a brief. There has been a development. As soon as you can, please."

Orvessa rolled off his chest and stood up. Gough stretched and got up. Kissed Orvessa once more and said,

"Let me wash my face and I will be there."

"The wash basin is in the shower room behind the mirror, darling."

"That's an earth term. You've been studying human archives again?"

"Later, my love. Take your meeting in the main room, as I have video links and sound. I will hear everything. I need to be unmade for a while longer."

Gough entered the doctor's medical facility, forcing himself into protocol mode. The doctor guided him through to the cave main room, without him having to consider the nurse and her stares. The nurse threw Gough a questioning glance–he should have been in his bunk, not here. But the Doctor gave no explanation, just led him forward from sterile lights to the smell of blood and burnt flesh.

The scene in the cave was reminiscent of a bloodspan rift. Syphera was sitting at the table in his chair. The stump of her left shoulder had been hastily sealed, the uniform sleeve blackened where the blast had torn through. Various guardians were on the floor with bits missing, serious Singeflesh wounds and various drips into parts of their bodies. Only a small number of the original guardians who were left for the base camp remained.

Blade came up to him, saluted and said,

"Captain, it was a gods-damned ambush! Humanoids–maybe even Harbour's Shards–they knew exactly where to hit them!"

Gough looked straight at Syphera and asks,

"What happened? Take your time, but tell me everything, please."

"Everything was going fine until we came into an undesignated checkpoint staffed by Marines. They pulled us over and I got out to talk with them. Showed them my papers and told them we were returning from a mission to seek and locate the Leader. They did not believe me and then everything went wrong. A squad of humanoid fighters appeared and started shooting up our transport. I lost my arm as the marine started blasting at me. They were expecting us. Someone knew our route–someone fed them our movements. Shards were in amongst the humanoids and torn into the team. Some of us used the escape pods to get out and away. Margo, my guardian, got me into a pod, but killed doing so. All we could do was to come back here."

Gough drew his breath in, holding it for a moment. Blade met his gaze, waiting, but said nothing.

"Who had access to the map in this briefing area? Who is alive and who is missing? Wounded take as alive? Find out for me, Blade, quickly. Doctor, please see what else can be done for Syphera."

Major Growton was standing in front of a large map of the local area, showing the Vilkyries' base camp, the mountains and Transit pads.

"Where have they gone? Come to that, where is Gough? This is unacceptable. Where is Gough? He's made me look like a bloody fool, and I won't stand for it. Tell me again what happened at the checkpoint, adjutant."

"Well Sir, difficult to say as a group of guardians arrived from nowhere, and then a group of humanoids and Shards arrived and all hell broke loose, so to speak. The guardians broke out, some killed, some marines injured and a good few of the raiders. The numbers of casualties is not yet fully known, Sir."

“Show me on the map again and mark it.” The adjutant drew red crossed swords on the map just about fifty clicks from the base camp. The major looked long and hard but could not see anything closer than the Valkyries’ base camp. “*Nothing near, nothing that would provide cover and the mountains were well over a one hundred clicks away. You would need special transport to get to them. So where had they come from? Who had taken the Leader and where was she,”* he wondered.

“Send out search and rescue teams for the Leader and to try to find Gough and his team. Do it bloody quickly! Full kit and ammunition for each team member, plus four days’ rations. Get to it, man.” Growton glared at the adjutant.

General Harbour stood in front of an identical map and looked at the terrain and the location of the fight.

“Where did you say the skirmish took place? How many did we lose? Where is the Leader? Is there any information? We did not kidnap her. Who Did?” His voice trailed off as he stared at the map.

“This fiasco looks like a poor planning of an operation. Who set this up? Bring them to me, now!”

A burly under sergeant came into the room. Stood to attention and saluted.

“You wanted me Sir? I planned the attack, but the troops did not follow my orders. Sir!” For all the man’s size and confident appearance, he was scared. Harbour could smell him. He did not like people making mistakes and then not owing up to them.

“You are responsible for piss poor planning, which resulted in piss poor performance, Gator.”

“Yes, Sir, but the troops did not follow my orders, exactly. Sir”

“The majority of them were humanoids and can only follow orders. So, you are trying to give me a load of old toffee.”

“Me Sir. No Sir. Not me.”

Harbour turned to the Howlfiend next to his feet and said,

“Enough. Kill.”

The Howlfiend tore the man's throat out from his neck, and then calmly returned to Harbour.

"That's the trouble number one. People spend too much time talking about killing and don't do it. It is very unfair to the person who is going to be killed. They think they might make a break, escape or something. Perhaps talk their way out of it. What I do every time is kill them. No mucking about, no hesitation, no useless chatter, just kill them, simple. Hesitation is the enemy. It breeds weakness. Weakness gets people killed. Do you understand number one?"

"Yes, Sir. I see," says number one. He kept his eyes on the dead body, not on the general."

"Call our operative on the planet. I need to know if anyone comes or goes at any time. Come fiend, it is time for our treats. You need some ruffage after that blood and I need my woman. Let's not keep either waiting."

Chapter Sixteen

Brief the Guys and Ask a Question

It was time to meet with the team and explain what was going on. Blade had assembled everyone in a small room of the main briefing and dining room. The troops quietened when Gough entered. Many looking to see what state he was in, as they had heard about the beating.

Both Gough and Blade sat down and looked at the band of warriors. Warriors that would put their lives on the line in the extremely near future. Gough cleared his throat.

"Right, let's get started. Our mission, as you know, is to get General Harbour and break up the Shards. This is the mission, but there are a few other things we have to do. Not the least is to find the traitor and eliminate whomever it is. The Vilkyries agree that someone is passing information to Harbour's group, and we have to find out who. That is why I got myself arrested and took a beating. We have all seen the results of someone's loose talk on the guardians. The security officer and Orvessa herself were kidnapped and, at the moment, still missing." He looked at the floor, not the troops, as he lied to them. He knew exactly where Orvessa was.

As Gough mentions the traitor, a warrior's grip tightens around their weapon–anger simmering beneath the surface. So, our job is to plan and execute the attack on Harbour's stronghold, without being given away. Then make the traitor give herself or himself away. Understood. You trust no one except the group, Blade, and me. Questions?"

"Why was it necessary for you to be the scapegoat, Sir?"

"I took the beating intentionally–HQ needed a ranking officer's arrest to sell the deception."

Blade remains unreadable, his expression fixed, jaw clenched—a show of unshaken resolve, whilst some of the troop shift in their seats, rolling their shoulders or cracking their knuckles. Blade's fingers tapped once against the chair, his only hint of impatience. A brief glance was exchanged between Blade and Gough.

"I cannot stress the need for secrecy or the need to know enough. Trust no one outside this room. Not even your usual contacts. Understood? Check weapons, kit, and grips. We move once planning and briefing are complete."

Gough got up and left the room without asking for any more questions. that Blade could cover in his absence. He wanted to visit Orvessa, but there were things to do first. *"Check on the guardians, and then plan the travel to the moon, Scar Grimmel. He also needed to check his kit and weaponry. The doc hadn't cleared him yet. If she didn't sign off soon, he'd be benched, and that wasn't an option. Not for this mission. Not when lives depended on him. A shower and change of clothes would also help,"* he thought. Reflecting upon the outcome, Gough knew that some of the team wouldn't make it. He knew that. Had accepted it. But there was no room for hesitation. No room for doubt.

Syphera was awake, her gaze steady as he moved into her view. Beds and curtains separated the injured, offering privacy but doing little to mask the weight of suffering. She looked a mess—her hair wild, her missing limb stark against the dim lighting. And yet, despite everything, she radiated something more than survival. She was becoming a beacon of hope for Gough, proof of the unwavering devotion of the Vilkyries that they held for their leader.

"What will you do Captain Gough? Do you know anything about our Leader, please? Fear is no longer an emotion for me. It is a force, a storm tearing through my very being. How can I help, please?"

"You need to rest and recover, Syphera, and allowing yourself to give way to emotion will not help your leader. I will call on you when I need you, don't worry."

A monitor let out a final, fractured chirp before falling silent. The guardian's breath shuddered—just a faint exhale—then nothing. The air grew heavier, pressing against Gough like the weight of the lives slipping away. He touched the doctor's arm as he went past her and she said,

"We've lost another guardian. Third, one today."

"I am sorry for the loss." His words felt hollow, inadequate. He did not know them personally, hadn't shared battle stories or victories. What else could he say? Yet, he felt the deep pain of soldiers lost in battle. He trudged towards the door behind the curtain in the medical facility and touched the pad. Orvessa met him as the door opened.

"It is tough, my darling, oh so tough. I share your grief for my people. Thank you, you are my loyal friend and lumina."

"I hate to see good people taken out with no real justification. We're military, but there has to be a purpose, angel. There has to be!" Gough took Orvessa in his arms and held her close. She wrapped her arms around his body, and it felt like they would never let go of each other. Yet, they both knew that his job and her position could lead to loss at any time.

They walked together to the sofa and looked into each other's eyes.

"The gateway to the soul," Gough whispered.

"Yes," replies Orvessa, "And your soul ... is good. You are a good man, Gough, and I am overjoyed you are my man. I heard all the conversations and your briefing. How much time do we have, darling?"

"I need to check my kit, shower, and then plan the attack. I will need the special transit pad locations from you for that, please."

"How about this order? We shower, you check your kit, I get the locations for you in code, and then you can plan the attack with my help?"

"Are you sure? I would love to be close to you. I have to ask, what does the water do to your hair?"

"It's not the water you need to worry about. The water is harmless. Me being next to you? That's another story! Shall we?"

Eagerly, they shed their clothes and stepped into the large shower. Warm water cascaded over them, neither too hot nor too cold–just enough to ease their tension. Steam curled around them as they lathered each other with wash crystals, their touches careful, lingering, exploring without urgency. They pressed together, so close that even a whisper of space would have felt unnatural. Washing gave way to kissing, which gave way to an even deeper embrace, as if closing the distance between them could erase the weight of everything outside this moment. Tenderness and relief intertwined, flowing between them in quiet understanding as warmth and gentleness became one. They dried each other and true to form Orvessa's hair was a dazzling glow of colours reflecting her feelings. Gough just uttered,

"I don't know what I'd do without you, Orvessa. You're everything I've ever wanted, everything I'll ever need. If I lost, you... I don't think I'd recover."

"I swear by the heavens above, you are mine. I will never leave you, Gough. Never!"

The term heavens struck Gough, and his gaze drifted to the patterns carved into the walls, shapes that felt intentional, almost reverent.

"That symbol... does it mean something? Do you have religion on the planet?"

"Yes, of course, my love. We will be married in the church of the angels here on Nebulon 17. We can marry as soon as your return from the mission, please. Do you agree?"

"Yes, but I actually need to propose to you formally and find something to share the occasion. On earth we give a ring and call it engagement."

"We call it a starsealed pact, and exchange Pulsebands. They are wearable bands that synchronise our heartbeats, allowing us to feel each other's pulse no matter where we are."

"Well, I don't have a ring or a pulse band, but it feels like I've known you forever?" He knelt down and took Orvessa's hand in his and looking into her eyes,

"Please grant me the greatest honour any woman can give a man, to be my wife, Orvessa. Will you?"

"Yes ... yes, yes! I want nothing less. And this moment–before battle begins–is the perfect time to declare it: my Captina, my friend, and my future lover."

He stood up, his breath uneven, drawn toward her as though gravity itself demands it. He kissed her, not a Velmari, but something more fragile, more aching. His arms tightened around her shoulders, holding her close, as if letting go would mean losing her to the unknown. The moment hung between them, charged, unspoken words trembling at the edge of his lips.

"There would be time later to cherish this moment. Now, duty called."

Gough dressed himself in Sentinel Shell and the weapons belt needed for transporting his personal weapon through the transit pad. He mentally ran through the checklist.

"Medical covers, weapon, spare cartridges, luminous terrain sheet, spare socks, respirator, WhisperNet for ultra-low-volume communication, and holoscribe."

Moving across to Orvessa, he took the viewscreen she had dictated the coordinates of the transit pads.

"One three and eight, are concealed, seven faces the complex and should be where you setup your covering fire. Nine and ten come up inside the complex near to their medical facility. I know that nothing has changed since we managed to obtain this plan. Does this help?"

Gough considered the diagram, and the transit pads uses.

"This helps me a lot, angel. Especially if it is accurate and current. Believe me I will be back. Because of you Orvessa, I have something to live for. I now do believe in love at first sight. It is you and me together forever."

Chapter Seventeen

SMEAQ (Situation, Mission, Execution, Admin & Logistics, Questions)

The team stood ready, Sentinel Shells locked in, and weapons belts fastened. Blade eyed Gough–something was different. Was that... joy? Gough wasn't a man who gloried in battle. Blade said nothing. He'd wait until after the brief.

"Please activate the local force field, Blade."

Blade placed the unit by the door and pushed the switch to turn it on. A blue haze filled the outer walls, floor, and ceiling.

"Force field up. Take notes. Standard SMEAQ format follows. The situation is the only moon of Nebulon 17 that supports humans, Scar Grimmel. The gravity is slightly less than earth, but not much. As you can see on this graphic, General harbour's is coloured in red and is about seven clicks by five. Intelligence suggests at least one hundred and fifty men, and assortment of humanoids and some battle gearings that use phase blasters. The walls of the complex are stock T fifty-seven plates of amourlight and can resist any field cannon, but they will buckle under the right amount of plastic. Transit pads marked green are fully concealed–entry or exit without detection. Brown pads surface just beneath the terrain; gives visual but not sensor contact.

Our mission is seeking out and destroy or capture General Harbour and cause as much chaos and disruption to the base as possible. Violent force is authorised.

Execution, we jump at 03:15 local Nebulon 17 time. Landing on Scar Grimmel at 03:17. Sun is already up–minimal shadows. I will give you the hack at the end of the brief. Make notes:

Stent you and I go in using this pad number 15 and come up in their medical area.

Carol-Anne and Eric you go in on brown six and place charges against the walls to create diversions. Once you have completed that use pad five to get into the parade area and hold off supporting troops for as long as you can. Get out and return to Nebulon 17. Do not get overrun or taken.

Renman and Blade you set up the attack weapons and use the control panel to operate them, do not get too close to the complex. Here again, you want them to come to you–not the other way around. Jenny, Rachel, and Gus you have to go in and get Harbour, using pad thirteen. Not superstitious, I hope. Come out the same way. No margin for error. Arthur back up at pad nine. Lethal force authorized. Extraction depends on success. No extraction kills him. We all know the transit pad tactics, so I am not going overt them again now.

Admin: break off is the bugout word. Harbour won't hesitate. He'll kill on sight. So, know your enemy. Blade takes command if I go down. Buddy, buddy check and then, questions?"

"What's Murphy's fallback if this all goes sideways? I mean what do we do if it goes wrong, boss?" Carol-Anne asks looking Gough straight in the eye.

"If it goes wrong get out. We can regroup and try again, only if we get out first. E and E through any pad and get back to here."

"Do we know for certain that Harbour is still there, Captain?"

"Yes, intel says he is at home."

"Intel's been wrong before, sir," Arthur muttered.

"We go with the info that we have Arthur. OK?"

Arthur was taken back that the Captain had remembered his name. He shut up.

"OK watch, time pieces hack in five, four, three, two, hack! Gather around."

Then, as one, they thrust their hands forward. "Semper Fi."

Chapter Eighteen
Shit What a Battle!

Blade and Gough checked their watches and moved everyone into place, without any word of command. Hand signals were the watch word. The watch ticked to 03h14. Gough held up one finger. The signal was passed to everyone.

Gough scanned Blade's combat rig—everything was in place. The high-velocity plasma rifle's multi calibrated scope hummed softly, auto-adjusting for range. The gravity-distortion charges clung to his belt, their dark shells shimmering with contained energy. Where was his monomolecular combat knife? He spotted it—sheathed on the opposite side of his belt.

He had opted for the Sentinel Arm Mounts - Forearm-embedded miniature railguns, triggered by neural impulse for quick-response fire.

WhisperNet Comm - Encrypted throat mic.

As number two he had the EchoDrone Scouts. The deployable micro-drones, feeding live terrain mapping and enemy locations into the Marine's HUD.

Finally, he was carrying the Kinetic Backup Shield, which were deployable energy shield, capable of absorbing direct impact for a brief time before it needed recharging.

"Yes, he had it all, good man."

03:15. They moved. Fluid precision, with their weapons snapped to targets—neural-linked, no hesitation. Breaths steady. Stances grounded, ready to pivot. NeuralSync flared alive, painting the battlefield in shared awareness. Every squad member is connected; their visuals, data, and battlefield awareness unified through NeuralSync.

As they deployed, it was not chaotic, methodical. Yet brutal, and unrelenting. Footsteps softened by VoidStep boots, phase carbines humming, EchoRounds ready to lock onto enemy heat signatures. They didn't waste movement.

Gough had just enough time to see that Carol-Anne and Eric were both equipped with Hyperkinetic Penetrators that are shaped charge rounds that accelerate to extreme velocities, punching through armour with precision.

Gough and Stent, disguised in white lab coats, entered the medical area. Lots of beds, no one in them. They moved slowly between each cocoon to check that each bed was really empty. Stent cut the throat of a single nurse in one single movement. No sound. Gough didn't pause–just nodded. They moved on, stepping over the lifeless form, mission ahead. Gough checking the layout on his arm view screen. They heard the explosions of the Hyperkinetic Penetrators hit the walls and the alarm sound within the complex, loud, very loud.

Arthur had arrived at pad nine only to find it full of Shards who torn him limb from limb.

Renman and Blade set up the Quantum Railgun. They would use their electromagnetic acceleration to launch projectiles at near-light speeds, delivering devastating kinetic impact. This would make the defenders imagine the force was much larger than it was. Noise, a constant noise is a constant in a battle, and it stops most people from thinking, frightens others, and makes some give up.

The hallways tremble under distant explosions. Carol-Anne and Eric's Hyperkinetic Penetrators tearing through outer walls. Smoky haze spreads, cutting visibility. Alarms scream, overlapping in different tones and security systems trying to compensate for the relentless assault, that simply failed.

Gough and Stent push forward, navigating through a mess of overturned tables, shattered screens, and flickering overhead lights. Every step carrying weight. They needed to not rush but be deliberate. Their NeuralSync overlays flash updates–heat signatures erratic, moving in bursts, stopping, retreating. Enemy squads fired in blind panic, unsure whether they're aiming at real threats or phantoms.

Inside the complex, defenders found themselves stumbling through corridors, desperately gripping weapons. Gunfire erupting in short bursts, but the shots were not accurate and hit walls, control consoles, sparks flying going everywhere. The sheer unpredictability of the attack had the Shards shooting at shadows, wasting ammunition, and most of all questioning what's real.

Stent gestured with a silent signal. Their destination is close.

A door swings open ahead, but no one steps through. Gough and Stent pause—scanning—no movement detected.

Then, the alarm shifts pitch to a deeper, more urgent tone.

Harbour's office is just beyond the next junction, its entry secured but flickering between red and green lockdown signals were easily seen by Gough and Stent. *"Where were the extraction team,"* Gough wondered. He called on his WhisperNet Comm but could not make out the answer.

Gough thought he could hear a muffle message, but the link went dead. At that moment they arrived at the corridor and were attacked by a group of Shard fighters. Everyone was involved as fists connect, Sentinel Shells absorbing partial impact, but not everything. Gough ducks under a wild swing, driving his elbow into an attacker's gut, feeling the crunch of ribs beneath his weight. Eric spins, slamming a knee into the side of another foe, sending them sprawling. The enemy isn't as organized and their desperation was starting to show, flailing, trying to hold the line. The Marines are trained killers, and it showed.

In a flash of heat, a screeching pulse, torn through the air. Gus staggered. The plasma round hit like a supernova—searing through his abdomen in a flash of molten light. Then came the wet, terrible rupture. His stomach split, spilling ropes of half-vaporized viscera across the deck. His breath comes in staggered gasps, eyes wide—not in fear, but in raw acceptance. He tries to say something to Gough, but nothing came out, only silence. Gough's breath locked in his throat. No time. No fucking time as he reacted first, launching forward, using that moment of fury to drive his HyperEdge Blade into the throat of the shooter. Yanking sideways, blood spurted in the artificial lighting, splattered armour, and stained the floor.

The battle compressed in seconds. It became instinct alone. Instinct to win and instinct to kill or be killed. The extraction team fought, harsher, faster, knowing there's no time to mourn, only time to finish the mission.

Harbour's door looms ahead, flickering, unsecured, waiting. Gough presses forward, adrenaline hammering through his veins. The door to Harbour's office looms ahead, but the moment they get close, the world erupts. A storm of phase fire blasts outward, impacting walls, chewing into debris, forcing the team back. Two figures stand inside. Identical and both moving coordinated, firing without pause.

"Doubles! Techno enhanced clones. Watch out!" Eric snarls, diving behind cover. Shot impacts sizzle against the floor, melting sections of plating. Pulse rounds scatter in every direction, wild and relentless, making any direct entry suicidal. Gough ducks low, his Sentinel Shell absorbing glancing blows, heat warnings flashing in his NeuralSync overlay. He doesn't hesitate as his mind is already calculating the possibilities. Which one is Harbour? Which one is the decoy? The enemy tactics are clear. Total suppression, with no gap in fire nor chance to rush them.

Jenny, Rachel, Eric, and Gough brace themselves, pinned down by relentless fire. The two figures, one real, one the decoy, hold their ground, blasting energy pulses through the thick haze of battle. A monitor is shattered in the chaos of shots. One of the doubles hesitated—just a flicker in its firing rhythm.

Gough's NeuralSync flagged the anomaly.

"Rachel! Right flank, suppressing fire—now! Jenny, Eric cover left!"" His voice is sharp, cutting through the chaos. Rachel pivots, unloading EchoRounds toward the right side of the room, forcing one of the shooters to duck. Echo Rounds use heat signatures, acoustic mapping, and trajectory correction to ensure near-perfect accuracy in combat scenarios. They were a godsend in this situation.

Yet, the second keeps firing, no hesitation. It was the decoy. The fake. They knew now who was whom.

Gough moving fast, dives toward the real Harbour. Phase blasts sear past him, scorching the floor inches away from his body. His Sentinel Shell absorbs partial impact, but the heat stings through his side. Doesn't matter. He's going in.

Eric slides under suppressive fire, knee driving into the decoy's ribs. The figure stumbles but doesn't react like a human would. It flickers, a synthetic projection overlay. At that moment Harbour tries to use a holo-shadow to confuse them. Jenny lunges, bringing her HyperEdge Blade up. A strike to the gut–nothing. The blade passes through.

"Dammit–he's using a mirage tech!" Rachel growls, snaps her rifle back into place.

Gough doesn't hesitate. "Then we go straight for the real one."

Harbour knows they've figured it out. His fire pattern changes with his evident desperation. His eyes flick toward the nearest exit, calculating an escape route. Gough sees the flicker of thought in his expression.

"You're cornered, Harbour," Gough growls, stepping forward, weapon raised. Harbour's grip tightens around his pistol, smirking as he takes a line to kill Gough, and get to his escape hatch. Harbour moves, his body shifting toward the escape hatch in a desperate burst of speed. Although his pistol rises, shaking slightly–not from hesitation, but from the raw instinct of survival. He does not shoot.

Jenny sees it., not waiting or hesitating. Her shot cracks through the air, phase energy tearing into Harbour's back before he can reach the hatch. His body jerks forward, colliding against the console as the blast burns through his spine.

His hand convulses, squeezing the trigger. The aim is off–skewed, uncontrolled. The shot goes wide, missing Gough entirely. Instead, it hits Eric.

For a half-second, Eric doesn't react, his body simply absorbing the heat–then, the pain registers. His breath halts, his chest convulsing as his stomach ruptures, liquefying beneath the plasma impact. His eyes widen, but in understanding of what has happened to him.

Rachel's scream tore through the comms. She lunged for Eric, gloved hands already slick with his blood. But the wound was a blackened crater, still bubbling at the edges. His lips moved, without sound. Then his body just folded, collapsing like a puppet with cut strings.

Gough's fingers tightened around his rifle. Later. Mourn later. Harbour, still alive, but choking on his own blood. Gough doesn't give him another second. One step forward–a single, merciless shot, which goes straight through Harbour's skull. The room fell silent, but the war outside still raged. At that point Blade was on the WhisperNet Comm, asking what was happening and where were they.

"You should be on your way out by now!"

They had to get out, but what about the bodies. Gough set incendiary charges to burn the bodies and took the two woman out of the chaos. It was then that he noticed Eric was in the room and there was no Carol-Anne. They should have been outside.

As they travelled down the corridors and back towards the medical area Stent swore.

"Mother freaking hell. Its Carol-Anne." Sten's curse died in his throat. Carol-Anne's Sentinel Shell–cracked open like an egg–revealed the ruin inside. Her face was frozen mid-snarl, one hand still clamped around a dead Shard's throat. Gough wrenched her ID tags free. No time for rites. Not here. He called Blade,

"We are coming out, casualties, but we are on our way. Get ready for final evac. Break-off, I repeat Break-off. Arthur get out, break out now." He could not break off as he had been finished off a while ago.

The transit pads moved them to safety as the firing and explosions continued. Jenny said,

"I picked this off the bastard's desk, is it useful, boss?"

Chapter Nineteen

Regroup, but nothing on the Traitor

As everyone arrived back at the cave, Gough made them strip off all their clothes. Much to the amusement of all of them, the nurses provided help to undress and towels for the woman to cover themselves. They then threw them into the portable force field.

Blade asks, "Why, Sir?"

"I need to check if anyone has been tagged to identify where we are." Four suits had locator beacons attached to them. It was from the hand-to-hand fighting.

The doctor went between each team member and undertook a quick triage. Everyone had wounds, some bad some not so bad. Gough wanted to get to Orvessa but had to stay with the remains of his team. Blade and Renman had been subject to crossfire and taken hits, so the call to break-off had been accepted with great speed. Jenny and Rachel had taken flesh wounds as had Gough. The majority of the hits had been soaked up by the Sentinel shell suits. Dead were Eric, Carol-Anne, Gus, and Arthur. Gough had all their dog tags with him. He would need that for his report. Each tag in his grip felt heavier than it should–like a weight beyond steel.

Blake commented that, "The silence in here is louder than the gunfire on Scar Grimmel had been.

Carol-Anne's partner stood alone, dejected as she had not returned. Blake's wife was there waiting for him to be stood down.

"After the medic has signed you off, stand down. Debrief tomorrow morning at 09h00 in the briefing room." After the medic had signed him off, Gough stood down.

The weight of names—those lost, those waiting—pressed heavy in his chest. Yet duty still called. He turned toward the medical wing. No time to waste.

He walked into the facility, pressing his finger against the keypad. The door slid open.

Orvessa turned sharply, breath hitching. Her eyes locked onto him—filthy, exhausted, but alive. Relief flickered across her face, but something deeper lingered in her gaze. Not just fear, but the weight of what could have been. What she might have lost forever.

She didn't hesitate. She ran to him, colliding against his chest, her arms encircling him so tightly it was as if she thought he might vanish if she let go.

"You're here," she whispers, voice cracking. Her fingers clutched at his uniform epaulettes, knuckles white, holding him as if to convince herself he was real.

Gough exhaled, exhaustion momentarily forgotten. He pressed his forehead against hers, closing his eyes for a fleeting second.

"Don't look so worried, angel," he murmurs, voice rough, filled with quiet affection. "I promised—I'm here."

She shook her head, fresh tears pooling in her eyes. "I thought—" Her voice broke.

"I know." Gough touched her face, brushed away a tear, his fingers lingering just long enough to feel the warmth of her skin beneath them. He kissed the path her tears had made, soft, grounding her in the moment.

"I need to wash," he says, voice lighter, trying to ease the weight that pressed between them. "But I do like that homecoming greeting. Will you do that after we're married?"

A half-laugh, strangled, slipped from her lips, but her hold didn't loosen. The tears kept coming, quiet, unrelenting Gough pulled her close, pressing his lips against her hair, then her temple—anywhere he could reach—until finally, he found her mouth, grounding them both in the relief of being here, together. Orvessa stopped crying and looked deeply into his eyes.

"I don't want to go through that ever again. I mean it, Gough. After we finish this assignment, I want you with me here. "I can find you a proper job. Like taking care of me. If you'll have me?"

Gough eased off his kit, still holding Orvessa as if the act of letting go might undo everything he had just come to understand. He had spent years chasing duty, answering the calls of others, believing that purpose was found in his missions, honour, and duty. Yet, here, now – wrapped in her arms, feeling her tremble against him–he realised how wrong he had been. This was the thing he never thought possible. A place to land. A reason to stay. Not just love, but a promise of something beyond fleeting moments–a future, a belonging he never knew on earth. At last, he was allowed to want–without guilt, without duty pulling him elsewhere. And now that he had found it, the thought of leaving felt like undoing something vital, like turning his back on the one thing that made all the rest worth it.

Gough let the water roll over his skin, his muscles aching but too wired to truly relax. The warmth should have grounded him, should have told his body he was safe. Yet something inside him still braced for impact, for the call to action that wasn't coming.

Orvessa was there–close, watching him with quiet intent. He caught her eyes, and for a moment, the world tipped. He wasn't sure if he was standing or swaying if he needed to hold on to her or if she was holding onto him.

She was speaking–soft, careful words–but they slipped through his thoughts like water through fractured stone. He struggled to grasp their meaning. Not because they didn't matter, but because they did–too much.

Gough blinked hard, tried to focus. Orvessa. Not a mission. Not a command. Her.

She touched his face, fingers skimming over skin rough from battle, tracing the battle-worn lines of his face, searching for the man beneath the soldier. That touch dragged him back, piece by piece, forcing him into the now. He exhaled sharply.

"I'm here," he murmurs, though even as he said it, he wasn't sure if it was meant for her or himself.

Orvessa washed him with crystals, traditional healing stones, and he let the water roll down his face and back. His hair was clean and so was he. However, the battle scars and lost team members would not get washed away. He put on pyjama bottoms and Orvessa wore his pyjama top. Gough laughed and said,

“There’s an old story from Hollywood. A couple walks into a shop to buy sleepwear–he needs the bottoms; she needs the top. It’s what they call a ‘meet cute.’ Well, my darling, this is ours.” Orvessa tilted her head slightly, as if trying to make sense of it, then smiles–a small, hesitant laugh escaping as she shook her head.

Gough lay beside Orvessa, his body clean but still carrying the weight of scars–seen and unseen. He exhaled, eyes tracing the dim glow of the room, his hand resting over hers.

“To sleep, perchance to dream,” he murmurs, voice heavy with exhaustion.

Orvessa turned her head, studying him. “Dreams should be beautiful, not something to fear,” she whispers.

Gough gave a faint smile. “You’d think so, wouldn’t you?”

She curled against him, one hand resting over his heart as if to tether him, to steady his breath. “Sleep,” she murmurs, fingers threading lightly through his hair. “If dreams come, let them be of me.”

Gough exhaled, the weight pressing against his ribs easing just enough. His fingers curled lightly around hers, grounding himself in her presence.

“Then stay close,” he murmurs, his voice hoarse, edged with something raw. “Make sure I don’t get lost in them.” Was he finding himself at last?

Chapter Twenty

The Picture Changes

Blade had been looking at the cameras outside after the debrief. As the transport slowed to a stop, he felt a pull–something about its arrival meant more than just cargo and passengers. It was marines and a dead body. He recognised the blade leader. Called the Captain and suggested,

"Keep out of sight, boss. I want to bring them in and see what we can find out. I also want to know who the body is, as well as why are they here. Did the tags get sent yesterday? Is that, OK?"

"Go for it but take the team with you and surround them. Bring the transport inside as well in case there are any drones supporting them."

"Good idea!" Blade quickly briefed the team around the monitor, giving positions and weapons required, and then they set off for the exit points. He walked casually up to the marines and said, "Hi Guys, what brings you out this far?"

"Oh, Hi Blade, I could ask the same thing. No, the boss said investigate a blip from yesterday and get rid of the corpse at the same time."

"The boss? Do you mean the major?"

The other blade leader laughs, "No, I mean the boss, the adjutant. The major is an old fart and a cover for the real boss. So why are you in this neck of woods?"

"No woods here. We're scouting for the Vilkyrie leader–lost our bearings."

"What troop are you? I don't remember your face. Are you new? I don't always see the new guys."

Blade pulled his Pulsefire X1 and replied,

"No, we came in a few days ago. Sorry, but I need you and your team to come with me, please!"

"You're gonna take all of us? I don't think so!"

"No, but my team and the X1 disagree, old chap. Start moving, please" With that, the rest of Blades team, Rachel, Jenny, and Stent moved into view and ushered the small group of marines to move into what looked like a solid wall. They walked through and the on-duty guardians took control of the marines as Blade went back to get the transport. He stopped and looked at the corpse. A female Vilkyrie, with bruises, compound factures, and a slit throat.

Gough had seen all of this on the monitor but stayed in the room with Orvessa until She saw the body. Screaming, she ran to the doorway.

"What is it, Orvessa? You need to remain hidden!"

"Not anymore! That is my head of security. What have they done to her?" She fought to open the door and ran through the medical facility to the transport, which had an open platform on the back holding the lifeless body. She was crying again, tears of vengeance and anger. Orvessa clutched the fallen guardian. Her fingers clenched over the body, desperate, searching–pleading for a reason that wasn't there." A ragged sob tore through her, shaking her frame.

"She was mine to protect," she whispers, voice splintering under the weight of failure and fury. "And I wasn't there." Turning to the marines who had been brought in, she shouted,

"Who did this! Which one of you did this?"

The marines exchanged uneasy glances, the confusion on their faces twisting something deeper inside Orvessa. They had no idea who she was–no idea what they had taken from her.

The blade stepped forward, his tone flat, indifferent.

"Sorry, Miss. She was interrogated by our second in command, accused of being a traitor. She died during her questioning. We were told to dispose of the body."

Orvessa's breath hitched–sharp, ragged. A traitor? That was a lie. A coward's excuse.

Her hand moved before she thought, snatching Blade's Pulsefire. The weight of it was solid, familiar. Her knuckles turned white around the grip.

For a fleeting second, the marines stiffened, eyes darting toward her, toward each other–recognition dawning too late.

She fired.

Two soldiers hit the ground before anyone could stop her.

The pulse of violence vanished as quickly as it had come, leaving only the sound of her uneven breath, the shaking of her fingers, the unbearable weight pressing against her ribs. The weapon fell from her grasp, clattering against the floor as she collapsed beside it–sobs swallowing the fury that had driven her only seconds ago.

Blade used the moment to amplify the tension by saying,

"Start talking. Now. I want everything–every detail from the complex. Because if you don't, you'll end up just like them."

Gough gently lifted Orvessa, cradling her as though she might break apart in his arms. He carried her through the medical area, each step slow, deliberate, shielding her from the world beyond the door. When he placed her on the sofa, her sobs did not ease. They shook her, raw and relentless.

He hesitated only for a second before kneeling beside her, closing the door behind him as if it might keep the grief from spilling further. Then, wordlessly, he reached for her hands–offering warmth, offering presence, offering all he had.

"She was my friend–my closest friend. We went to school together. She held me the night my mother died... took a shot for me during the Shard raids. And now–now she's gone, Gough. Gone."

This was a moment when words were not enough, Gough understood this, as you can never really understand another's grief. He held her in his arms and let her continue to speak between the shudders and sobbing.

"I thought she had gone undercover... like me." Her breath hitched, trembling against Gough's arms. "I will kill that bastard, Major. No more marines. Not one. I will drive them all out myself. How could they do this? How? Why?" Her fingers clenched over the fallen guardian's body, desperate, searching, pleads for a reason that didn't exist. "All she ever did was protect me. Why?"

"The reason did exist if she had found out who the traitor was and was coming to tell Orvessa." Gough calmly repeated his thought.

"There was a reason," Gough says evenly, his voice cutting through the chaos. "If she uncovered the traitor and was coming to tell you... why else would she be silenced?"

Orvessa stopped, sat up, and looked at Gough's face.

"Do you think so?"

"Yes, I do, I really do. We'll see what Blade gets from the rest of them, but not much, I think. Yet I do believe this is the reason. We need to check her clothes and tidy her up, to offer her some dignity in death."

"Don't leave me, Gough, please don't leave me yet." The sobs and tears slowed and stopped, whilst Gough continued to hold Orvessa in his arms.

Blade had split the marines up and was grilling them individually. Slowly, but surely, the picture began to emerge, and he could piece the story together. A specialist group of marines took the security head. Led by the adjutant on the orders of the major. They broke her down, piece by piece–her body, her will, her silence. The truth came only when she had nothing left to hold onto, though she never gave any information, no names ever surfaced. In the end, the adjutant and major dismissed the troops before they could hear what mattered most. By then, her shattered frame had endured far more than words could mend. Once she had spoken, there was nothing left–nothing but the quiet end that followed. Her death. Blade would have strangled the marines, but that was not the answer at the moment. I need to brief Gough and Orvessa. He mused, "*At least Orvessa was safe. How long had she been in the back of the cave? He did not really care—she was safe."*

The debrief, to Gough, revealed the horror without the detail. Orvessa sat perfectly still, and her hair had gone the purest white. Then said to Blade,

"Please ask my doctor to make the necessary arrangements. I will undress her myself in a few moments. Can your people bring her into the medical facility?"

"Yes, ma'am. Of course." With that, he left the room and quietly closed the door. Orvessa clung to Gough like a drowning woman to a piece of wood. He stroked her hair and kept her close to his warm body. She had gone cold.

"I have never needed anyone like I need you now. You must not fail me, Gough. If you do, I will fall–and I cannot fall, my love."

"I am here for you now and forever, my queen, my friend, and my love. Forever!"

They both went out and pulled the curtains around the body on the doctor's examination table. Gough took the clothes and checked them for anything inside, whilst Orvessa washed and covered her friend's body in plain white linen sheets. In the lining of the tunic, Gough found a scrap of fabric, upon which were written some characters, which he could not understand. He carefully folded the fabric and put it inside his tunic.

Chapter Twenty-One
The Puzzle Pieces

Jenny asked Gough if he had a chance to look at the book from Harbour's desk.

"Not yet, but I have not forgotten it. Did you read any of it?"

"Yes, it looked like a code book for something. So, I thought it might be useful."

"OK, I will read it and add it to the information we already have. We still have to locate the traitor, and quickly." Gough walked back into the room behind the medical facility and took out the piece of fabric and the notebook. Turning the pages, he could not make much out, as it appeared to be in a cryptic code. The fabric has symbols, but no proper words. It was not much help. He would have to disturb Orvessa. He kept turning the pages, noticing fragmented words and bits of diagrams until he saw a picture of a phoenix and this was one symbol on the fabric. *"What did it mean?"*

He typed AI search on the computer and asks for details of traditional or historical uses of a phoenix in Vilkyries' history. He found the following story:

The phoenix was once a guardian of truth, appearing only when the balance of power was threatened. Centuries ago, during a great betrayal, the phoenix burned away an entire faction of corrupt warriors, leaving behind only those loyal to the cause. Since then, the Valkyries have regarded it as a divine judge. When the phoenix returns, it judges them, and when corruption festers, it reveals the guilty.

So according to the tradition, if the phoenix returns it would identify the traitor if they were Vilkyrie. Gough then asked if the phoenix real or just a symbol, today?

Historically, the original story revolves around a real phoenix. However, over the last few hundred years, the phoenix has been as a hooded figure that arrives, and remains until the Vilkyrie, who is causing the problem, has been judged.

Orvessa same into the room and moved directly to Gough. Placing her hands on his shoulders, she asked,

"Whatcha doing?"

"Gosh, your English is getting really good. I am reading about Vilkyrie traditional and history."

"Why?"

"I found a piece of fabric in the tunic we took off the guardian and one of my team found a code book in Harbour's office. The only thing I can make out is a phoenix and writing that I can't decipher. Can you help me, please?"

Orvessa looked at the fabric and could understand it straight away.

"It's an ancient Vilkyrie scrip. We learnt it in school. No one uses it now. So, no one can read it, except a few like Rosalind and me."

"What does it say, please?"

"The phoenix will rise, its flames illuminating the darkest corners, forcing the evildoer from their lair. A soul tainted by betrayal cannot withstand its gaze, and those unworthy will be cast out, stripped of their false allegiance. They are not true Vilkyrians–only those who stand in honour will endure the trial."

"Great, what about the code book, by any chance, please?"

"Frequencies on the Valkyrie's emergency communications networks and dates written in Ploti. That is the ancient script for Christians used when the monks brought Christianity to the region. Does that help?"

"I think so."

"I need you to break off for a moment, please? We need to catch up on us! I want us to declare publicly and then we can wear the Pulsebands. I am afraid of losing you and the bands will help me. I want to be close to you, Gough, and nothing and no one is going to stand in my way. I hope you agree!" See stared at his face, trying to read his expression. All she could see was joy and happiness.

"So be it–Starsealed," says Gough, and kissed her neck. "Do we need to wear something special? To whom do we declare? Can my team attend as well?"

"Yes, everyone here and yes! Tonight, at first sunset, in the chapel, with the ancient minister of faith."

"That quick?"

"Are you not sure? Have you changed your mind?" Orvessa's hair went flame red. Gough saw the change instantly–the vivid shift in her hair's colour, a blazing signal of her emotions. *"Flame red."* His heart jolted. "*Had he made her doubt him? Had she thought, even for a second, that he wasn't certain?"*

Without hesitation, he reached for her hands, his grip firm yet careful, anchoring them both.

"Orvessa, no–listen to me," he says, his voice steady despite the rush in his pulse. "I want this. I want you. Nothing has changed. You just caught me off guard for a second, that's all."

He held her gaze, refusing to let uncertainty settle between them.

"You're right–we should declare it publicly; we should wear the Pulsebands. I just didn't expect it to be this soon, but that doesn't mean I don't want it. I do."

A pause. Then softer–almost reverent. "With every certainty I have, I do."

The fire in Orvessa's hair didn't fade–it flared, searing into him like an unspoken accusation. Gough felt his pulse hammer against his ribs. He had been careless, too caught in his own thoughts to realise how his hesitation might wound her.

"Orvessa," he says, voice quieter now, "I was wrong to say it like that. To make you wonder, even for a second. I should have never made you doubt me–not for a second. I was caught off guard, but that doesn't mean I hesitate. This promise, this bond–it matters to me. You matter to me. I won't let anything shake that."

He stepped forward, no hesitation this time, pressing his palm against her chest, right over her heartbeat. It was fast–sharp with emotion. Had he done that?

"You deserve certainty, and I should have given it to you immediately. So here it is, clearly: I want this, I want you, and nothing will change that. As God is my witness. I don't take the Lord's name in vain, ever."

Her gaze searched him, testing the truth of his words. But he didn't waver. Slowly, the flames in her hair flickered, shifting, not fully gone–but softer now, no longer a wall between them.

"I need to hear you say it again," she murmured. "Not just that you want this, but that you know what it means. That you understand."

Gough exhaled, letting the weight of the moment settle fully between them. "I do," he says, his palm still pressed to her heart, his own beating just as fiercely. He moved her hand over his heart and placed it firmly there.

Orvessa held her breath.

"I'll prove it to you–every day, and every night, in every way you need me to."

Her hair went to its normal sparkly colour. A critical moment passed.

But Gough didn't move immediately. His thumb whisked against the back of her hand, lingering in quiet reassurance–an unspoken vow, as if sealing his words with touch alone. Orvessa exhaled, slow and steady, then finally nodded.

"Then we are Starsealed, tonight" she murmurs, a hint of softness returns to her voice.

Relief flooded through him–not just because the moment had passed, but because she had chosen to trust him again. He lifted her hand, pressing a kiss to her knuckles, knowing that words had done their part, but actions would prove the rest.

Gough asked Blade to stand with him during the ceremony and Orvessa had asked the Doctor to stand by her. All part of the custom. The troops were in clean uniforms and Blade had somehow found a set of blues, the number one uniform for the Captain. Gough had polished his shoes, just like that had been taught in training. You could see Orvessa's face in his toecaps. They both had Starsealed caps over their clothes. Orvessa was in a pure white shift, no buttons, no straps. It just seemed to hold up on its own.

At sunset, they walked down the aisle in the chapel together, with Doc and Blade walking behind them.

The minister welcomed everyone, guardians, troops, and the happy couple in Vilkyrian. Then he switched to English.

"In this Starsealed chamber we meet to offer to God our two people here present, Orvessa of the house of Ancients and Gough of the house of the House of Drasken, Earth. They will bind together from this day forward in the eyes of Our Lord and the eyes of both planets. Never shall they be parted, and never to remove the Pulsebands until they day they moved into God's heaven.

"Orvessa, do you wish to be Bound to Gough?"

"Yes, I do."

"Then place the band on his right wrist, please. Gough, do you wish to be bound to Orvessa?"

"Yes, I do."

"Then place the band on her right wrist, please. Do you feel the beating of our one heart?"

"We do," they say together.

"Then you are bound for now and ever. Your marriage must occur before twelve moons."

As the bands clicked into place, a hush fell over the chapel. It wasn't silence–it was something deeper. A moment suspended in reverence, where time itself seemed to acknowledge the binding between them.

Orvessa stared at the band on her wrist, fingers grazing the edges, as if testing the reality of it. The pulse beneath it thrummed, steady, synchronising with Gough's, as if their very hearts had woven together.

Gough exhaled slowly, feeling the weight of history settle onto his shoulders. This was more than a vow–it was a link between worlds, between two destinies. He glanced at

Orvessa, and in her shimmering eyes, he saw understanding, acceptance... and something even stronger.

Then, like the first breath after a storm, she smiled. The moment broke open, and the gathered troops erupted into cheers, sealing their union in celebration, and Gough kissed Orvessa softly, but deeply. Blade and the doctor threw pieces of thin green snowgrass over their heads. Gough's smile was not just ear to ear; it covered his entire face for the first time in his life. Orvessa's face transformed, the tension melting away as warmth flooded her expression. Her eyes, shimmering like liquid gold, caught the fading sunlight's brilliance that made them seem almost ethereal. Her lips curved into a radiant smile, soft yet full of certainty, like the first bloom of dawn after a storm. A quiet glow settled in her cheeks, the faintest sparkle tracing her skin—a reflection of the deep emotion coursing through her. She wasn't just smiling; she was glowing with quiet triumph, with trust restored, with the undeniable strength of a heart that had been tested and found unwavering.

"You're shining like the stars we have sworn by, Orvessa," he murmurs, watching the glow of her expression, the quiet brilliance that transformed her features. "I don't just see joy—I see your strength, trust, something unbreakable. I swear, I will never take you and our love for granted."

The after fare in the main cavern was a feast beyond measure—tables so laden with food that they seemed to bow under the weight.

Gough leaned in, his voice warm against her ear. "What a meet cute... but no pyjamas tonight."

Chapter Twenty-Two

Now the Detective Work Starts

The entire group returned to the citadel–Vilkyries and humans alike–transported together, with Orvessa leading her guardians. Many arrived in hospital transports or carried on stretchers. The citadel's garrison of marines did not greet the returning party; Major Sarik was still bitter over Gough's acceptance and praise by Orvessa and her retinue. Both he and the adjutant were visibly displeased with the success of the assault on General Harbour's camps–and his death.

Gough's reduced troop of marines were now housed in individual rooms within the citadel. Blade's wife stayed with him, while Gough himself occupied the leader's suite with Orvessa. His Pulseband continued to draw compliments, though it felt more a distraction than an honour. The focus needed to be on finding the traitor. Yet diplomacy had become just as crucial.

Since the Starseal ceremony, Gough had been pulled into endless diplomatic meetings. Elders, commanders, and key political figures all demanded his presence, treating him less than a military commander and more as an Earth's unofficial envoy. Every time he attempted to advance the investigation into the traitor, another obligation surfaced–guardian troop movements, cultural integration strategies, Vilkyrie traditions, or discussions on his newly assumed role. His frustration grew. He was Orvessa's Starseal first, a soldier second, a strategist third–and now, unwillingly, a diplomat.

Gough had sent a message to Colonel Zarek Tarrin, asking for permission to marry, and attaching a detailed report on the battle, including casualties and outcomes. He had written personal letters to the families of the fallen–a painful duty–and recommended several of his marines for commendations. But Tarrin's response had been brief approval for the marriage, and an imperative–find the traitor.

Orvessa entered his duty room and saw him slumped behind the desk. It didn't suit him. She walked over, touched his hand gently, and said,

"Gough, I know what you're feeling. You want action, answers, justice–you hate wasting time. But diplomacy isn't just talk. It's about positioning, trust, and strategy. Push too hard, too fast, and doors will close instead of open. We don't need more enemies–we need information. So, breathe. Be patient. Let me help you navigate this before we make a move we can't take back."

Gough nodded and took a deep breath.

"You're right," he mumbles. "I know you are. But it's hard. I couldn't do this without you, my love. I just couldn't."

Orvessa left but didn't as the Pulseband tells Gough that their heart rate was up. They were both feeling the stress.

The intercept room was monitoring calls and heard a transmission from Nebulon 17 to somewhere. It was in clear and said,

"Get me out before I get caught. I have done all I can here. Evac quick. I repeat evac quick." The airwave went quiet. It was an emergency frequency not used by most of the Valkyries. The operator wrote out the message and addressed it to her superior and handed the message off. The message eventually goes to Orvessa. Who read it and sent it to Gough.

As she was dispatching the note, her communications unit sparked into life, and she was told that an inter-galaxy call was coming through. It was Colonel Zarek Tarrin.

"Colonel Tarrin, how may I be of assistance," Orvessa asks.

"Outstanding leader, I trust that you are well and safe. I have been reviewing the reports from my captain. We need to bring the perpetrators of the murder of your security minister to justice. Do you agree?"

"Yes, I do. I can run a court under Vilkyrie law, but your two marines in the main barracks can argue that they are not governed by our law, but military law."

"Just so. I propose that we setup a court martial on Nebulon 17 and that trial can recommend death for a case of murder. A court-martial on Nebulon 17 would allow us to try them under Earth law–unless you insist on Vilkyrie justice. But I'd need your cooperation to make it work. Would you agree to this, please? I will arrange everything, Judge Advocate General, military lawyers, defence, and prosecution. Also, if you agree, I will promote Gough to acting Lieutenant Colonel to ensure that Growton cannot override Gough's orders. Yes?"

"They are your troops, Colonel."

"On another matter, please. If I may take up your time. Gough has sought permission to marry and cite you as his future wife. Is that the case, please?"

"Yes, very much so. We have already taken the Starseal vows and wear Pulsebands."

"If I can arrange it, would you like him as your liaison officer permanently, with a promotion, of course? One condition, please. I want an invitation to the wedding, please, and for my plus one."

"Of course you are already on this guest list. You had better ask Gough about the promotion. I know he wants to be here, with me."

Tarrin asked for the call to be transferred to Gough, and Orvessa hung up. The smile on her face was as big as after the Starseal ceremony. She sat and waited as the Pulseband showed their heart rate increasing. Minutes passed and Gough appeared at the door.

"Honey, I have just spoken with Colonel Tarrin and she ...."

Orvessa cut across him,

"So have I, darling."

"May I come in, please?"

"That's so nice you don't take me for granted, do you?"

"No, I gave you my word and my heart. I will never take you for granted in anything, Orvessa." Gough sat down and looked at his beautiful soul-mate. The bands responded to the feeling.

"She wants a court martial. I will arrest the major and the adjutant a little later on. The Blade leader is still in prison with his team, so it's only the officers left. It sounds like Tarrin is ready to travel to Nebulon 17 soon. What did you take from your call, Orvessa?"

"Oh, so we're already shifting to formal addresses and distant decorum. The 'love' and 'darling' are gone, and we're not even married yet." She chuckles.

Gough blushed and was truly embarrassed.

"No, I mean, I think I mean. Hang it all, this is work. I still have to catch the traitor or traitors to keep you safe, my beautiful darling." He pushed his lips forward as if he would kiss her, even though they were a desk and a space apart. Orvessa laughed aloud. Walked from behind her desk and kissed him on each cheek.

"My friend, my lover, and my guardian."

Gough stood up, holding Orvessa close as he returned her kiss. He lingered for just a moment, his gaze tracing the familiar contours of her face, before exhaling softly—something unspoken, something only she would understand. Then, with a slight smile, he saluted her and said,

"I must go and arrange for some arrests. Care to have dinner with me this evening? Be my date?"

Orvessa grinned, tilting her head playfully.

"Oh, so now I'm a formal dinner guest? My love, you'd better not bring an arrest warrant to the table. Just you!"

Gough left and went to his office. Called Blade and explained the arrest and the need for the troop to be with Blade.

"Pick up the arrest warrants from my office before you leave. You have better be tooled up. Bring a secure vehicle, to be on the safe side. I will be there to sort out the remaining troops as their new Colonel. 13h00 at my office. Will you book transport for me as well, Blade?"

Gough checked the team before they entered the marine barracks. Everyone was armed, except Blade, who was holding pairs of plastic wrist cuffs. Wearing his new badges of rank, Gough strode into the complex. Chastised the guard for failure to salute and put him on an immediate charge. Proceeding to the major office with Blade, he pushed open the door and entered.

"What the hell do you think you are doing Captain," screamed the major. The adjutant shot up and moved to grab Gough.

"Pursuant to the laws governing military conduct and under the authority vested in me by the United Earth Armed Forces and allied Vilkyrie command, you are hereby ordered to detain and secure you both under the following charges:

Obstruction of Justice - Wilful interference in an ongoing investigation concerning the assassination of the Vilkyrie Security Minister.

Dereliction of Duty - Failure to uphold the ethical and operational standards expected of officers in the United Earth Armed Forces.

Suspected Treasonous Conduct - Potential collusion with external entities that pose a security risk to both Earth and Vilkyrie forces.

Involvement in the murder of a Vilkyrie national, namely the head of guardian security, and

Conduct unbecoming an officer who is serving in the United Earth Armed forces.

We are so authorised to conduct the arrests, ensuring that both individuals are placed in secure holding under the jurisdiction of the Nebulon 17 Tribunal. Upon execution of this order, I will notify Tribunal Command and submit an official statement regarding compliance with arrest protocols. Arrest them, Blade, and take them out to the prison transport." Blade placed both men in plastic wrist cuffs and pulled them tightly around their wrists. The major was swearing and threatening Gough, whilst the adjutant glared and hissed,

"Dead man walking Gough! You'll beg for a bullet before this ends... but they'll make you watch her die first."

Gough's Pulseband was unnaturally steady, not a flicker. Picking up the base intercom mic, Gough said,

"All personnel, off and on duty, to report to the mess hall immediately for a briefing by your new Lt Colonel, commanding officer." Jenny and stent walked beside Gough as they marched briskly to the mess hall.

Wearing his formal headdress barracks uniform, and a marine on either side. Gough looked the part of a new officer taking over command. The troops arrived in dribs and drabs, some uniformed others, just as they were when the message was transmitted. Everyone waited for the reaming marines to arrive.

"I am Lieutenant Colonel Gough of House of Drasken. Appointed by Colonel Tarrin of the United Earth Armed Forces to take immediate command of this detachment. I accept command. All blade leaders are to assemble after this short introduction for my orders concerning the role and readiness of this detachment. Understood? Good dismiss."

The amazed troops filed out of the mess hall, whilst the Blade leaders peeled off and sat at the dining room tables, whispering between themselves. Gough joined them, still with his two troops by his side.

"OK, the whole troop is under suspicion of aiding and abetting the two officers of murdering the Vilkyrie national, namely the head of guardian security. Every blade leader will write up their troops' activities during the past week. No one is to leave this base without my express permission. The armoury will be sealed, and no personal weapons will be allowed in the barracks. Personal can use the gym, and the mess hall, or remain in their barrack rooms. Video surveyance will be twenty-four-hour and anyone disregarding the orders will be removed to the citadel prison complex. If you were involved, tell the truth, if you weren't, tell the truth. I will be available for a private interview to all the troopers, through your request. Dismiss." No discussion, no frills, just business!"

Chapter Twenty-Three

Colonel Tarrin, Traitors and more

The pieces were in place! All the blades had submitted their reports, and some were now on minor charges, but the majority had not been involved, as could be verified by activity logs on the base activity recorder. Lawyers had arrived for the prosecution and the defence. The junior and senior member of the courts martial panel were transited in from Jupiter and Cronos 5, respectively. The arrival party was awaiting the Colonel and the judge advocate general's judge from Earth.

The luggage arrived on the logistics pad first. Everyone looked and then moved their glance to the personnel pad. Then Tarrin and Judge O'Dell of the house of Advocacy were standing on the personnel pad. Both dressed in informal clothes for the trip to Nebulon 17. Gough saluted but held his ground, knowing that formality mattered here." Orvessa and two of her guardians moved towards Tarrin and offered her a Velmari. They knew each other, and this was Nebulon 17, her planet. The judge received an offer of a handshake.

Tarrin returns Gough's salute and says, "I'll speak to you later." She glanced around, taking in Nebulon 17's skyline before turning to Orvessa.

"Feels good to be back. The planet keeps developing, but *Starlight Haven*–that place never changes." She smiles at Gough. "Twin suns over endless emerald plains, crystalline trees bending light like glass. It's home." Orvessa nodded.

"It will always be your home, Tarrin." With that, Orvessa and the arrivals were gone.

Gough was talking to Orvessa about the open transmission they had sent to them. No definitive location had been put forth on the message. Their discussion was interrupted when the intercom computer chimed in with, "Colonel Tarrin wishes to enter and speak with you both, please? Do you agree?"

"Orvessa moved and opened the door to her office. Tarrin walked in not in uniform, but wearing a flowing Veilspire made with Lumisilk, a futuristic fabric woven with micro-reactive filaments that subtly shift opacity based on ambient lighting.

"Sorry about the gown, but my one plus loves this."

Orvessa laughs and, seeing Gough's amazement, she replies.

"My younger sister always had good taste, Tarrin. How are you? It has been such a long time since you have been to Starlight Haven." Nestled within the rolling emerald plains of Nebulon 17, Starlight Haven was a breathtaking ranch that blends classic charm with futuristic elegance. Expansive fields ripple like liquid jade beneath the twin suns, bordered by towering crystalline trees that refract light into dazzling prisms at dusk.

The heart of the ranch was a sprawling villa constructed from bio-enhanced stone, its surface subtly glowing with embedded energy channels that regulate temperature and lighting. A network of gravity-assisted paddocks allows native creatures–sleek, luminescent, equine-like beings–to move freely, their hooves never quite touching the ground. Streams of iridescent water carve natural pathways, lined with sculpted flora that bloom in response to ambient sound, creating an ever-changing tapestry of colour. The nighttime sky unfurled into a vast cosmic canvas, with nebulae visible to any naked eye. It was Tarrin and Edessa's home.

Tarrin giggled and offered a Velmari to Orvessa and to Gough.

"You are almost family now, Gough. Surprised?" Tarrin and Orvessa embraced as Edessa entered the room. Gough was speechless as an almost identical woman came into view. Gough's Pulseband spiked–first at her resemblance to Orvessa, then at her disregard for protocol. Orvessa smiled at him, she understood. A little shorter than Orvessa, but physically the same, except for the hair. Edessa's hair is a striking contrast to Orvessa's, marking not only their individuality but subtle nuances in their heritage and roles. Where Orvessa's hair flows in controlled, silken waves–tempered by her disciplined life as a leader–Edessa's is wild, voluminous, cascading in thick spirals that catch the light, reflecting deep auburn undertones beneath its primary silver sheen.

Here again, unlike Orvessa, whose hair carries the weight of tradition and careful presentation, Edessa's untamed locks symbolised her freer spirit, a younger sibling not yet bound by the same duties. Genetic variance caused the additional volume and texture within their lineage. A trait that was inherited from their maternal side, where hair was considered a marker of vitality and inner strength.

Though bound by sisterhood, their hair reflects their differences: Orvessa, composed and deliberate; Edessa, untamed and radiant. She moved effortlessly towards Tarrin and kissed her on the lips, ignoring protocol.

"Tarrin, your message was so short and gave no reason for your visit. I can't believe it is because of me," she teases.

"Business first, then us, then their wedding."

Edessa asks, "May I stay or is it secret squirrel stuff?"

Tarrin, Gough, and Edessa looked at Orvessa,

"Yes, I will seal the door and prevent listening in. We can't break up the party now; it has just started. When we are finished, we'll have dinner together." It was a command, not a suggestion. Orvessa pushed a button on her desk, and a group of four Orbis Rests appeared. PolyMesh-Memory Foam Composite with kinetic, alloy frame, which adjusts to the individual's shape based on the user's biometric feedback. That allowed both lumbar and spinal alignment.

"This open transmission is worrying," Tarrin started, "No location, and names, no detail. Is it real or a hoax?"

Orvessa replies, "The operator confirmed that it is a real transmission. Yet?" A long pause occurred, which was broken by Gough's intake of breath.

"We don't know who the Traitor or traitors are. If we get another panic message, then we don't have the real traitors in custody. Thay are the murders, but they may not be traitors."

"Was this tri-angulated, Orvessa?"

"Yes, it put the call near the marine barracks, but outside, not inside."

"I have not had time to go through all of the stuff from the major's office and the adjutant's desk. I think we will know more tomorrow before the trial starts. We still have the fabric swatch and the codebook, plus the message about the phoenix." Gough's mind still churned with legal protocols, but the scent of spiced Veluta wine and Edessa's sudden appearance made it hard to focus. War and weddings, treason, and tenderness–Nebulon 17 demanded both.

Edessa's back arched, and she blurted out,

"I don't like the phoenix ever at any time. Mumbo Jumbo if you ask me."

Orvessa's fingers tightened around her glass. "The Phoenix isn't superstition, sister. It's a warning–one we ignored last time."

No one spoke for a few moments, then Tarrin broke into laughter.

"That's my lady! I love her. Have we one as far as we can? I'm hungry, bloody famished, really."

Gough was seeing a new side of "his" family. They moved to the private dining room, which he and Orvessa used regularly since they had been back at the citadel. Guardians were all around the room and one moved the chair for Orvessa to sit down, then everyone else could join her.

Dinner was Cryo-Seared Lunar Egg Medley. The eggs were flash-cooled in cryo vapor, stabilising proteins before an intense plasma sear locks in flavour. The accompanying vegetables were local dishes of stellar-grown kale and exotic aurora squash. These were vacuum-steamed in hyper-pressurised chambers, ensuring precise texture while preserving their bio-enhanced nutrients. Glasses of a pale green liquid, non-alcoholic, were served, and the discussion broke out concerning the upcoming wedding.

"So, when did you know about Gough, then Orvessa?" Tarrin asks. "I said nothing to him about my links of this world." Edessa chipped in, "Yes, do tell, all the gory details." Gough was starting to feel as if he should not be there. His Pulseband was reacting. Orvessa felt it, too.

"I met him from the transit pad, and we talked in a skiff. It was then that time it hit me, like a punch in the stomach, but of course it was my hair. I could not believe it. I couldn't control it. It was so embarrassing. Yet. So real." She paused, "I just knew it. I don't think he did, though." Both Pulsebands were going crazy, lighting up and showing the level of emotion between Orvessa and Gough.

"So, when is the wedding, Sis?"

Chapter Twenty-Four
Courts-Martial is Different, Yes Different

"Order, Order, Order," the judge banged his gavel on the solid wooden block. "Come to order, please. March in the defendants." The court room was like many others all over the galaxy. A dais at the end of the court, higher than the desks for prosecution and defence. Both areas encased in Plexi material, so that people were visible but could not throw things or attack anyone. Witnesses seated outside and a stack of military law manuals on the clerk to the court's desk.

The two defendants marched in, crisp uniform number ones, no caps, no belts, and no shoelaces. Marine guards, armed, were at the doorway and on either side of the dais. The polished metal gleaming under the sterile glow of overhead lighting. The rhythmic thud of boots against the floor as the defendants march in. Everything was metal, except the gavel and the wooden block.

The major and his captain were not standing next to each other. In a military court-martial, the separation of the major and his captain is deliberate—ensuring their individual accountability is unmistakable, preventing any suggestion of shared culpability or coordinated defence.

"Read the charges, please."

"Pursuant to the laws governing military conduct and under the authority of the United Earth Armed Forces and allied Vilkyrie command, you are hereby charged as follows:

Obstruction of Justice - Wilful interference in an ongoing investigation concerning the assassination of the Vilkyrie Security Minister.

Dereliction of Duty - Failure to uphold the ethical and operational standards expected of officers in the United Earth Armed Forces.

Suspected Treasonous Conduct - Potential collusion with external entities that pose a security risk to both Earth and Vilkyrie forces.

Involvement in the murder of a Vilkyrie national, namely the head of guardian security, and

Conduct unbecoming an officer who is serving in the United Earth Armed forces.

The judge asks, "How do you plead?"

The defence lawyer got up and says, "Not guilty for each of my clients." A murmur rippling through the assembled officers and ratings sat in the courtroom.

The prosecution lawyer got up and opened the proceedings with details of the murder and the testimony of the Blade leader who saw the beatings and eventual outcome, where he was told to bury the body.

"The defence will try to allege that Blade has some personal ill will against the officers. However, the blade leader has not been charged with any offense by either officer or has been stationed on Nebulon 17 for only five months."

The defence lawyer got up, and in a very cocky manner, started his opening remarks,

"The defence will show that this is nothing more thana travesty of justice. That Captain Gough came here to cause trouble and was arrested for his insubordination. Escaped and cause upset to the local inhabitants on a nearby moon and then suggests that these two upstanding offers are responsible for a murder they did not commit."

The prosecution presented and admitted into evidence autopsy reports, DNA from the body, and security footage from the barracks. All of which the defence had to accept. The first witness for the prosecution was, of course, the Blade leader, who had been part of the planning group to kidnap Orvessa's security chief. He explained the method of kidnap in detail and moved on to her stay in the marine barracks cell, where she was degraded by cutting her hair, merciless beatings, and eventually killed. All the assaults were led by the adjutant, z troop, and the major looking on.

Orvessa sat stoically still during this. Her face did not move. Her hair remained white, as were her knuckles. Tarrin was sitting on her left side as Gough had to remain outside as a witness. The Pulseband glowed crimson red on both Orvessa and Gough wrists, showing their own involvement and feelings in the trial.

The cross examination was of little help to the two officers, as the lawyer could not break his story and his recollections. Although he did challenge the Blade leader's reliability by pointing out his involvement in the kidnapping. Stating that a co-conspirator's testimony should be seen as inherently suspect. Yet, no actual evidence to support this assumption. The judge allowed him to return to his prison cell, rather than sit in court. The next witness was Gough's blade leader, who recounted meeting the z troop Blade and seeing the broken body on the back of a troop carrier. Here again, cross examination proved hopeless, and the defence had to accept that the remainder of the troop would agree with Blade's story and, therefore, should not be called.

Finally, Gough was called and had to explain why he had been sent to Nebulon 17 with his troop. He commented upon the trinkets that the major worn, well outside the pay grade and his normal earning capacity. He offered the court copies of his orders, which the major had refused to read. Finaly, he recounted his beating at the hands of the adjutant and some troopers.

The defence lawyer took a slow, deliberate step forward to start his cross examination was based upon the fact that Gough had planned all of this and had produced fake orders to get into the barracks and provoke the major, who rightly accused him of being a traitor and locked him up. He was going to get Gough to admit this but failed. However, the defence could not explain the written medical evidence of his beating and why it had occurred. With a tightened jaw, an impatient shuffle of documents, the lawyer returned to his desk and fell into his chair.

The judge ordered a recess for thirty minutes but did not explain why. Tarrin knocked on the judge's chamber door.

"What is happening, please?"

"Someone has kidnapped my wife and has sent me this box, with her ring finger in it. I can't go on." Tarrin looked at the box and says,

"This is not a real finger, the ring is real, but the finger is a piece of made-up prosthetic." The judge looked harder and felt the "finger."

"You are right. But what if my wife has been taken?"

"Keep your cool, listen to the facts and judge on that. I will set the wheels in motion and confirm that your wife is safe, trust me." The judge nodded and allowed Tarrin to go out and try to contact people on Earth.

The court resumed, and the defence opened its response. They called members of the remaining troops from the barracks who sworn statement where that no beatings ever took place in the barracks. However, all the marines under cross-examination, confirmed that they were nowhere near the cell blocks when the head of security was there or captain Gough.

The defence decided to put the Major on the stand. Who refused to answer questions, just kept saying that his was setup designed to discredit a senior officer, him. Eventually, the defence lawyer offered his statement that they would rest and sum up at the judge's convenience.

There was another recess. The Judge sat alone in his chambers, the weight of the proceedings pressing down on him. Sweat gathered at his temples, his fingers twitching against the desk. The air felt stifling–too thick with the unspoken consequences of every ruling, every hesitation. He was worried, not just about the case but about the fallout, the power struggles unfolding beyond the walls of the courtroom. Outside, the trial loomed like a storm he couldn't outrun. *"Was Tarrin right, was his wife safe or."* He could not think about the outcome.

Tarrin came in with a screen and communicator. The person at the other end of the comms link was his wife. Happy, smiling, sitting in their garden, drinking Earl grey tea from her favourite China teacup.

The judge reconvened and the summing up became a list of complaints from the defence, saying that they had proved their case when they had not. The prosecutor reminded the Bench that the case against the two officers was murder. The Judge allowed the panel of officers to withdraw to consider their verdict. The two junior members of the court-martial panel spoke with the judge to confirm the maximum penalty for this offence. The clerk to the court had a few papers to offer the judge if they were found guilty.

Everyone rose as the panel of officer came back into the court.

"Have you reached a verdict of you all?"

"We have your honour. Major Growton of the House Varok guilty on all counts. Adjutant Captain Hugo Moncrieff guilty on all counts." The foreperson of panel, the jury, sat down. Not a sound could be heard in the court. The clerk, then broke the silence with the previous offences' sheets for both men. The judge and the other members hear the sheets read out.

"Major Growton of the House Varok, three counts of embezzlement, four counts of theft of other officer's kit and equipment, and one charge of assault against a senior officer. Captain Hugo Moncrieff, four counts of physical violence against junior officers under his command, one year in detention for attacking a female marine officer in her room, and one count of robbery with violence."

"In view of your passed offences and the guilty verdicts put forth today, the panel of officers finds you, Major Growton of the House Varok, guilty as charged and it is punishable by death. You, Captain Hugo Moncrieff, are found guilty as charged and it is punishable by death. So ordered by firing squad on Wednesday morning at 08h00 hours. There is no right of appeal in this case. However, you may receive last rites from the priest on the planet." The judge slammed his gavel down and then left the court.

Chapter Twenty-Five

Death by Firing Squad and the comms traffic stops

Killing is never easy–even when ordered by your government in defence of the realm. The courts-martial had ruled, the sentences carried out, yet Gough couldn't shake the doubt gnawing at him. The warm Nebulon 17 breeze felt almost mocking against the weight of the moment. Gough sat behind his desk and pondered the situation. They had been found guilty on all the charges, but no one was closer to finding out the traitor. Yes, the messages had stopped, which pointed to the Major and the captain. Yet Gough was not sure. He stood up, brushed down his uniform, and placed his dress hat on his head. He was still holding the acting rank of lieutenant colonel, so he was responsible for the firing squad and its actions.

Outside in the courtyard of the barracks were the marines who would be the firing squad. Not a task anyone wanted to do. However, many things in the military are plainly difficult. A marine came up to him, saluted and said,

"*Sir, the major—he insisted you read this now.*" Gough opened, unfolded the note, and read the following lines scribbled on the paper. *"I know I have done wrong, but I am not a traitor, look for Davani."* Gough read the note in his head. Gough reread the note, jaw tightening. "*Who was Davani? No time to dwell—the execution was set. Answers would have to wait as the two officers were charged and found guilty of killing the Security Guardian, not treason.*"

The traitor was still out there, elusive. Gough adjusted his cuffs–a habit when uncertainty crept in. The officers were marched out and offered blind folds. The Major accepted the offer. The captain rejected the blindfold, his expression defiant. As he was led forward, he sneered at Gough, spat at Gough's feet, his voice a razor's edge.

"You didn't kill Harbour – you killed a shadow. Watch your back, twat." The rifles cracked before his laughter faded. The duty was completed quickly, and the bodies were taken away. Gough returned to the citadel, fingers tightening around the note. This wasn't over–not by a long shot. He found Orvessa in her office. Orvessa barely glanced up, her fingers pausing over her holoscreen.

"Your Pulseband's been buzzing like a hornet's nest. It's driving me crazy this morning."

"This," Gough placed the note on her desk.

"Where did it come from, please?"

"The major before he was shot."

"Umm, do you know who Davani is?"

"No idea, not a clue. Do you know anyone called that?"

"Hang on a moment... I think that was her given name. If it's who I think it is, you've got a real problem–she's Blade's wife."

"Didn't I see her when we arrived?"

"Yes, her and Blade went off to their home. If it is the same person. Do we need to find out quietly or make a fuss? Can you deal with it?"

"First problem is that she is one of yours, not a marine. So, I will not have any authority unless Blade is involved."

"I see. Yes, that's true. I suppose the question is why–and to what end–if she was passing secrets. It's a real bother. This is a mess, and I don't have time to deal with it. No one is helping–not the staff, not the council, and certainly not you, Gough. I have heads of state to coordinate, security to arrange, and a wedding that feels more like a political summit than a celebration. I can't deal with this right now. You'll have to take it on. Please."

"I see it now, Orvessa. This is a lot. I'll take care of this, I promise. And about the Pulseband–I didn't realise how much it was getting to you. What's really going on?" He moved around her desk and stood close to her, putting his arm on her shoulder.

"I am sorry, baby. It's just... my security guardian would have handled all of this, but she's gone. I haven't appointed a new one yet. And now–there's no one. No one stepping up, no one handling it for me." Then her voice faltered.

"What if we try something?" Gough says soberly.

"You're drowning already. You are up to your armpits in intrigue already."

"No baby, listen. You know the guardian who lost her arm? Can she do paperwork and answer the telephone and that sort of stuff? You know Syphera, that's her name. Is she up to this to help you?"

"That's a damn good idea, my love. I will check with the medics. She would be a great help. Did I use 'damn good' right?"

Gough replies,

"Zai, velam tu." (*Yes, you did.*)

She smirked. "Adorable effort, but you just told me 'Yes, you dance.' It's 'velan,' not 'velam.' Try again."

"Zai, velan tu Orvessa. Mia zareth'len valora." (*Yes, you did Orvessa. My most beautiful darling.*)

She got up and kissed him on his cheek, "More tonight, my wonderful soon to be husband."

Gough left her office, like a small child leaving a sweet shop with a bag full of candy. Colonel Tarrin walked past him. He saluted, and she asked,

"You look happy. What's happening?"

"Sorry boss. I just got a kiss from my future wife and a promise." He laughs.

"Sounds fairly good to me. I hear there was a note from the firing squad this morning. I was looking for you to give me a quick brief."

"Let's take this to my office."

Gough explains the note and Orvessa's comments and her asking him to deal with it. Tarrin agreed that it really was not a military matter if it was Blade's wife. However, she understood the situation and agreed to work it with Gough. A shadow flickered—passing without sound, despite the sealed doors and windows. The figure glided toward them, its movements deliberate, unnatural. Then it stopped.

"Its voice was sharp, reverberating in the stillness: "Look to mistakes, not treachery!" Then, as suddenly as it had appeared, it was gone. Both Tarrin and Gogh were shocked and looked at each other.

"Did you see that too, Colonel? Was it real?"

"You tell me. Did you see it too? Was it real?" A few moments of silence before Tarrin said,

"First thing, Gough, is to get Blade in with his wife, now if you can. We can put it to them and see the reaction together. Would you mind my sitting in?"

"No, colonel I would welcome it, please."

Gough sent a comms message to Blade saying,

"Have to see you and your wife immediately. In my office, in the citadel." After about thirty minutes, there was a knock on his door.

"Enter." Blade marched in, saluted and then looked hard at the Colonel. His wife walked in behind him.

"Sit down both. I believe you both know Colonel Tarrin, yes? Let me get straight to the point, please. We have a lead on the traitor, Blade, and I believe that you and your wife might help. Like you did for the setup before the raid on Scar Grimmel.

"Of course we will help, anyway we can. Don't you agree Davani?"

Gough passed the note to Blade, who read it and stopped dead. Looked hard at his wife and then said,

"Is this real, please Sir and ma'am?"

"I'm afraid that it is, Blade. From your reaction, you know nothing of this. Am I correct?"

"I don't believe it, Sir. She would not put me at risk." Colonel Tarrin then jumped in, saying,

"Well, woman to woman, I would like to ask her, please?"

"Davani, you use your maidan name still? Only between my husband and me. What is the problem, please?"

Tarrin continues, "You work in the comcen near the marine barracks, yes?"

"Yes, I have been there ever since I married Blade. It was to allow me to talk to him whenever we could. I miss him terrible when he is away."

"Would you want to put your husband in danger, please, Davani?"

"No, no, of course not. I love him so very much. He is my life. Well, him and the baby."

"The why did you send ghost messages to the Shard group and a message to say get me out of here?"

Blade broke in,

"You did what, you stupid Velkar faldora. (*Hopeless idiot.*)" His wife burst into tears. Her shoulders vibrating with her sobs.

Davani's breath hitched. "I—I only used the safety frequency. I thought... if they recalled him, I wouldn't be alone with the baby. Not somewhere in the galaxy." Floods of tears came down her face, and Blade looked hopelessly at the Colonel and the Gough.

"Ma'am, Sir. I swear I did not know. I swear it on the good book."

Tarrin calmly says,

"Well. That's it, then. We've found the source. But I don't think this is over yet. We will submit a report to the disciplinary council. It is not our decision."

Davani was placed in a holding cell, in the citadel and Blade could do nothing.

Gough and Tarrin authored the report explaining the stupidity of Davani. Confirming that she had not actually transmitted to anyone. She had used a safety frequency to get her husband home. Although they should not have made any recommendation. They did so. Fine and reduction in military rank, but no prison time. Gough stared at the report. Justice or mercy? Either way, Harbour's shadow still loomed.

Chapter Twenty-Six

Build up to and the Big Day

Syphera felt as if she had a role and was needed once more. Losing her arm had threatened mandatory retirement, a future of uncertainty and loss. Yet, when Orvessa, her leader, personally asked her to help organise the wedding, everything shifted. The request had reignited something in her–she felt alive again. She was enjoying answering comms, talking with the senior leader's staff, and getting the diagrams and layouts for arrivals, residences, and returns organised.

Every morning, she checked in with the leader and gave her updates, dates, and diary changes in terms of who had agreed and who had not. It was more like who had not been invited, as everyone wanted to comet to the wedding.

This morning, Orvessa had stayed in bed with Gough. She said that they had needed a rest together. They sat up in bed, munching on croissant and coffee. Gough had arranged for the croissant to be delivered from France in Europe, Earth. The croissants flaked apart in her hands, buttery and impossibly light–like they'd just left a Parisian bakery, not a transit pad.

"God, I needed this," Orvessa mumbles into her coffee. "You're a miracle worker, getting these croissants and we have a lie-in."

"No, tired, really tired. Do you think we could abscond and get married on the quiet somewhere, like Venus 9?"

"We could do whatever you wish, my Angel. However, you might upset a few of the eiders and some of the galactic dignitaries."

"Oh, bother them. All of them I want to be with you."

"Not to put too fine a point on it, baby. You are with me. Granted, it is your bed, and I am yours, Pulseband and all. We are together, and I love it every single second of it."

"So, you want your bed, not mine, do you?"

"No, my love, I just want you anywhere, anytime, when you want me. True!"

"Do you mean that, Gough, really?"

Gough moved closer to her in the bed. His gaze steady on Orvessa's face. He wasn't just offering reassurance; this was an oath, a declaration. His voice, usually sharp with command, softened–but held an unshakable certainty.

"Zai, veyth raloth'ka, mia zareth valora." (Yes, I truly do, my beautiful darling.)

The words landed with quiet intensity, and Orvessa's breath hitched. There was something about hearing him say it, in her language, with absolute conviction. It wasn't just a promise–it was understanding. She reached for his hand, gripping it tightly, as if grounding herself in the certainty of the man before her.

A pause stretched between them–charged, full of meaning. Then she exhaled slowly, a small, weary smile breaking through the weight of everything.

She sighed, weariness bleeding through her usual command. "I needed to hear that," she admitted–a rare concession. "Not just the words, but the way you said them." Orvessa held his gaze, searching for hesitation–but there was none. His words had landed with the unwavering certainty she needed. Relief, love, and exhaustion warred in her expression, but love won.

"Zai, veyth raloth'ka." (Yes, I truly do.)

She moved even closer, placing both hands on his naked chest, feeling the steadiness of his heartbeat. A breath, deep and grounding, and then the words came, not rushed, not uncertain, but spoken as truth.

"And I need you to know–I am yours, Gough. Entirely. Without condition, without fear. No matter what's ahead."

A pause, heavy with everything they had been through, everything yet to come. Then, her voice dropped to something almost reverent.

"You will never walk alone, again ever."

Her hands slid to his shoulders, fingers tightening as if anchoring him. A promise, one neither of them could break. They lingered, tangled in sheets and quiet promises, until Orvessa groaned.

"As much as I'd love to stay here forever, the galaxy won't run itself." She pressed a kiss to his collarbone. "And neither will our wedding. We need to get to work, my one and only. I have a dress fitting and you need to see the tailor for your blues last fit."

Gough jumped out of bed, then came back to tickle Orvessa and run his fingers through her gorgeous hair. She swooned and pulled him back for one last cuddle.

Syphera was waiting at the office door for Orvessa. The seamstress was also standing with various dressmaking bits in her hands.

"Sorry guys, but I needed a break this morning with my man."

The seamstress was an older lady and just smiled. Syphera blushed a little, and they all went into the office and got to work. Syphera's fingers hovered over the guest list. So many names, so many alliances–and one glaring absence. Davani. *"Where was Blade's wife?"*

Gough was walking along the street to the tailor when Blade caught him up.

"Sir, Sir, a moment, please."

"Yes, blade, what is it? I have an appointment."

"My wife, do you know what will happen? Who will deal with it the colonel or yourself, sir?"

"Well, it is like this. Colonel Tarrin and I have sent the report to the Vilkyrie High Command, as your wife is not a member of our force. So, although we investigated it. We don't get to decide. Sorry, that is all I can say, Blade."

"But she is not a spy, sir. Really, just a silly woman in love." Blade's voice cracked. "Sir, please–they'll execute her if High Command rules wrong!""

Gough hesitated. "Blade, I've done all I can. But I'll signal you the second I hear. We have made our report."

The tailor's shop smelled of ozone and pressed wool, its holographic mannequins flickering as Gough entered.

"Colonel Gough, your last fitting, Sir. May I say it has been a perfect pleasure to work with you on your uniform for the wedding. We are so proud that you chose us as your tailor and did not go back to Earth." The uniform was an excellent fit, and smooth so that the creases were in the right places. The jacket was not snug or pinching. *"A truly professional piece of tailoring."*

Gough complimented the tailors and their skill, paid the bill by Quors from his recently opened Quor account on Vilkyrie and asked for the Uniform to be delivered to his apartment at the citadel, no later than Friday at 10h00. He had a dress rehearsal on Friday morning for the wedding on Saturday. As Gough admired his uniform, Orvessa stood before her seamstress, the weight of her own attire settling like destiny. He stood outside of the shop, and it hit him. *"He was getting married to the most wonderful, beautiful woman in the galaxy on Saturday. Married to be with her for the rest of his life. How could one man be so lucky?"*

Orvessa's wedding gown was a masterpiece–a reflection of tradition, leadership, and the future. Embedded within the folds were delicate silver filaments, weaving ancient Vilkyrian ceremonial motifs into the modern design–a quiet homage to those who came before her. The train flowed behind her, cascading like liquid silk, but structured in layers reminiscent of Vilkyrian warrior robes, adding a regal sharpness to the elegance. It was more than decorative–it carried meaning, each layer representing a stage of duty and devotion.

Her veil was no ordinary cloth–it was a marvel of craftsmanship. Semi-transparent, infused with luminous filaments, it glowed faintly, as if woven with stardust. The effect wasn't ostentatious, but mesmerising; a celestial aura that whispered of tradition and transformation.

Everything about the attire spoke of power, grace, and legacy. She was not just a bride–she was a leader, standing at the threshold of a new chapter, uniting duty with love.

Next, she tried the dress for the rehearsal. Gough was not going to see this masterpiece until he saw her in church on Saturday. She changed into the number two dress. Her sister could not believe the designs, fashions, materials, and style. Orvessa's second wedding gown was a breathtaking fusion of tradition, authority, and futuristic elegance. The iridescent fabric shimmered, shifting between deep royal purple and midnight violet, catching the light like liquid metal. It wasn't just beautiful–it was symbolic, woven with delicate silver filaments that traced ancient Vilkyrian ceremonial motifs, honouring the legacy of those who came before her.

The split design gave the gown a commanding presence, allowing for both regal movement and practicality. The structured layers, reminiscent of Vilkyrian warrior robes, cascaded behind her in a flowing train, each fold representing duty, devotion, and the weight of leadership she carried.

Her veil was no ordinary cloth–it was a marvel of craftsmanship. Semi-transparent, infused with luminous filaments, it glowed faintly, as if woven with stardust.

Edessa stepped back, pressing a hand to her mouth as her eyes shimmered with emotion. For a long moment, she couldn't speak–only stare.

"Orvessa... I–" She exhaled sharply, shaking her head, as if words weren't enough. Then, her voice came, soft at first but growing stronger.

"I have never seen you like this. Not just beautiful–commanding. Like you were never meant to stand beside power, but to be power itself." She gestured at the gown, at the shimmering glow of the veil that framed Orvessa like stardust.

"You look like everything you were meant to be. Like our ancestors would rise just to bow to you. Like the universe itself had to stop and stare. I can't–" Her voice caught, breaking as the weight of it hit her. And then, the laughter spilled through the tears–too much emotion, too much love. She wiped at her face, shaking her head.

"Oth mia valora'len sathai, tu velar az zareth'kai." (Oh, my darling sister, you look like a radiant queen.)

Orvessa laughed through the tears, shaking her head.

"Look at us–a mess."

But what a beautiful mess it was. Edessa touched her sister's face gently and then touched the train on her shoulders.

"If this is the standby dress, Gough will go crazy. Are you sure it is him and only him?"

Orvessa responded quietly with,

"Let me ask you something, sister. How did you feel about Tarrin and you're getting married? Is she the right one for you? Would you change her for another?"

"No, I would not no, no, never. She is my soul mate, my kindred spirit. I am so lucky to have found her and have the relationship we have."

"Thought so. Exactly. That's how I feel about Gough. He is my fate, my future–and I would choose him, always, and he chose me."

Friday came, and Gough was pacing up and down, waiting for the uniform to arrive. He did not have a best man as this was not part of the tradition on Nebulon 17. Tarrin stood by him at the church and tried to calm him down. He was all over the place. His Pulseband was on the verge of short out.

The church layout was vastly different to Earth. People came into the church from either side, not at the back. There was one aisle in the middle, and The bride came in from the left, whilst the groom came in from the right. No organ or piano, just piped music. An altar and kneelers in-front of the cross. Plain wood, oak and polished. The minister was in a black smock for the practice, save for his minister's white stole.

Gough could not take his eye from Orvessa and her dress. He was speechless and in total awe of Orvessa's beauty, grace, and style. The practice went off, and the couple were not allowed to see each other until Saturday at ten o'clock for the wedding itself. Both found this difficult, but they knew it would be worth it.

Saturday morning came, and Gough was very carefully shaving. He did not want to cut himself. Had he really thought about it, he could have used an Andie, who would not cut him. He drank one small coffee from his Nespresso machine, which went everywhere with him, and then sat waiting to get dressed and arrive early at the church. There was a knock at his door.

"Sir, I wanted to express my gratitude. Davani has been invited to the wedding, and I cannot thank you enough. Best wishes for your day."

"I would love to say it was because of me. However, I know it was not. Enjoy yourselves and thank you for your support on our operation together. You're a good man, Blade. Enjoy the day with her."

The local computer told it was time to get dressed and move to the transit pad. "Don't forget your headdress, Sir." His polished shoes gleamed, the toe caps reflecting the soft light. His uniform was crisp–pressed cotton shirt, corps tie neatly aligned. The last thing he attached was his ceremonial sword. He had permission to take it through the transit pad.

He stood in the church looking at all the dignitaries and heads of state, here for his wedding. He could have never believed it. As he turned around, he saw his mum and dad in the front row of pews. He had asked them to attend, but they said they were not sure. Yet here they were. Tarrin says,

"Your folks look happy."

Gough's reply was simple, "Thank you, Colonel."

Standing there, surrounded by dignitaries, heads of state, and family, the weight of the moment settled over Gough. This wasn't just a ceremony–it was a promise, a new era. And in mere moments, she would step into it beside him. The music started up as Orvessa moved towards the centre of the church. The minister was wearing his Quantum Apostle Attire - Valkyrie Ceremonial Robes. Made from Valkyrie Battle Silk. A nano-weave originally designed for officers' dress uniforms, now ceremonial. Light as gauze but with the tensile strength of starship hull plating. The minister's robes shimmered, fractal hems dissolving into Valkyrie flight paths–a living map of battles turned blessings.

The music built up to a crescendo as Orvessa came into view. Gasps could be heard from the gathered crowd. Her gown, the iridescent fabric shimmering and shifting between a deep royal purple and midnight violet as it was caught by the light. It symbolised her balance between wisdom, authority, leadership, and femininity. Embedded within the folds of the dress were delicate silver filaments, weaving ancient Vilkyrian ceremonial motifs into a modern design. She moved with the grace and poise of a national leader. Yet, her eyes were on Gough, no one else. She acknowledges no one except him.

As the final notes of the music faded into reverent silence, Gough and Orvessa stood side by side, facing the altar. Gough couldn't help himself. His eyes flicked to her–not just at the gown, not at the shimmering silver filaments, but at her. She was looking at him. Only him.

The weight of everything settled into his chest. The battles fought, the worlds changed, the duty accepted–and yet, here, standing before him, was the only future he had ever truly chosen.

"Zai, mia valora'len, tu velar az mia zareth'kai. Raloth'ka, zareth, valora. Mia thal'kai, mia thal'len, mia thal'vesh–tu mia, raloth'ka." Yes, my most beloved, you look like my radiant queen. I vow. I see. I cherish. My heart, my soul, my future–you are mine, forever.

A single tear escaped–rolling down Orvessa's cheek, catching the glow of her iridescent veil. Gough reached out, his white-gloved fingers moving with infinite care, brushing it away. No makeup. No embellishment. Just the tear.

The minister started the service in English, as many would not understand Vilkyrian.

"By the grace of the Stars and the Light of Earth's traditions, we bind these souls. Marriage is one of life's glorious moments–a time of solemn commitment, as well as good wishes, feasting, and joy. St John tells us how Jesus shared in such an occasion at Cana and gave there a sign of new beginnings as he turned water into wine. God intends marriage to be a creative relationship, as His blessing enables spouses to love and support each other in good times and in bad, and to share in the care and upbringing of children." He paused and then looked at the couple.

"As tradition dictates, you are asked to pledge your love for each other in your own words. This is your moment to speak from the heart, to honour the bond you share, and to declare your commitment before all who stand witness. Orvessa, you are invited to begin, followed by Gough."

"I, Orvessa Sandri Que, take Gough of the House of Drasken as my lawful and wedded husband. I make this pledge freely, without hesitation or doubt. Before God, this congregation, and my beloved Gough, I vow my love and devotion."

"I, Gough Ivor William of the House of Drasken, honour the bond between Orvessa and me. I choose her now and forever. For as long as we live in harmony and love. I make this pledge before this congregation and my one and only Orvessa. So, help me God."

Gough mother, Edessa, and Tarrin were now in floods of tears, as were many of the dignitaries in the church. The minister then asked for prayers.

"Oth raloth'ka, keeper of the stars and guardian of all paths, we stand before You in witness of a sacred union. Bless Orvessa and Gough as they weave their lives together, bound not only by love but by honour, duty, and the legacy of those who came before them. May their hearts beat as one, their souls entwined in the eternal dance of devotion. Let their love be as steadfast as the Vilkyrian moons, unwavering through the tides of time. May their words be truth, their hands be strength, and their journey be guided by wisdom.

As they pledge themselves before You and this congregation, may their bond be written among the stars, a testament to love that endures beyond the limits of fate. Bless them, now and forevermore.

Zai raloth'ka, veyth valora, veyth thal'kai. So, it is spoken, so it shall be." (Yes, great guardian, we see love, we see devotion. So, it is spoken, so it shall be.)

"May the Lord go before you, guiding your steps in love and unity. May His light shine upon your marriage, filling your days with joy and understanding. May your home be a place of peace, your hearts forever bound in faith and devotion. Go forth in love, strengthened by His grace, and may your union be blessed now and always.

In the name of the Father, the Son, and the Holy Spirit. Amen

They were married. Bound in faith, love, and the promise of forever. Together, they walked down the aisle, leading the way toward the wedding breakfast ahead of the congregation. Yet, as they stepped forward, Gough paused–unable to resist.

Before they could leave the aisle, he turned to Orvessa, cupping her face gently, and kissed her.

A ripple of applause spread through the church, soft at first, then growing–a shared moment of joy from those who had witnessed their vows. As applause swelled, Gough's eyes flicked to Blade in the crowd–his wife's hand clutched tight. Davani's name hung unspoken between them. Some laughed, others cheered, but all felt the weight of what had just begun.

Orvessa smiles against his lips, whispering,

"You couldn't wait, could you?"

Gough chuckles, his forehead resting against hers for just a second longer.

"Not a chance."

Gough had found his love, his life, and himself–anchored in the embrace of one woman, Orvessa, and in the galaxy he now called home.

DYING IS NOT SO FINAL:

THE SEYLIRA WAR

(Book II)

Chapter Twenty-Six
The Honeymoon

Not everyone on Nebulon 17 was happy about an earthling marrying their leader, but this did not deter Orvessa and Gough from planning their honeymoon.

"Where do you want to go, honey?" Gough asked, the holographic map of the galaxy shimmering between them.

"Oh, I don't know the galaxy as well as you do, sweetness," Orvessa replied, her silvery eyes twinkling. "Tell me where you would like to go – or we could try Regal 7. It's a beautiful honeymoon spot. Let's go there."

"You sound like you've been there before."

"Yes, when Tarrin and Edessa got together."

"Oh."

"Problem?"

"Not really. I just thought we could find somewhere of our own. You know what I mean. *'Zhen'kai?'* Angel."

"*Valkari,* to please me, please Gough."

"I can refuse you nothing, my precious one. Where is this place?"

"Regal 7 is in the Dravh'Nar galaxy – 'the place where light was exiled.' Despite the name, it's a beautiful world of purple seas, hidden beaches, and private villas. You'll love it."

"As long as we're together, I will love anywhere. Do we need guards, or just your marine husband?"

"Both, baby. One small thing: there are no transit pads, simply good old-fashioned spy craft. We'll fly there in a Valkyrie stealth Starbird." Orvessa laughed. "Do you get space sick?"

"I don't remember the last time I flew in one of those things – I can't remember if I do."

The door to the office swished open and Tarrin entered. Both Orvessa and Gough looked up and said in unison, "Problem?"

"Yes, Orvessa, there is. A marine patrol has captured a small group of rebels who have been preaching dissent – because of my acting Colonel here."

"Don't you mean my husband and marine liaison officer to my court?" she teased, a sly smile on her face.

"Sorry – that thing," Tarrin said, pointing to Gough as she sat down and fixed Orvessa with a long, hard stare. Gough's relaxed posture straightened almost imperceptibly.

"How many? And what were they armed with?" he asked, his voice shedding its honeymoon softness for a tone Blade would have recognised instantly.

"Are you really going to go off-world for your honeymoon with all this trouble brewing, Orvessa?" Tarrin asked.

"Yes – and you and Edessa are both coming for the second week. That is an order from your leader and your partner's sister. Is that clear?"

"Oh, are you sure? Has Gough agreed to this?"

"He is my man, and he has agreed to please me, *Valkari*. Besides, we will be on our honeymoon – he can't command the troops, so you are required. I can't have him spending time on work when we are on our honeymoon. Can you imagine if he were hurt?" Orvessa's voice dropped to a whisper. "*Dying is not so final* – but loving you, Gough, feels eternal."

Tarrin sighed, finally conceding. "Fine. A honeymoon. But just remember, trouble has a way of following you two." She paused. "Actually, trouble doesn't follow you, Orvessa. It waits for you to arrive. I'll have the guards on high alert." She turned to leave, pausing at the door. "And Gough? Pack your sidearm."

Chapter Twenty-Seven
Regal 7

The Starbird spy craft was an interesting piece of equipment that Gough had never seen before. The device appeared metallic but functioned as a living being that expanded when used. Its light thruster engines were incorporated into the hull, and it seemed to relate to its pilot, responding to spoken Vilkyrian phrases. The control panel was simpler than Gough expected – a screen, a wheel, and glowing veins that pulsed with the pilot's emotions: blue in peace, amber or red in tension.

Saying *"Kitamar"* activated a protective shield and made the ship invisible. Gough felt the weaponry on board was sufficient to handle any attack should one occur.

They landed on Regal 7. With no requirement to register, Orvessa and he, along with a platoon of her personal guards, were whisked along a dusty track to a magnificent villa.

The villa was built into the gentle curve of a crystalline cliff, overlooking an ocean of shimmering purple water that glowed softly under the planet's twin moons. An invisible protective shield-maintained quietness and peace.

"Well, at least for the first week," Gough thought. The Infinity Lagoon was a private swimming space that flowed into the distant ocean view, filtered through Regal 7's moonstone system, which produced soft illumination and therapeutic effects.

Upon their arrival, they discovered the main room offered a complete ocean view through its sunken lounge area, memory-reactive lighting, and a fireplace with a temperature-controlled flame. The bedroom combined music and visual displays, with heart rate-controlled background sounds and walls that displayed their collective memories.

Orvessa was thinking of their wedding, and a full-splendour image of the ceremony appeared on the wall.

The guards placed their bags inside before departing. The door closed softly after them. The villa produced a soft humming noise while the purple sea created a whispering sound in the distance. Gough embraced Orvessa before delivering a gentle kiss to her lips, their breaths mingling in the quiet.

"I love you, Orvessa," he said. "In you, I have found everything I have ever wanted, dreamed of, or cared for. I am grateful for our marriage because it has brought me the happiness of a complete life."

She replied, "I already told you that my grandmother named it the Zyphir's Call. Yet today we call it the Seylira bond. It is reinforced by our Pulsebands. The biological link between Vilkyrians enables them to select their perfect match during specific moments in particular locations. You are my love, my lover, and my friend, Gough. You are my perfect match."

Different coloured Pulsebands appeared in the air until they united into a single radiant beam of light. Now was the moment, and they sank onto the huge bed. The villa was silent, save for the rhythmic breath of the sea and the soft glow of the Pulsebands still shimmering on their wrists. Gough cradled Orvessa in his arms, feeling her warmth and the unexplainable, eternal bond between them.

She placed her hand gently on his chest, over the beat of his heart.

She whispered, "This is the musical design of the Seylira bond. Our love exists in perfect harmony with the values we both hold dear. Spirit to spirit. Destiny to destiny."

Gough closed his eyes. The villa responded – its walls dimming to a soft indigo as the ceiling opened to reveal the stars above. The two moons illuminated their bodies with silver light while the ocean produced a deep, resonant sound.

He spoke both to the universe that had united them and directly to her. "I was a soldier. A wanderer. A man of duty. You have become my safe haven, Orvessa. If the Creator of stars had written my life story, he would have written it to end in this exact verse."

Orvessa smiled through her tears, which glimmered like morning sunlight. "The Vilkyrian people believe that souls select their echoes before they enter the world. You are my echo, Gough. My answer to the Zyphir's Call."

The two stayed still, listening to the sounds that surrounded them. The villa generated a soft musical sequence that seemed to synchronise with their heartbeats. A soft bell sounded from the distant Covenant Garden – a signal that a new memory seed had bloomed.

Orvessa turned her face toward his and spoke softly. "We should bury this night deep in the earth, where it will remain forever."

So, they did. Not with hands, but with hearts. The villa remained still in complete silence. Their physical closeness and the deepening of their spiritual bond made their connection stronger than ever.

Chapter Twenty-Eight

Week Two

They had spent the first week going to the wellness spa, swimming, and making love at various times during the day and night. Gough had asked the villa about the line down the middle of the building. The villa explained that it allowed the house to exist in both day and night at the same time – simply walk from one side to the other or remain in one zone to experience a full cycle of day or night. That had come as a surprise, but they used it to extend nighttime and daytime as they wished.

Edessa and Tarrin arrived at the doorway and rang the entry button. The door slid open and Edessa walked in without waiting to be invited.

"Sis, where are you? Are you decent or doing rude things with your man?" she cried out. Tarrin set the bags down and left the Andie to deal with them. Both women were dressed in cool, flowing robes of matching colours, their Pulsebands glowing with the same colour and intensity.

Orvessa appeared in a small but beautifully designed bikini – bio-silk woven from Regal 7's native moonvine, a fabric that shimmered with her emotional state. When calm, it glowed gently; when passionate, it pulsed with light. To her sister, it seemed to mirror her very mood. The bikini was high-cut with wraparound side ties that resembled the wings of a Starbird, adjusting automatically to her movement and offering both comfort and allure. Gough followed her into the vestibule in his Hydra Flow swimmers. They stood together and looked Tarrin and Edessa up and down, slowly, as though they could scarcely believe it was already time for them to arrive.

"Join us at the infinity lagoon. We're about to have a snack and something to drink. Slip into something comfortable." The two women knew the layout well, having been there before, and quickly joined them at the poolside.

Edessa wore a translucent, heat-reactive fabric woven from Regal 7's volcanic silk vines. It clung to her like firelight on water, shifting in crimson waves with her movements and forming a beautiful wave pattern as she walked. The back of the bottoms displayed a strong micro-cut pattern, designed to enhance self-assurance and leadership presence. She wore it like a declaration:

"I am visible. I am in control. I fear nothing and no one."

Tarrin, by contrast, wore a one-piece of Shadowlace mesh – a semi-sheer fabric that moulded to her body and used memory-based responses to sense her emotional state. The colour darkened when she was lost in thought and showed a faint glow when she became active. A deep V-shaped neckline hinted at vulnerability, while the structured shoulder design projected authority and composure. A dramatic open back featured a single vertical glyph-thread running down her spine, etched with the Vilkyrian word *"Seylira"* – a symbol of her sacred bond and chosen destiny with Edessa.

Their preferred sunbeds were Solara Drifts – floating loungers with a crescent design that used micro-gravity stabilisers and magnetic levitation pads to stay suspended in the air or above the water. The surface adapted gently to body shape, automatically adjusting its firmness according to both position and emotional state. The system collected emotional data from users at rest and during intimate moments, allowing them to relive memories through touch-sensitive vibrations and light-based effects. When used together, the beds harmonised their light and music settings for shared relaxation.

The afternoon sun was pleasantly warm. An Andie arrived with trays of snacks and a cream-coloured liquid – Lunavella. A creamy vanilla base with hints of spiced orchid and a whisper of mint. Among the Vilkyrian people, the faint shimmer it left on the lips was a sign of romantic interest.

Edessa wanted to know everything about the first week.

"OK, Sis – give me the full up and down!"

“I suppose, my dearest sister, the best way to describe it is this: I love this man more than I have ever loved anyone or anything in my entire life. He truly is my Seylira bond, my partner, and my soul.” Gough, for his part, blushed a deep red and took another long sip of his Lunavella. Tarrin let out a slow, deep sigh, then turned her attention to the blushing Gough.

“You’ve got yourself a real woman there, my friend – and my family. Look after her, or you will deal with me.” She smiled as she said it. Yet Gough knew she was serious.

Chapter Twenty-Nine
Dinner and Details

They dressed for dinner – al fresco, in reduced light but not darkness. Posh frocks for the women and chino slacks for Gough. Candles lit the table, and an interesting sculpture occupied the centre as a display piece. It was a crystal orchid glowing with shifting blues, purples, and golds, a quantum spark pulsing at its heart and releasing a mist of light that vanished before touching the table. A real talking point.

Dinner was exquisitely ordinary. Gough had ordered burgers in seed buns with lettuce, onion, tomatoes, and a large dollop of Heidelburg cream mayonnaise.

"What is this stuff?" Edessa asked.

"Just eat it, passion – you'll love it," Tarrin responded. "Earth food. Not a roast, but filling."

Talk eventually turned to work when Gough asked, "How are things back on Nebulon 17?"

"Fine, on the whole," Tarrin replied. "The real problem appears to be coming from this quadrant – the Varkalon Dominion, the rulers of this region. They have been quiet for many years but seem to have awoken since you two came here for your honeymoon." At the mention of the Varkalon, the centrepiece's blues and purples flashed to a sudden, sharp red for just a second before settling back – reflecting the shift in the emotional field at the table. A silent alarm bell, perhaps.

Gough paused, a burger halfway to his mouth. "Awoken how? Increased patrols? Or something else?"

Orvessa said quietly, "They always play up after a few years of silence. We have always managed to beat them in combat. Yet you are right to mention it, Tarrin – thank you. Don't worry about them, honey. We can deal with this when we get back."

Gough set his burger down and seemed wistful. Orvessa touched his arm and glanced at her Pulseband. It was the same colour as Gough's. Both were a pale red.

Dinner continued, but with much less banter, and a general feeling of foreboding settled over the remainder of the meal. Even the Andie sensed it and asked, "Madam, Sir – is anything wrong with the meal or my service?"

"No, thank you – that will be all," Orvessa said. "Please clear up once we retire to the lounging room."

"As you wish, Madam. It is always a pleasure to serve."

Chapter Thirty
Varkalon Dominion

Varkalon is a scarred world, its jagged volcanoes forever hidden beneath ash storms that drift like mourning veils. One Earth mission put it bluntly: *"What a dump. Even cockroaches file complaints."* The planet endures harsh extremes – scorching heat by day, freezing winds by night. The air is breathable only through filtration masks, and even the natives bear scars from exposure. Varkalon Dominion is not a place of life. It is, however, a crucible of survival. Its cities are built into cliff faces and crater rims, more bunker than home. Towers rise like spears, and streets are paved with alloy and bone.

The population, known as the Synthborne, are a grim fusion of organic and synthetic parts – humanoid in shape, but any semblance of humanity ends there. They stand tall, an elegant fusion of flesh and alloy. From a distance, they might pass for human, but up close the illusion fractures. Patches of synthetic dermal mesh stretch across organic muscle, shimmering faintly with embedded data veins. Where flesh remains, it is pale, scarred, and marked by surgical integration and battle wounds. Most strikingly, each Synthborne carries one human eye alongside a glowing lens that shifts colour according to emotional state and tactical input. Yet the Synthborne retains a soul. It dreams. It mourns. It loves. Its emotions, however, are filtered through layers of algorithm.

These ruthless expansionists coveted one thing above all else: the biological link within the Vilkyrians – the Seylira. They believed it would enhance their fighting capability and that it could be extracted from the Amazonian race and transplanted into their own being.

Long ago, the Varkalon home world had been lush and vibrant, ruled by a council of philosopher-kings who believed in balance and cosmic harmony. Then came the Shatterfall – fragments of a dying star raining across the planet, poisoning the soil and warping the minds of its people. It left Varkalon the last place in the universe anyone would choose to survive.

Under their leader Vorrak the Unyielding, the Dominion had entered a new phase. No longer content with conquest, they now sought purification. Worlds that resisted were not enslaved. They were simply erased. His famous maxim: *"Mercy is the lie of the weak. Strength is the only truth."*

Vorrak turned to his number three. They never used even numbers.

"Are we ready to launch an attack on Nebulon 17 yet?"

"In a few weeks, Lord Vorrak – in a few weeks."

"How many, cur? Five? Three? Perhaps sooner?"

"Our transport platforms are being upgraded to accommodate the larger numbers and the necessary equipment. The Shards are also attempting to regroup in support of our attack, but their trans-pads are not compatible with our platforms. Our local operatives are preparing new installation sites. Once that is complete, we will be ready, Lord Vorrak."

"And the Virexion Lance – have we developed it fully?" Vorrak's voice dropped to something quieter and more dangerous. "A Vilkyrian name. Perfect for blowing Vilkyrian souls to dust. It does not fall. It hunts. Once launched, it glides with intelligent pathing, evading defences and selecting impact points with surgical cruelty – no sound, no heat trail. It creates only a faint ripple in space-time, detectable mere seconds before impact."

He paused, savouring the thought.

"Yes. Just what the Vilkyrians deserve. I do not seek peace with them. We seek to harvest their essence – to graft soul onto our steel."

Vorrak laughed, amused by his own savagery.

Chapter Thirty-One
Back to The Grind

Gough sat in his office, just down from Orvessa's suite, and looked at his in-tray. Blade tapped on the door.

"Enter."

"Boss, you're back. Can you spare me a few minutes? We need to talk about the training situation in the garrison."

"Go ahead."

"It's the garrison changeover. The new men won't have proper training facilities – no assault course, nothing adequate. What can we do?"

"Not your problem, old son."

Blade stiffened. "What do you mean, Boss? Training is my problem. Or has my post been changed?"

Gough leaned back. "No, your post hasn't changed. You have. You're being posted back to Earth, accompanied by Davini and your toddler."

Blade froze. "But Sir – Davini – after everything..."

"You've been selected for officer training. My recommendation. You, Davini, and the child will be accommodated on Earth during your course. Paid move. Full clearance. No more whispers. No more shadows."

Blade's voice cracked. "Sir, they called her a traitor."

"I called her loyal. That's the difference. Go tell your wife the good news. In twelve or thirteen months, your team will be calling you 'Sir.'"

Blade saluted, eyes wet but proud. "Thank you, Sir."

He turned and marched out, the weight of accusation finally lifting behind him.

***

Blade stood outside their quarters, the door half-open, the soft hum of the house systems echoing in the hallway. He hesitated – not because he feared her reaction, but because the weight of the past still clung to his shoulders.

Inside, Davini was rocking the little one, her eyes tired but alert. She looked up as he entered, her expression unreadable.

"You're back," she said softly.

"I am," Blade replied, stepping closer. "And I've got news."

She raised an eyebrow. "Good or bad?"

He knelt beside her, resting a hand on the baby's blanket. "We're going home. Earth. All three of us."

Davini blinked. "What?"

"You've been cleared. Fully. Gough made it official. I've been selected for officer training. We'll be housed on Earth during the course. Paid move. No more whispers. No more suspicion."

Her lips trembled. "They called me a traitor."

"I know," Blade said, his voice thick. "But the boss didn't. He saw the truth. And now he's giving us our own future."

Davini looked down at the child playing with her fingers, then back at Blade. "Do you believe it?"

"I do. For the first time in a long time, I do."

She reached out and touched his face. "Then let's pack. Let's go where our child can grow without shadows."

Blade nodded, holding back tears. "Where you can be seen for who you are – not what they feared."

The baby cooed softly, and the house lights dimmed in response, casting a warm glow over the small family.

***

The next knock on Gough's door was Colonel Tarrin. He stood up.

"Sit down. Have you got a minute?"

"Of course. How may I be of assistance?"

"We never really cleared out the rebels on that moon, did we? We never properly trained the marines here for close combat, and we've never run invasion drills. Have we?"

"No, Colonel – but do we need to?"

"Yes. Let's talk strategy and geopolitics, shall we? This planet sits central to the route from Diego 9 to Earth. Correct?"

"Yes – because it cuts out Varkalon."

"And what if Varkalon took this planet? What would that do to the supply routes to Diego and beyond?"

"Simply put – they would stop functioning entirely. People would be cut off from Earth and from every alliance we currently hold. So, not good."

"Worse than that. The Vilkyrians are Amazons, but they haven't had to fight for a great many years. We lack adequate planetary defences and the machinery to repel a full invasion. So what can you and I do about it, Gough?"

Gough was quiet for a moment. "You're not describing a possibility. You're describing a worst-case scenario that we are completely unprepared for."

"Think weeks rather than months," Tarrin replied sombrely.

Chapter Thirty-Two
Is There a Time for Every Purpose?

Gough got Davini, their child, and Blade off the planet within four days. He appointed Rachel as the new Blade Leader and Arthur as the Marine Regimental Sergeant Major.

The team was summoned to a briefing with Orvessa, Colonel Tarrin – now Security Leader for Nebulon 17 – and Gough. Tarrin presented all necessary information before opening the floor to questions. Orvessa sat completely still, observing everyone at the table. Some looked so young, so untested by conflict or battle.

"I will activate the war defence plan. Everyone will be called up for military service, training, and combat. Major, assist with palace guard training. Security Leader, coordinate with Colonel Tarrin to prepare both the palace guard and my personal bodyguard. Sergeant Major, identify potential ground defence battery locations. Blade Leader – Gough needs a quick reaction unit positioned at the palace as a rapid deployment point. Questions?"

There were none. The meeting ended.

Gough continued to watch his wife and leader as the room emptied. Orvessa had responded with both speed and force, drawing on expertise honed through previous encounters. She hadn't trained on Earth, but she didn't need to. Her instincts surpassed any formal training. The teachings of her faith and her deep commitment to her people went far beyond the requirements of her official role. She stood ready for what was coming – and she could sense it.

The training yard fell silent, morning sunlight casting long shadows across the stone floor. Rachel positioned herself at the front, her new insignia catching the light. Those nearest her showed a mixture of curiosity and doubt. Blade had been their anchor. Now, she was the storm.

She stepped forward, her voice composed and certain. "I am here to carry on what Blade started – to honour his work and ensure it continues. The three core values of the Marine Corps are discipline, readiness, and loyalty. *Semper Fi.* The training ahead will test you as never before. You will reach speeds you never imagined possible. We will be the first to answer the call when it comes."

No one spoke. Heads nodded. The transformation had already begun.

While the military forces readied themselves, Orvessa stood alone beneath the silverleaf tree, its leaves dancing softly in the wind. She held her Pulseband, watching its soft red glow flicker. Gough approached carefully, not wanting to break her silence – but he could not help himself.

"You were brilliant in the briefing."

She didn't look up. "I noticed fear in their eyes – youth, inexperience. But also resolve."

Gough sat beside her. "You gave them purpose."

Orvessa turned to him, her voice barely above a whisper. "Is there time for every purpose, Gough? Time to love, time to lead, time to fight?"

He reached for her hand. "There is. And you're living all of them."

Her expression carried the weight of the day's countless decisions.

Everyone was now in fatigues, the team racing against a silent clock. Each hour slipped away like atmosphere from a compromised hull. Gun emplacements were discussed and built at breakneck speed, tests repeated multiple times. Ammunition dumps were established – accessible yet safely distanced from the buildings and the palace. Pulse cannons were mounted along the walls surrounding the palace grounds.

The twin suns of Nebulon 17 hung low, casting golden light across the marble spires of the capital. The atmosphere grew heavy with expectation. All focus narrowed to preparation, to breaking old procedure, to the single goal of defence. Temple bells and market melodies fell silent as palace guards marched in unison and ships returning from outer sectors rumbled their deep warnings across the sky.

From the high balcony of the Citadel of Echoes, Orvessa observed the city she had dedicated herself to defend. The streets were alive with movement – recruits marching in formation, elders deep in prayer, engineers working tirelessly to reinforce the shield grid against aerial bombardment. Nebulon 17 was no longer simply a home. It was a fortress – a sanctuary and a target.

Deep beneath the city, the war room and bug-out bunker served as both survival sanctuary and strategic nerve centre, its circular layout integrating holographic displays, memory crystal interfaces, and Pulseband-operated technology. *Would they be ready in time? Is there time for every purpose under heaven?* Orvessa thought.

The last piece fell into place when the trans-pads notified both the Colonel and the Major that the 83rd Brigade were moving into position on the planet to provide additional support. Tarrin's message had got through.

What Tarrin did not yet know was that she would not be allowed to stay and fight.

Chapter Thirty-Three

The Hell of War is the Waiting

Gough sat on a chair and watched Orvessa sleeping. They were settled in the leader's bedroom of the bug-out bunker. The smell was distinctive – he had experienced it so many times in training and on exercise. She was beautiful, her hair glowing softly in the darkness. He could not understand how any one man could be so lucky. Yet it was true: Orvessa was his wife and his soul mate. She shifted in her sleep, and he was grateful for whatever blessing allowed her to rest. Life had been chaotic, and it would not change anytime soon.

Before the communications blackout, Colonel Tarrin had been called back to Earth to advise and help coordinate the response. It had been a difficult goodbye for everyone. Edessa, unwilling to leave her sister, had chosen not to travel to Earth even though she could have. Orvessa was losing her military expert, and Gough was losing his mentor.

Gough had been a substantive Lieutenant Colonel but was now acting as a full Colonel, working alongside the Vilkyrian security team and the marines positioned around the planet. The weight of command sat uncomfortably without Blade beside him or Tarrin at his back. He had wanted to go into battle with Arthur and Rachel. But here he was.

Orvessa called his name in her sleep. He moved to the bedside, touched her arm, and she drew it to her chest and held on tightly. He had no choice but to sit beside her and let her keep hold. He wanted her to rest as peacefully as possible.

Gough checked his watch. 05:15. He replaced the cover and took a long look at Orvessa.

Then it hit.

The first bombing raids from outer space struck the palace areas. The ground shuddered beneath a cacophony of sound. Orvessa jolted awake and Gough held her in his arms until she was fully with him.

"I must go, angel. Please stay here until I know what we're dealing with – then we'll assess together. You're safe here." He moved quickly towards the door and heard her voice behind him:

"Zha'reth valen, en'kai toran." Hold safety. Return to me.

But he was already through the door, rushing past the sleeping rooms toward the command centre.

He scanned the view screens to survey the damage. The pulse cannons had brought down several spacecraft, though the debris had caused additional destruction to buildings on the western side of the city. Marine sections checked in with damage and casualty reports. Gough studied the airborne scanners and noted a handful of ships retreating from the planet – only to be intercepted and destroyed by the fighter detachment on Scar Grimmel. They had not expected that. Gough allowed himself a wry smile.

Then, as suddenly as it had begun, it was over.

He was handed a cup of coffee and drank it slowly, listening to the casualty reports coming in from both the marines and the Vilkyrian forces. *How many*, he thought, *is not too many?*

Orvessa appeared at his side. He turned and gave her a brief report, then added, "You were supposed to stay in the bunker room."

"Yes, but–" She stopped herself and studied the screens. "First wave. No landings, no troops yet."

They both understood what that meant. The Varkalons wanted live bodies to experiment on, not dead ones. A landing had to come.

The main bunker door opened and Orvessa's head of security stumbled over the airtight ledge.

"Sorry, Leader – I was outside when they hit. Our emplacements took out a great many of them, and Colonel Gough was right to station a squadron of attack fighters on Scar. We obliterated them on their way home. Casualties were lower than I feared, ma'am." He paused, almost as an afterthought. "Colonel – are you all right?"

Gough didn't mind. Arthur's voice came through on the communications panel, requesting to speak with him.

"Go ahead. What is it?"

"Sir, we've found what appear to be transit pads – larger than ours, with beams at each corner. We've tried to rip them up, tried to blow them up. No joy. We're not sure what they're for."

Orvessa stepped forward. "They are transit platforms for the Varkalons – their technology is incompatible with our trans-pads. This is how they will invade. They have done it before. Locate every one of them and ensure you have sufficient men surrounding each platform."

Gough cut in. "You hear that, Sergeant Major? Get to it. And make sure you have Karnex Tal'vorr units primed and targeting grids ready – a cone of death the moment boots hit those platforms."

"Yes, ma'am. Sir. Will do. Thank you."

Chapter Thirty-Four
Things that Go Bump In the Night

Sereth Ka'vorr, a seasoned Varnak-Tier – a non-commissioned officer – had been sitting and waiting at a remote transit platform her group had located and surrounded. She stood about one fifteen cyms tall, with golden hair: an anomaly in Vilkyrian society. She had served across various theatres of conflict and was well accustomed to the pace of battle. At that moment she felt the familiar itch at the back of her neck that always meant something was about to happen.

The platform began to glow a faint blue. She readied her force. "Hold fire until you see their shapes materialise. We may be able to take one alive for interrogation." She fell silent and trained her night vision goggles on the centre of the platform.

The colour shifted to orange. The four corner posts activated a force field to protect whatever – or whoever – was about to arrive. Sereth watched as what appeared to be a mortar tube materialised on the platform. The moment it stabilised; it fired a grab net out into the darkness. It landed on one of her troopers, entangling them and dragging them back toward the force field. Sereth recognised the trooper – a school friend. Yet she did not hesitate. She fired, sparing her from becoming a lab rat on Varkalon. History was not a reason to wait.

The platform then produced two Varkalons seemingly out of thin air. Both looked for the grab net and appeared confused to find only a body. In that moment they dropped the shield, and the Vilkyrian battle cry rang out across the darkness:

"Drav'korr ven'tal!" – Strike death upon the cursed.

A hail of pulse fire erupted alongside a Xereth V-9 Talon shot. The V-9 marksman – the unit's sharpshooter – wielded the weapon with surgical precision. Nicknamed the Whispering Fang, its micro-guided rounds tore into the first Varkalon. The second managed to return fire, but only into the empty night. Two troopers finished the engagement with their pulse lancers to devastating effect. It was over in less than three particles. No survivors. No Vilkyrians taken.

As Sereth called her people to their feet, the platform exploded, engulfing the three nearest troopers in flame. There were no extinguishers, no cover blankets – the troops had never faced such a weapon before. The troopers died from shock and third-degree burns.

Sereth stood motionless in the midst of the carnage. Was it her mistake, or simply the foul work of an enemy that gave no thought to butchery or collateral damage? She had to call it in. The platform's self-destruction needed to be reported – it might save others.

Close to the palace, a group of marines guarding the ammunition dump came under attack from a rebel force. Then, as if from nowhere, a Varkalon unit arrived in support of the rebels. The firefight was intense and the marines were holding their own – until the Varkalons brought forward a subspace-core entropy cannon. It fired a destabilising energy beam that unravelled matter at the quantum level. Varkalon war doctrine called it the Silence Maker, and it lived up to its name. Marine resistance ceased instantly.

The only reckoning the Varkalons received came from the ammunition dump itself. The overload triggered a catastrophic explosion that killed everyone left standing.

Chapter Thirty-Five
Echoes Beneath the Skin

The display screen in front of Gough failed to hold his attention. His thoughts were with the dead marines and Vilkyrians. The command centre was unnaturally silent – the alarms and shouting had stopped, and the backup power systems continued at a low hum. The stillness made it feel as though the war had withdrawn into quiet before launching its next assault on Nebulon 17 and its people. But something was happening. He was certain of it.

Orvessa hadn't spoken since the last report. She stood at his side, watching the casualty grid climb, arms folded, eyes locked on the display – her fingers making small, brief movements as though reaching for something invisible. Gough understood that entirely. Death at this scale attacked your inner being as much as your mind.

A warning alert appeared on the screen: *Remote Post 7 — Signal Lost.* No coordinates. No distress code. Just silence. He moved to the display and muttered, "Another test. Watching how we react."

Orvessa finally turned to him. "Are they already inside my palace and coming for me?"

"Over my dead body," Gough replied.

"No – to be more precise, it will be over my living body if they catch me."

The Varkalon command post was concealed behind one of Nebulon's moons. Lord Vorrak was not content with how the conflict was unfolding. He was losing troops at every stage of the attack, and the loss of ships in the first wave should not have happened. He had not anticipated the storm fighters from Scar Grimmel – and that was his mistake. Not that anyone would dare tell him so. Not if they wished to keep living.

"Are we inside the palace yet?"

"No, my Lord. We had hoped to use the ammunition dump as a passageway, but the explosion destroyed the tunnel and we cannot get through. We are now using the sewer system. Progress is slow – the sewers are fitted with guard nets across the tubes, and our Skreth'naal is not cutting through the armour plating or dismantling the fortifications quickly enough."

"How long?"

"Some three hours, my Lord."

"How long?"

"At least three, my Lord."

Vorrak studied the screens. No live captures.

"We are here for bodies – live ones, not dead Threx'gul. Dead husks are of no use to our scientists. Have we located the position of that Velkrith, Orvessa? Only a Velkrith like her could turn the minds of a battalion without a single shot fired."

Orvessa's head of security, Gemenith, requested permission to visit the main hospital centre to assess the casualties. Orvessa agreed. *"Vesh tal'kai, zhar'en thal'vora et zhen'kai."* Yes – go and ensure everything possible is being done for the wounded and those who give them strength.

Gemenith stood in the triage area and observed. Edessa approached and spoke quietly in English, so others would not understand.

"Gemenith – look at the nursing sister dealing with the bodies. I think she is writing patients off as dead when they are still alive. Could she be a rebel harvesting bodies for transit?"

Gemenith watched for what felt like a long time, then spoke again in English. "Get some of the team around the makeshift mortuary and let no one remove anything – while I arrange troopers. Do it now."

She called her safety patrol into the medical facility and briefed them swiftly, then dispatched the Tarnak-Vel – the frontline keeper – to arrest the nursing sister with maximum force.

"All personnel – stand still and stop what you are doing. Even if it causes a medical emergency. We have a traitor in this facility, and she is to be removed immediately."

Every head looked up – except the nursing sister, who moved quickly toward the emergency exit. The Tarnak-Vel stepped in front of her. The sister seized the servicewoman and pressed a knife to her throat.

"Anyone moves and she dies."

She had not noticed that Edessa had slipped back into the room from the mortuary, placing herself directly behind her. Edessa picked up a scalpel and drove it into the small of the woman's back, working it like a saw. Blood spurted. An agonised cry rang out. The nursing sister collapsed and was immediately shot by the Tarnak-Vel with her phase pistol.

Edessa straightened. "The bodies were being prepared for transit pad transport – off to one of the moons. I can't determine which one yet. I'll keep checking."

"Thank you, Edessa. You are a true Amazon warrior. I will tell Orvessa."

Gough turned from the motionless screen to face Orvessa. "Post Seven is a trap. I'm certain of it."

Orvessa listened, her expression composed.

"But we need to understand what we're dealing with," he said, lowering his voice. "I'm requesting permission to send Rachel and the old team to investigate. They're the best tools we have for this kind of reconnaissance."

Orvessa's expression tightened. "You're asking me to authorise a mission that could send them into that trap. What if they're killed?"

The weight of his responsibilities pressed down on him. "They will take on this duty if you grant permission. But the decision is yours to make."

She held his gaze for a long moment as the command centre grew quieter still. Then a single nod.

"Do it. But make sure they understand the risk."

"Thank you." Gough opened the channel to Rachel and delivered his orders with characteristic clarity. "You have a go for Post Seven. Get out there, verify the situation, and come back alive. That is an order."

Chapter Thirty-Five

One Trap Leads to Another

Rachel surveyed the hills on either side of the former post and gun emplacement. The gun barrel had been blown apart, rendering it useless. No movement, no apparent camouflage draped over anything. A few bodies lay near the entrance – too far away to tell if they were Varkalon or Vilkyrian. She offered the field glasses to her number two.

"Can't see much, Boss. What do you think? If we follow the track it's perfect ambush country. If not, how in the void do we get above anyone to look down on the road and any possible enemy?"

"How indeed. Interesting conundrum. Give me a moment."

Arthur wasn't there anymore to help, and Rachel had no intention of making quick decisions that could go drastically wrong. Her number two said, "Got a drone, if that gives us a look at the higher ground."

Rachel called a Vilkyrian trooper over and asked if she had any local knowledge of the terrain.

"Yes, Commander Rachel. I used to live near here – that's why they attached me to your recce troop."

"Good. Tell me what's special about this place."

"The gun emplacement is new. We have many new emplacements, so that could mean nothing – but it wasn't here last year when we exercised in this area. This used to be a wadi, with an entrance to a series of tunnels running through the hills. Just beyond the emplacement is a dead end – sheer rock face, nothing like the hills on either side."

"Can we get into the tunnels from here?"

"I think so. We'd need to do a quick sound survey to find an entrance. One problem, Commander – if we can think of it, so can the Varkalons. We could still be walking into a trap."

Rachel knew she could not withdraw and wait for more time to evaluate. She had to act, and quickly.

"Do you know these tunnels?"

"Yes. I used to play in them as a child – in the summer, to escape the heat."

"Right. Listen up, everyone." Rachel gathered the group. "Rob and number two – move forward as though you're the advance party of the recce group. Make enough noise for anyone watching to believe more people are coming behind you." She turned to the trooper. "What's your name?"

"Thalassa, of the clan Vorn'kai, Commander."

"I'll call you Sandy. Sandy, you and I and the remaining troop will find an entrance and try to get into the post from the inside. If we make it, I'll flash the comms panel once. If not, twice. Understood, number two?"

The brief was done. Rachel was ready to move when Sandy said, "I'm sorry – I need to go, and I can't do that in the tunnels. Wait for me." Without waiting for a reply, she stepped away from the group, dropped her trousers, and relieved herself.

"Right," Rachel said when she returned. "Are we ready now?"

While Rob deployed the Whisper Wheels – a compressed alloy pod, standard marine reconnaissance issue, weighing around eighteen kilos, capable of hovering over unstable ground and running across dust plains, rocky outcrops, and shallow craters – Rachel pressed the mind recorder attached to her temple and sent a situation report back to Command.

They were ready. Rachel's group moved off first to locate an entry point. Number two gave them a full five teks before she and Rob mounted the Whisper Wheels.

The wheels moved off at a measured pace, running parallel to the road but not on it. Number two drove while Rob used the locator to scan for life signs. The scanner picked up two inside the gun emplacement and nothing in the outer area. He briefed number two through his throat mike. She guided the Whisper Wheels to a position just far enough away that whoever was inside the emplacement could not determine whether they were looking at one person or two, human or Vilkyrian.

"Frontal assault?" Rob asked.

"Why not play their game – and end it fast."

Number two eased the wheels closer and stopped. She climbed out and left the cover shield up on the front of the vehicle so that anything beyond the obvious remained hidden. She strolled toward the entrance, glancing at the bodies as she passed. All dead. All Vilkyrian. One had a terrible gash across its chest, as though something had attempted to extract a part of the body before death. She drew her short-range hyper blaster and switched it to kill.

The two Varkalons came out of the emplacement on either side of her and reached for her arms.

"She's human – no krath'zul way!"

Rob's blaster was already out. He dropped the first one instantly. Number two took down the second with cool efficiency.

"Too easy," Rob said. He glanced at her. "By the way – what's your name, number two?"

"Ruth. Wondered when you'd ask."

The entrance to the tunnel complex was wider than Rachel had expected. Sandy led the way, with Rachel two marines behind. She swept the tunnel for heat signatures. The air grew colder, but the scanner pulsed red – two heat signatures, just around the bend. She motioned to the team and signalled with traditional hand signals: kill, not stun. The Varkalons never saw what hit them. The team moved on, leaving more dead enemy behind.

Sandy stopped and signalled Rachel forward. She drew two paths on her palm – a fork ahead. The scanner showed multiple life signs in both branches. Sandy wrote on the scratch pad that one tunnel led nowhere, while the other was the path back to the emplacement. Rachel knew both tunnels had to be cleared, or they would have Varkalons ahead and behind them.

She called three marines forward and pointed them to the left tunnel. She indicated to Sandy that they would take the other and assigned the last marine to cover the rear. Rachel drew her hunting knife. The marines silently did the same.

Moving up to the fork, the approaches were dark, but the Varkalons had placed lights to illuminate the tunnels they occupied – not to shine back toward anyone coming in. *Fatal mistake*, Rachel thought.

The three marines hugged the walls until the last moment, when one stepped forward and walked directly up to the Varkalons.

"Hi – I was out cave exploring and got a bit lost. Any chance you could help? I'm new to this planet." The Varkalons stared at him, thrown completely. They had been briefed on capturing Vilkyrians, not humans. All four turned to each other, speaking in a language the marine didn't understand. It didn't matter. He drove his knife into the nearest one, and the other two marines took care of the rest.

The noise, however, carried. The Varkalons in the other tunnel turned toward it – just as Rachel and Sandy came at them from behind and slit their throats. Purple foam and a foul smell oozed from the wounds, and both Varkalons fell, clawing at the women as they dropped.

The team regrouped and pressed further into the tunnels. The scanner showed more bodies moving ahead.

"Oh, truffles," muttered one of the marines, doing his best to express his frustration at their lack of progress. Then a Breach Lance fired – a spiralling energy bolt that destabilised molecular cohesion on impact. The two rear marines crumpled and fell, dead before they hit the ground.

"Run!" Rachel shouted to Sandy and the others. "Escape plan gamma."

Every person for themselves. The Varkalons had used their own people as bait to draw the humans in, and it had worked. Rachel and Sandy sprinted down the tunnel and threw themselves behind a large rock. The rest of the troop were not so fortunate – the Breach Lance accounted for them all.

Rachel heard movement behind her and braced. She glanced back to find Rob and Ruth running toward them, carrying a Reaper Array – a Karnex Tal'vorr. Ruth took aim and hit the sniper in a single shot. The Reaper's multi-band detection – infrared sights and auto-lock targeting for cloaked or camouflaged units, using heat bleed and micro-vibrations – did exactly what it was built for.

The tunnel fell completely silent. The acrid smell of ozone and blood hung in the cold air.

Rachel rested her back against the stone wall, her breathing breaking into ragged, uncontrolled gasps as the adrenaline drained away. She looked at the three survivors – Sandy, Rob, and Ruth – and saw the same hollow expression of shock on each of their faces that she knew was on her own. Clearing this nest had come at a permanent cost to the terrain and the people in it. The sector was taken, but war had already left its mark across Nebulon 17 in too many places to count.

"Come on," she said, her voice rough. "We establish a safe perimeter before we contact Command. This day isn't over yet."

Chapter Thirty-Six

Varkalons in the Palace

Gough and Orvessa decided they had to take turns – one staying in the command centre while the other slept.

"Toss you for it. Heads or tails?"

"I'm sorry, Colonel – what are you talking about?"

"I flip a coin, you call it, and whoever gets it right chooses. It's a fair way to decide."

"Why?"

"What do you mean, why? It's an old Earth custom."

"Gough, we're in the middle of a war. Can we skip the games?"

"Sorry. I just thought it might ease the tension a little."

"It doesn't. Get yourself some sleep and I'll wake you to take over."

Gough moved reluctantly toward the door of the command centre and along the corridor to the leader's quarters in the bunker. He was tired – his shoulders sagged, his muscles ached, and his legs seemed to want to go in directions he wasn't asking them to. The last time he had felt this exhausted was on his second camp during officer training: seven days of little sleep, constant attacks, and counter-attacks. Still, this was the job he had chosen over diplomacy.

He fell into the bunk and was asleep before his head had fully hit the pillow. His last thought: *Another day, another dollar. But I must protect Orvessa.*

Orvessa worked through the situation reports and drew battle lines across the screens. They had survived the first day without being too severely damaged. No additional bombing runs – the fighters had seen to that. Reports mentioned possible new missiles, but none had arrived yet. Some rebel activity, a few set-backs, but small wins were entirely acceptable. She had been in situations like this before.

What troubled her was Vorrak. She could not determine what he would do next. She suspected he was thinking exactly the same of her, given that the fighting response he had encountered was clearly not what he had planned for. Many Vilkyrians and Varkalons were dead. As far as she knew, no one had been captured. The biological link was safe. She noticed that every person in the control room had the same colour on their Pulsebands as she and Gough.

She looked at the empty chair and thought about her response to him.

Oh well. I can't change it now. He'll understand — he's my man.

The sewers beneath the palace had always served two purposes: sanitation and escape. Not entry. The Varkalons were still working their way through the grids but were getting closer to the openings set behind the palace walls. A comm link crackled, and the voice of Lord Vorrak's deputy came through, requesting a situation report.

"You promised me three hours. Where are you now?"

"Just approaching the first of the entry hatches inside the palace, behind the outer wall, Sir. Not much longer before we can deploy."

"Good. Get on with it."

"May I ask one question? Where are all these humans coming from? We have killed a number of them, but they are of no use to us. Should we kill them or avoid a confrontation with Earth?"

"Don't kill them unless you have to protect yourselves. Out."

Orvessa was tallying the casualty data when she felt an odd pulse move through her body. She looked up and saw the Phoenix shining down on her. She frowned, then carried on. This was inside the palace – inside the command centre, inside the bunker. No one could reach her here.

"Did anyone else see something strange just now?" she asked.

Murmured replies of *No, Leader* came back from around the room.

She wondered whether to wake Gough, just in case. She was unsettled and, if she was honest with herself, a little afraid. Gough had seen the Phoenix before, with Tarrin. She touched her wedding ring and thought of him.

Gough was woken by a banging on the floor of the bunker bedroom. He rolled over to find a panel being removed from beneath him. He was still dressed. He got to his feet and drew his personal weapon – the Vornex Edgecaster, capable of slicing through armour, forged from a rare Vilkyrian metal known for its resonance with command-grade Pulsebands. His team had coined a verse for it: *If Gough draws the Fang, it's already too late. That weapon doesn't miss — it chooses you.*

A Varkalon head appeared through the panel and seemed genuinely surprised to find a human where it had expected to find Orvessa.

"Get out – all of you – and put your hands where I can see them."

"We are not here for you, Earthling. Step aside or we will cause you great harm."

Gough backed off. As more Varkalons began climbing through the hole, he made a dash for the door, slammed it shut behind him, and jammed a nearby chair under the handle. It wouldn't hold long, but it might give him enough time to reach Orvessa. As he ran, he heard the banging on the door, then the splintering of wood and metal as the Varkalons blasted through it. Palace guards were running toward the bedroom, only to be captured or shot. Gough had no time to stop. His thoughts were fixed entirely on Orvessa – his lady, his love, the reason he had found himself.

He burst into the command room, slammed the door and spun the locking mechanism.

"The Varkalons are in the palace – inside the bunker. We have to use the escape duct."

Orvessa stared at him. "Have you just woken from a nightmare? I would have seen it on the screens."

"Not the bedrooms, you wouldn't."

The screaming and weapons fire from beyond the door settled the argument. Orvessa looked at him.

"Come here. Now. Place your Pulseband on mine – quickly."

He did as he was told. Orvessa issued a rapid command in Vilkyrian to the room, then pulled Gough close against her. He was about to ask what was happening when they found themselves in the cavern he had used before the assault on Scar Grimmel. Others arrived around them in pairs as the Vilkyrians teleported out from the palace.

The Varkalons burst through the command room door to find their quarry disappearing before their eyes. One lunged for a couple mid-transport and found himself deposited in the cavern instead. Gough dispatched him without hesitation, then turned to take in what had just happened. Orvessa was not flustered – simply and calmly directing an evacuation that Gough had known nothing about.

"Orvessa – what just happened?"

"I'll explain once we know how many made it out. But you are safe, my love. You are with me."

Chapter Thirty-Seven

Rebind the Arc

Fall back and phase down. Rebind the Arc at the cellar. Pulse-check your squads — then regroup at the cavern. The order had been issued to all Vilkyrians. Some had Pulse-banded with marine husbands, and the motley crew had gathered in the cavern's main chamber.

Sandy had Pulse-banded the remains of the team and brought them through. She and Rachel made their way to Orvessa and Gough.

"They're rounding up the humans to use as bargaining chips – offering to trade one human for one live Vilkyrian, Madam Leader. What can we do?"

"We will address that once we have taken a census and established who is here. Colonel Gough, would you organise that, please?" She turned and moved toward the medical cavern. Gough knew she was heading for the room behind it – to recover and do her own quiet regrouping. He set the marine team and Sandy to work, then followed her.

"Orvessa – your message said *Rebind the Arc.* What is the Arc? And why did I not know about the Pulsebands and teleportation?"

"I'm sorry, Gough. There are still many things about us – about me – that you don't yet know. I thought we had time. We don't. We have a chaotic situation to resolve and no time to bring you fully up to speed with the intricacies of our world. I need time to reflect and re-envision the Arc of our people. It holds the power of this planet and of ourselves."

"But what is it?"

"Come with me. I will show you something no outsider has ever seen or experienced."

Orvessa pressed what appeared to be a solid rock wall. A circular stairwell opened before them, well-lit and descending into darkness. Gough was about to step forward when Orvessa said, "Remove your weapon."

"We're still at war. I can't."

"Now, Gough."

Reluctantly, he did as he was told and followed her down. After a long descent they emerged into a vast underground complex – enormous, with a flat floor, and at its centre a massive curved wooden vessel buried in the cavern like a fossilised wave.

Orvessa tossed a small piece of metal toward it and they both watched it vaporise instantly. Gough stared. He stayed close to her. The structure was a living entity, responding to the emotional and moral state of those who approached – its colour shifting to reflect the atmosphere of the room. At that moment, it glowed bright green.

Orvessa touched a panel at the base of the slope leading up to the wooden structure, and a door opened.

"This is the bridge between our world and the ancient people of Nebulon 17. It allows for the transfer of the physical and the spiritual – past, present, and future. Without it, the memory of who we were and the hope of who we might become would be lost to the void forever. But it is still more than that, my love. It is the fount of the Seylira Bond. It is everything that makes us what we are as a people. It is activated by resonance – by chanting, thought, and vibration. Come inside the Arc with me, Gough."

As they moved forward, both felt a tremendous joy – toward each other and toward the Arc itself. Orvessa had felt it before, but for Gough, experiencing it for the first time, the force of it nearly brought him to his knees.

They entered, and a wooden door closed softly behind them. The air shifted as they crossed the threshold. The scent of aged wood and deep silence wrapped around them like a cloak. They climbed a short flight of stairs and found themselves in what could only be described as a ship's cabin – three window spaces on each side, one at the front, an oversized captain's chair, and a ship's wheel. Everything was dark oak or teak. No metal. Nothing on the walls.

Orvessa spoke quietly.

"Before we sit, our bodies must remain in contact and one hand each must rest on the handle. Do not release it – if you break the link, you will interrupt everything. I have never heard you curse, but know this is sacred ground. All will be well. We will rebind the Arc ourselves. Are you ready, my love – my life, my being?"

"Yes, Orvessa. *En'cael aeneth lye.*" She knew then that he was bound to her.

They sat together, bodies pressed close. Two hand-bars emerged from the wheel. Orvessa took the left; Gough took the right. Their free hands clasped tightly together as they pushed forward, their bodies touching. In the window before them a red flame came to life and burned brightly.

A voice emerged from the flame – vast and unhurried, like something older than language.

"Orvessa. You did not follow the stated tradition, and you broke the link. Please explain why to the council of Nebulon and to the Creator."

"Oh, spirit of our nation – I did not understand the significance of bringing my one true Seylira bond to you for the Vethen. I seek your forgiveness and to repair that which is broken. I have my soul mate here. Oh, Mighty One."

Orvessa was not as composed as she appeared. Gough looked at her, deeply concerned. He did not yet understand what was happening or why.

"Young Gough – do you believe in a supreme being?"

Gough blinked. "You know my name?"

"Please answer the question."

"Yes. I believe in a supreme being as set forth in the holy book of my people."

The flame burned brighter when the voice spoke again – this time addressing them both in Vilkyrian:

"Aen'valaen En'cael vethar il'naer, aeneth'seren il'vethen Alencar en'kai."

"Do you both seek the Arc reborn in the image of the divine, and your souls joined in love and care for the land? Answer in the tongue."

Orvessa murmured to Gough, "Follow me." Haltingly at first, then together, they repeated the rebuilding phrase:

"Aeneth'seren il'vethen ael'caer, en'nar il'veneth. En'vethen, en'caer, en'sael."

We wish our souls to unite in love and care, for the land and the nation. In love, care, and truth.

"Gough will now be reborn, as you have been – oh great and mighty leader of the ancients and of the present Nebulon's, whom some call Vilkyrian."

Gough felt his heart stop. His breath left his body. He was no longer certain he could hold the handle as his head fell forward onto his chest, which had ceased to move. Time seemed to fold inward, and memories he had never lived flickered behind his eyes.

"Naer'vethar il'seren. Ael'cael en'veneth, aeneth'vethen il'valaen. En'sael, en'caer, en'vethen ael'lara."

The supreme being is with you and your rebirth. Bringing truth, mercy, and love to all.

Gough gasped for air. A white glow moved through his entire body. He felt as though Orvessa were touching every part of him, and he every part of her, though neither had moved. The flame roared – and then fell silent.

The final words were directed at Orvessa alone.

"Experience my truth as the Nebulon's have. Many chose to believe, and that is why your profession of faith and love for this human has been heard and accepted. I say this now in his tongue, so that Gough may understand: *Your faith has mended the fracture. Healing will come — not swiftly, but surely. The blessing of the Supreme Being is upon you both. Peace is your keystone. Grace and mercy shall walk beside you all your mortal days.*"

Everything went silent. The flame died away.

Gough was drenched in sweat. Orvessa, for the first time, had lost her composure entirely. They had both experienced something that went far beyond words.

They felt it completely – *Nareth seren* – kindred spirits, as though each now knew what the other was thinking and feeling without needing to ask.

Chapter Thirty-Eight

The Bond Can Not be Transferred.

The cavern had become a hive of industry. It seemed every Vilkyrian with a Pulseband had been brought to the location. Under the direction of the Vilkyrian guards and the few remaining marines, people and couples were being organised, and spaces for sleeping and eating were being secured.

Gough and Orvessa lay on their bed, and eventually Gough said, "So dying is not so final. Is it, Orvessa? Have you gone through that yourself?"

"Yes, beloved – but alone. The experience with you was shatteringly different. Much stronger, much more meaningful, and closer. Thank you, my precious one. Thank you for your trust and your faith in us. Blessings be upon us and our nation. May the Seylira shine upon us and our people."

He held her close, absorbing her words. "You're right. You always are." After a moment, the weight of command settled back onto his shoulders. "But we must turn our attention to the conflict – and to the humans in captivity. Not forgetting any Vilkyrians the Varkalons may have taken. You've dealt with them before." He paused. "I can't stop thinking about the children. Where are they? Why haven't we heard anything?"

"Do you remember when I mentioned the Varkalons being in the palace?"

"Yes."

"Everything went quiet shortly after that. The children were moved to a safe place – similar to this cavern, but not here. They are on the other side of the mountain ranges, near Zareth'Kai – built beneath the twin moons, carved into the cliffs of memory. It is said that every whisper spoken in its halls is heard again in dreams. The city holds the archives of the Seylira Bond and is guarded by those who have walked the Arc and returned."

"That is a great weight off my mind. I had been very worried – there had been no word at all." He squeezed her hand. "Let's get back to the conflict."

The moment passed, and duty reclaimed them. They rose together and returned to the command centre in the cavern, making their way to the briefing room for a full update on the general situation.

Lord Vorrak was still not content with how the conflict had unfolded, even as he marched ceremoniously into the palace complex. Very few Vilkyrians had been captured alive, no children had been taken, and Orvessa had simply vanished. They had not secured sufficient Vilkyrians for their scientific research to continue. He was *Grav'thakar* – and number three knew that if the Lord did not calm himself, he would *Thakarin* – unleash his fury on everyone within reach. Things were not disastrous, but they were far from good.

Vorrak strolled into the area set aside for research and surveyed the bodies that had been used and discarded. He turned to the senior researcher.

"We are successful?"

"I am terribly sorry, Lord Vorrak, but our results suggest we will never fully understand how to transfer the bonding. We do not know how it occurs naturally – and therefore we cannot reproduce it. The experiments on the Vilkyrians have proved deeply unsatisfactory. I am truly sorry, my Lord. But we still have hope."

"Ah, yes," Vorrak said softly. "We always have hope." He paused. *"Throkar en'vethar. Let the blood speak. The blade is drawn. Let truth be revealed."*

He spun and drew his jewel-handled Throkar across the man's throat in a single motion. Blood splattered across number three, who used the edge of the researcher's white coat to wipe his face clean. That was not enough for Vorrak. He raised the blade again and split the body from throat to navel. Blood, gore, and pieces of the man fell to the floor.

He turned to number three.

"If we cannot take what we want, then kill them all – humans, Vilkyrians, everyone and everything. I will require proof of the death count. Let no stone stand. Let memory itself burn." He thrust the blade toward him. "Get to it."

Chapter Thirty-Nine

Where Is the Cavalry?

Tarrin was pacing her office, waiting for the top brass to commit to a rescue plan – not just for the people, but for her partner, her soul mate, Edessa. *When would they decide?*

A knock at the door broke her chain of thought.

"Go away – I am extremely busy!" The knocking continued. Tarrin's patience snapped. She threw open the door, a sharp rebuke on her lips – which died instantly. Her mind, racing with strategies and frustrations, screeched to a halt. It couldn't be. It wasn't possible. The figure before her looked a little like a *vezof jin azantys* – a damaged warrior – but it was. It was Edessa.

They threw their arms around each other, and tears fell onto Tarrin's uniform.

"Come in, come in, my love." The Pulsebands blazed a shocking green as they clung to each other.

"How – when – are you hurt? Do you need anything? Food, drink?"

"I don't suppose you have any Drakarys Ember?"

"I do – hang on." Tarrin pressed the beverage panel and ordered a Drakarys Ember and a strong black coffee, hot.

"Sorry about my hair."

"It's cut short. Why?"

"After the Varkalons got into the palace – once I was certain Orvessa and Gough were out – I cut my hair and dressed like a doxal. I talked my way onto a cargo ship bound for Scar. One of the crew offered me a great many credits for company. I told him I was going to the hospital on Scar because I had contracted Zaldrīzes Ānogra from letting marines use my body. He left me alone after that."

Tarrin laughed despite herself. "What a brazen *Seryna.* An excellent cover story."

"At the hospital I showed my credentials to the doctor, and they appeared on every screen in the building. For a moment I thought I was finished – but a pilot from your fleet, sitting in the waiting area, grabbed my arm and pulled me into an admin office until the marine guards moved on. To cut a long story short, I trans-padded to Earth using the code you gave me and arrived downstairs. To everyone's considerable surprise." Edessa allowed herself a small smile. "I asked for Colonel Tarrin. The guard said, *Brigadier, do you have an appointment?*"

"I'm sorry – I should have updated you."

"You've been promoted?"

"Yes. One star general now." Tarrin looked her over carefully. "How are you feeling? Do you need food? A change of clothes?"

"Both, yes – and anything warm. Even one of those bun things from the honeymoon that Gough made. It is freezing here."

Clothed and fed, Edessa was about to ask about Earth's plans for support when the comms unit requested Brigadier Tarrin's presence in the General's office.

"You're coming with me. We need to brief the commander." They entered a well-appointed office – leather chairs, a wooden desk, family photographs, and a wedding portrait of General Pridou and his wife on the wall.

Tarrin saluted. "Sir, I present the Vilkyrian Deputy Commander in Chief, Zorvakar Ulthien. She has just evaded Varkalon capture and carries current, critical intelligence. I deemed it necessary to bring her directly to you."

The General nodded. "Protocol be damned – we need every advantage we can get. Sit down, both of you. I was just about to brief the Brigadier on the rescue operation to clear the Varkalons from the planet."

He leaned forward. "We have encouraged our allies, the Rogens, to deploy their forces. They are already mobilised and awaiting the final execute order – and they carry an intense hatred for Lord Vorrak and the Varkalons. Our ground forces will trans-pad directly to locations previously identified by Leader Orvessa, under Brigadier Tarrin's command. The attack is timed for 03:45 local time. It should achieve surprise – morning will not yet have broken, and we are known to attack at dawn."

Tarrin spoke. "General, I recommend sending a message to the OR Lords on Deacon 4 requesting their assistance. Use the codeword *Peace Breaker* – that will authorise their troops to mop up the more remote areas of the planet. A further message should go to Nebulon 2, directing them to strike the Varkalon home base. With their entire force committed to Nebulon 17, they will not be battle-ready to defend it."

"Consider it done. Brigadier – what about the marines already on the planet? The 83rd?"

"We assess on the ground, Sir. Most will have gone to escape and evasion. If any are being held together in a single location – which I consider unlikely – we break them out and fold them into the assault. I will go in first, secure space in the Nebulon caves for our incoming troops, and link up with the Deputy Commander, the Leader, and Colonel Gough. Once the position is established, I will transmit the release codeword – *Ark Fire* – to initiate the attack." She paused. "It may prove costly. But it is necessary. Lord Vorrak needs to be brought down – one way or another."

They left the office to prepare for the return to Nebulon 17.

Chapter Forty

What's Left of the Marines

Many of the marines had gone for escape and evasion when word reached them that the palace had fallen to the Varkalons. However, a significant part of the Brigade had been corralled into a makeshift camp, contained behind a high force field fence that electrocuted anyone who attempted to touch or climb it. The conditions were appalling – filth and excrement gathering in corners, the Varkalons having done nothing beyond erecting the force fields. No food, no water, no facilities of any kind. The marines had marked out sanitation areas as best they could, but the open piles of waste stank in the elements. The rank structure held. Non-commissioned officers sorted fighters into one group, the wounded into another, and the dead into a third. They waited – for Vilkyrians, for anyone – to attack the compound so they could attempt a break-out.

The escape troops spent their time evading Varkalon patrols, hiding in tunnels, digging *Zarveth* – warriors' ditches – and setting up camouflage positions near trees and thickets. One group had cut reeds and concealed themselves in a river near the second city, remaining hidden from search patrols for days. They had no idea whether a rescue was coming. They maintained their drills and watch rotations regardless. It was all that remained of the routine that kept them marines.

Vorrak was furious. A great number of the marines could not be traced, and he had ordered them dead. Results were not coming fast enough. He lay back on the bunker bedroom bed and ate some sweet green pollens – *Veshkar thalorin.* They tasted of green dust, and he liked it. Number three entered.

"May I disturb you, my Lord? I need to know where you wish the bodies to be left after execution. There will be too many for a simple pile."

Vorrak didn't look up from the green dust on his fingers. "Why must I be bothered with such details? Incinerate them. Dump them in a ravine. I don't care. Just make certain they are found – as a warning."

"Sir – I have a human who claims he can show us where the Vilkyrians have disappeared to. He says he was the Shard leader on the planet. His name is Harbour. General Harbour – an ex-marine general."

"Oh, that scumbag." Vorrak looked up for the first time. "Bring him in."

Number three dragged in a man ravaged by exhaustion and days without food or water. His lips were cracked; sores covered his face, arms, and legs. He wore military shorts, desert boots, long socks, and a battledress top torn and stiff with dried blood.

A group of marines lay under cover on either side of a dirt road on the approaches to the second city. No Blade Leader – but a sharp corporal who had decided that attack was the best form of defence. Briefed and ready, they were invisible as a column of Varkalons moved along the road, carrying a consignment of Virexion Lances intended for the marine compound. The corporal did not know that. He simply wanted to fight back.

The stage was set. The first hoover carrier rounded the bend in the track and the marines opened fire with their Thornspikes – tactical handheld weapons that fired armour-piercing darts with explosive tips. The corporal's heart hammered against his ribs as he waited for the lead vehicle to be perfectly silhouetted in the kill zone. He took a breath.

"Fire!"

The first transport disintegrated. The second was close behind it before the Varkalons could understand what had hit them. As troops poured out of the third vehicle to return fire, the marines switched their Brimshards to Shardstorm mode – a wide-burst setting designed for exactly this kind of crowded target. It was over almost before it had begun. The ambush site was littered with dead Varkalons and the wreckage of their vehicles – all except one hoover truck that still appeared operational.

The corporal gathered the troop, offered his congratulations, and asked if anyone could get the vehicle started. A voice behind him made him spin, weapon raised.

"I can work it. I not speak your language well. We are Vilkyrian troopers. We need to go to this location. It is – hope."

"It is hope?"

The corporal had not seen the three troopers concealed in the rocks, watching the ambush. He pulled out his translator. "You are Vilkyrian? If so – who is the leader's man? Her husband?"

"Colonel Gough of the House of Draken. We must get to hope. Please."

"Show me on the map."

The trooper pointed to a spot near some mountains – far enough from the palace for no one to bother with it.

"There's nothing there."

"No – hope is here. Hope, we go here. All of us to hope."

The corporal looked around at his marines. Nods all round.

"Right. Let's move before more Varkalons show up."

They piled into the transport and headed in the direction of hope.

Orvessa and Gough had woken together, fully dressed, boots still on. A banging at the door had pulled them from a deep and much-needed sleep.

"Leader, Commander – quickly, please. The view screens. Come now."

They came into the briefing room and looked at the observation screen to find a hoover carrier transport parked outside the entrance, with three Vilkyrian troopers trying to collapse the force field to get in. Gough noticed the marines still in the vehicle.

"Check them out, Blade Leader. Carefully," he said.

Rachel came around the back of the transport and listened to the conversation before stepping into view, her weapon held loosely but ready.

"Where in the name of God's green apples have you lot come from?"

The corporal dropped down from the transport and saluted. "Corporal Angelo, Blade. We went E&E from a gun emplacement near Zareth'Kai. Picked these troopers up after an ambush on Varkalon fighters. They asked us to bring them here and called it Point Hope."

Rachel raised her weapon a fraction. "Everyone out. Slowly. Weapons on the ground. Now."

Troops and marines climbed out. Everyone was walked into the cavern. The weapons and transport were secured, and the force field fully reactivated.

Gough met the marines and turned to the Vilkyrian commander. "Check detail – name, rank, and numbers. Get them food and water. Debrief them and then brief me."

One of the marines stared as Gough walked away. "I've just been eyeballed by the eagle. An actual eagle – Colonel Gough." He shook his head slowly. "Wow."

Gough was making his way back to Orvessa when an alarm began to sound – a wailing tone he had never heard before.

"Quickly, Colonel – we need to check the trans pad," Orvessa told him, already moving.

"What trans pad? Where?" he called after her, bewildered, as she disappeared into another level of the caverns. Something else she hadn't told him about. He ran to catch up.

Chapter Forty-One

The Pendulum Swings, but Which Way?

By the time they reached what looked like an empty hangar floor, lights were strobing and an alarm blared, creating a wall of sound in the vast space. Two figures stood in the middle of it, dressed in military uniforms – one carrying full webbing and a personal weapon, the other carrying nothing but a paper bag.

Gough drew his sidearm. "Turn around now and place the weapon on the ground!"

"That would be *turn around, Brigadier, Colonel Gough.*" Tarrin laughed. Orvessa recognised them instantly – Tarrin and Edessa. Edessa was already reaching into the paper bag.

"These are incredible, Sis. They're called doughnuts. I don't know where they originally come from, but they taste wonderful. Hello, everyone!" The guards lowered their weapons. Most came to attention. Edessa began offering doughnuts around.

"Please stop that, Edessa," Orvessa said. "Where have you come from, and how are you here together?"

Tarrin answered. "She got out of the palace dressed as a doxal, made it to Earth somehow, and found me. We're the advance party for the counter-assault. Needed to confirm you had sufficient space for the troops and equipment arriving in approximately two minutes. So – shall we move?"

Gough opened his mouth. "How did you–"

"Shut up, Gough, and listen. You might learn something." Tarrin was already moving.

They cleared the space, and sure enough – light weaponry and marines began arriving in cadres. Orvessa's guards directed each wave off to other caves to make room for the next. It continued for some time before Tarrin suggested they withdraw to a briefing room.

Tarrin pointed to a holographic map hovering above the table. "The main assault is synchronised to begin at 03:45 local – when the Varkalon guard shift is at its lowest alertness. Our first objectives are to simultaneously disable the force field generators here and here–"

An aide handed her a data pad. She glanced at it, her expression hardening.

"Which we need to do sooner than planned. Signals intelligence is showing a localised power fluctuation at the main camp. The prisoners are getting restless. They may try something drastic before we're in position."

The marines in the prisoner camp had grown restless and had no way of knowing when – or whether – a rescue was coming. A group of Blade leaders arranged a confrontation with the guards: partly to test the integrity of the camp's defences, partly as a genuine attempt to break out and fight another day. They had dug *Zarveths* close to the fence, as the Vilkyrian troops had shown them, and scraped together what weapons they could – penknives, the odd hunting knife, piano wire garottes. The plan was to provoke the Varkalon guards into entering the camp and use that opening to break out. The Blade leaders would start a disturbance, draw the guards toward the gate, and attempt to get them to touch the electrified wire.

It was not a spectacular plan. But it was simple enough to work, provided the guards believed the trouble was genuine.

They debated the timing. One Blade suggested twilight – the guards had limited night vision, only one bionic eye and one human. Another argued for just before dawn, when the guards would be tired and the shift change approaching. They settled on 03:50. Dawn was at 03:55. The changeover was at 04:30.

Gough was leading the Brigadier's forces. They were in position and ready, the compound visible ahead, its guards thinly spread. A set of Shadowveils waited in reserve to extract the living and wounded once the compound was breached. All was set.

Gough checked his watch in the darkness. 03:35. Nearly time.

He sent the message through his mind recorder: *It's almost dawn. Synchronised to attack at 03:45. Moving into position now.*

In the camp, the prisoners were supposedly asleep. The break group lay ready in their *Zarveths*. The Blade leaders moved back and forth to the latrine area a few metres away, watching.

Then the camp Blade leaders saw the guards grouping, eyes turned toward the horizon.

"Someone's out there – go now, go now. Distract the guards. Go, go, GO!"

The Blade leaders hurled stones and debris at the fence. It crackled and shimmered as the current surged with each impact. The guards looked back, uncertain.

Through his long-range stereoscope, Gough caught the flashes on the fence and watched the guards turn away from the perimeter.

"*Ark Fire. Ark Fire.*"

The attack on the camp began. The Varkalon guards did not know which threat to answer. Some moved toward the wire; others turned toward the sounds of the assault. Those heading for the wire signalled for the gate to be opened and stood at the entrance, weapons ready – which meant the electricity was off. The marines charged.

Gough's troops charged with them. Lances of destructive energy crisscrossed the compound, slicing through the pre-dawn darkness.

"Get the marines out – keep the gateway clear!" Gough's voice carried across the chaos.

The camp was fully awake now. More guards were coming, but more marines were fighting their way out. Weapons became useless in the press of bodies and hand-to-hand fighting broke out. The Varkalons were built for exactly this – and the captive marines, weakened and unarmed, were no match for them in close combat. It was beginning to look as though everything was going to go wrong.

Gough called the Shadowveils forward and used them as a barrier against the incoming fire. His leading troops reached the gate and passed small arms through to the Blade leaders, who used them to cover the marines as they pushed out of the compound and away from the hand-to-hand fighting. Marines carried their wounded comrades into the backs of the Shadowveils, and as soon as each transport was full it departed, immediately replaced by an empty one for the next batch of prisoners.

"Use the destructor packs – throw them toward the oncoming Varkalons, not into the camp!" Gough urged his troops. Massive explosions erupted and stopped the Varkalon advance, fragments of bodies flying past Gough and the transports.

He moved to the gate and found a Blade leader. "How many more? Do you know?"

The Varkalon guards were shouting orders that no one was following. The majority simply surged forward in a frontal assault – but throwing themselves at the Shadowveils achieved nothing. As more and more marines seized weapons, the balance shifted. The Varkalons began to fall, cut down by the hail of fire. Their human tissue was being torn away, and the mechanical components could not function without flesh and muscle to support them. The Varkalons tried to regroup and charged again – one time too many. They were cut down by Gough's force, by armed prisoners, and by the growing light in the sky that made them perfect targets for the marines and Vilkyrian troopers.

Gough had been the first into the battle. He was the last to leave the field. As he climbed into the Shadowveil, right hand gripping the internal handle, a single stray plasma bolt ricocheted off the bulkhead and tore his left arm clean off.

In the transport, he looked at his arm in his right hand.

Then he passed out.

The pendulum had swung to the liberators. The Shadowveils continued their runs until the very end.

No one living was left behind.

Chapter Forty-Two
One Battle Does Not Win the War

The Shadowveils had avoided the palace and travelled as quickly as possible to the caverns, taking care not to be followed. Edessa, Tarrin, and Orvessa watched as each transport came in and unloaded its casualties, former prisoners, and fighters. Many were rushed straight into the medical facility; others wandered about in a daze. With each transport that arrived without Gough, Orvessa grew more and more anxious.

The last transport in seemed to carry a Phoenix above it – visible to everyone. Orvessa let out a *Kra'veth ul'zorra* – the soul is torn – and rushed to the transport. She saw the damage and blast marks on the back doors.

"Oh God, no. He promised me. He promised me – *Thren'kai! Thren'kai!* No. Not this. Please God, not this."

Gough was brought out on a stretcher, still holding the remains of his arm, not moving.

"Or'vethan, zorrakai ul'zorra. Creator, please guard my soul."

At that moment Orvessa realised she could not feel her own left arm. She could not leave his side. As they carried him, his eyes opened and in a faint voice he said, "I am yours. Not going anywhere without you." Then he was gone again.

Tarrin and Edessa rushed forward and held Orvessa, who refused to move from his side. The doctor examined him and took him directly into surgery. A nurse gently removed what was left of his arm from his hand and prepared him for immediate, life-saving surgery. Others were in a bad way too – but this was the leader's man. Her soul mate. They could not get this wrong.

Time moved without mercy. Orvessa remained motionless outside the operating room, her left arm numb, a temporary sling holding it still. She refused pain medication. Her eyes never left the sealed door. Around her, the cavern filled with the sounds of medical staff, the distant deployment of Shadowveils, and the muffled cries of the wounded.

A medic approached quietly and offered her a ration bar and a hot flask of broth. Orvessa took neither.

Tarrin sat down beside her and spoke softly – the patient was remarkably strong, he had come through difficult situations before.

"Not like this," Orvessa said. "Not with me broken too."

Edessa sat on her other side and placed a hand gently on her shoulder. "Your bond with him makes this pain so intense. You feel everything he feels."

The surgical lights flickered briefly, then steadied. A nurse stepped out, her face carefully composed, and gave Tarrin a brief, reassuring nod before returning inside.

Orvessa drew a slow breath. "He is more than a soldier. He is a symbol. And symbols have a way of resisting death."

On the tactical display outside, red zones pulsed and blue zones flickered. The battle continued beyond the cavern walls – but in this corridor, time had condensed into a single heartbeat on the other side of that door.

"When he wakes," Orvessa said, her voice rough, "I want him to know that the line held. That we fought on. Together."

They wheeled Gough out of surgery and the doctor came to Orvessa.

"He is stable. We have fitted the most advanced prosthetic arm we have. He will not be exactly as he was – but he will be all right. We will teach him to use it. His right arm and hand are unaffected."

Orvessa tried to stand and fainted. She came round on the gurney beside Gough's, close enough to see his pale face and the shallow rise and fall of his chest.

"My Seylira. My love. My life." Her voice was barely a whisper. "Please don't falter now, angel. Please. You cannot die."

Tarrin took command. Edessa stayed close to support her. And Orvessa remained where she was – at Gough's side, where she would stay until he came back to her.

Chapter Forty-Three
Rehab and Reflection

The next two weeks became a blur for Gough and Orvessa. The off-world attack was held up, giving the Varkalons time to regroup and prepare.

Lord Vorrak was pleased that a battle was coming but equally displeased at having lost the humans as a bargaining chip. Things were not going well. His scientists were still attempting to replicate the Seylira from Vilkyrian bodies, without success. Reports had reached him that the homeland was under attack, but he refused to allow any troops to return to defend it. Number three was not bringing him the results he wanted. Frustration was building, and he needed action – something to reassert his dominance. He ordered his men to deploy the Virexion Lances against Zareth'Kai. Any sanctuaries or places of worship were to be targeted specifically. Crush the city until nothing remained but rubble.

Number three stood to attention. "Lord Vorrak – if we do not win this, the damage caused could come back to haunt you."

"Nothing haunts me, Number Three. Not mystics, not laws, not history. The only thing you need concern yourself with is when I decide to kill you to stop your incessant questions. Do you understand?"

"As my Lord requests, so shall it be done."

Zareth'Kai was obliterated. Old men and women, priests and lay preachers, members of the Council – and all the animals. Gone. The Virexion Lances had proved devastatingly effective, and this pleased Vorrak greatly.

During the final week of his recovery, Gough had been sitting up in bed, studying his new arm. He flexed it, rolled each finger in turn, and when he knocked something from the table his hand shot out and caught it. The problem was that he caught it – and crushed it to pulp.

He was not suffering from phantom limb syndrome. He had a new limb. But he was terrified that if he touched Orvessa, he would hurt her. She could not understand the sudden absence of his usual tenderness, the lack of contact. Until she looked him in the eyes and said, "Tell me."

"What if I touch you and hurt you? That would be terrible – not just for you, but for me." He held up the metallic arm. "This thing may be a symbol of survival, but it is a burden to me. You married a whole man, and you don't have that anymore. I don't have that anymore. I need to fight, and I'm not sure I can. I am scared – properly scared. Scared that when all this is over, you won't want me."

"We are joined through the Seylira. Don't you still feel that? I do. Don't you feel the spirit flowing between us, through our love? The Seylira is a blessing from the Creator, and it will never fade. Has your belief in that – your faith – faded?" Her voice softened and fell quiet.

Gough looked at the prosthetic arm in the dim light. It caught the glow like a cold mirror. Beneath his skin it produced a sensation he could only describe as a heartbeat – and when all other sounds faded, a soft whisper at the edge of thought. The loss of his limb, the sheer finality of it, arrived in full at last. Everything else vanished from his mind.

His jaw tightened. Then he let it go. When he spoke, his voice was deep and measured, his eyes carrying both exhaustion and resolve.

"When you married me, you married a warrior. A fighter. The body of a fighter will eventually break down – that is what fighters do. You chose differently from what you perhaps expected, because you chose a soul mate. I am that soul mate, and I always will be." He paused. "Please – let me hold you. Both arms."

They held each other. Gough was careful, deliberate – but no less tender for it. Feeling Orvessa close against him, both arms around her, said everything that words could not.

Vorrak had grown tired of waiting. He called number three into his quarters.

"Where is number five? Get him in here. Now."

As number three turned to confirm that number five was on his way, Vorrak hurled a hunting knife into his forehead and laughed as the man died in front of him.

Chapter Forty-Four

Poor Planning Makes for Poor Performance

"New Number Three – what is the state of our defences? I have a feeling we need to ship more defensive weapons from the homeland, and quickly."

"My Lord, I am still trying to establish what remains after the initial fighting. My predecessor did not brief me fully. I believe more is always better than less – yet I would not presume to tell my Lord what he should do."

"You are a real toady, aren't you, Number Three? You may go far. *May*. Order another delivery of Virexion Lances – and some of those intergalactic blaster things."

"As my Lord commands, so shall it be done. Blessings upon my Lord Vorrak."

The fighter squadron on Scar had been keeping close watch on the supply routes from Varkalon to Nebulon 17, successfully intercepting most of the resupply coordination before it could get through. On patrol around some of the outer moons, a series of signals were picked up from the surface of a moon almost indistinguishable from Nebulon 17. Scans showed structures and transmission pylons.

"Control – I've found another rebel base. Definitely not one of ours. Permission to shoot the S H 1 T out of it?"

"Where is it?"

"Almost behind Scar, Sir. Invisible unless you're right on top of it."

"Wait out." A brief pause. "Yes – good target practice. Tally-Ho."

The pilot fired air-to-ground missiles, then dropped destructive ordnance. The buildings vanished. His screen showed no living signatures. Unknown to him, he had just killed the real General Harbour.

"Lord Vorrak – I have the pleasure of informing you that General Harbour is no more."

"Good news, Number Three. I hope it was painful."

"Shall I destroy the record of your meeting with him?"

"No. Bring me the mind record. I want to know whether he was telling me the truth or simply buying himself time."

Tarrin, Gough, Orvessa, and Edessa were poring over maps of the space above the palace, working out the best approach for the strike force before ground troops went in.

"It has to be a timed attack, Brigadier," Gough said. "Otherwise, we risk losing troops to friendly fire."

"Agreed. I will take half the marines in through the sewers and tunnels Vorrak never found. Edessa – you take the guards and move in from east and west, cutting off anyone attempting to escape. Orvessa, you will hold the reserves here until they are needed."

Gough looked up. "And me, Brigadier?"

"You are responsible for defending this complex – on every level. Vorrak has been too quiet for too long."

Gough said nothing. The task was valid, and he knew it. Protecting Orvessa mattered on more levels than one.

"When do we move?" Orvessa asked.

"Troops rest tonight. We move in the early hours – 04:30 for an on-site assault at 05:00. The outer space strike begins at 04:30 and ceases at 04:59. Questions?"

"The fighters on Scar – will you use them for air-to-ground support?" Gough asked.

"If needed, yes. Brief them to be ready at the appropriate time."

Orvessa sighed. Everyone looked at her.

"Sorry. I was thinking about rebuilding. Our two cities – our only cities. What we will have lost. What we can do to prevent this kind of devastation in the future."

No one had an answer for that. Not yet.

Lord Vorrak was listening to the mind record of Harbour. It contained information the man had not volunteered during their meeting – interesting material. He heard Harbour's voice:

"The entrance to Point Hope, in the mountains west of the palace, is impregnable. Two small doors either side, opening only from within. Take your forces to the front entrance and you will fail. I'll keep the next part as a bargaining chip — but four hundred metres down to the left, as you face the main entrance, there is a service exit built for fire evacuation. Roll the stone away and you gain access. The door opens inward.

If you get inside, there is a gallery running around the main area — food, briefings, a parade ground. Below the centre section is the hospital complex. Sliding doors close automatically and can only be opened from inside. The Commander's room is somewhere in there. I was shown around on a goodwill visit when I was still in the Corps."

Vorrak sat back. Remarkably interesting.

"Number Three – prepare a battle force for immediate deployment. I will lead it personally. Full kit: fighting rations, double ammunition, mountain camouflage, personnel carriers, and my armoured vehicle – the one that doesn't require wheels or tracks. Move."

The Varkalon column left the palace and headed for the mountains. A routine overflight by the fighter squadron picked up the movement on scanner. The following message was relayed to Tarrin just as she was preparing to enter the sewers:

"Foxtrot Charlie One to Ground Control. Foxtrot Charlie One to Ground Control. No Duff message for Brigadier — urgent, No Duff. Varkalon column moving toward the mountain area west of the palace. Large force on scanner. Advise you consider defence of Point Hope. I say again — consider defence of Point Hope. Roger, out."

No Duff. The only time anyone used those words, it was real.

Tarrin contacted Edessa immediately and shared the message. "What do you think?"

"If it's genuine, we have no choice – we respond. And it means fewer Varkalons in the city. Redeploy half of each of our forces back to Point Hope and notify the Commander and the Colonel. Agreed?"

"Agreed. Who will you put in command, Edessa? This is fundamentally a Vilkyrian operation."

"Velmaraak Absus. Battle-hardened – three campaigns."

"Good. Issue the orders. I'll dispatch half the marines to Point 4376, 9796 now."

"Copy – Point 4376, 9796. May the Creator guard us all. Out."

Chapter Forty-Five
It's Going to Hit the Fan

The Palace

Tarrin had brought her force to the entrance to the sewers and tunnels beneath the palace, ensuring that every platoon of marines had a Blade Leader and a junior officer – experience distributed through every group.

Edessa had used the Shadowveils as cover to mass her forces close to, but not too near, the main palace entrance.

The barrage began exactly on time. Fighters launched air-to-ground plasma bolts that shook the walls and tore apart the entrance. By the second wave, the gates had ceased to exist. The cannon emplacements and Virexion launchers were useless against an attack from outer space – outside their range-finding capability entirely. What fire they managed to return went back to their launch positions inside the palace and caused almost as much damage as the aerial bombardment itself. The barrage lasted exactly twenty-nine minutes. Then, as abruptly as it had started, it stopped.

Silence – where moments before there had been *Drav'khaal.* It replaced the violent, discordant surge of sound that had been something like war drums, screams, and metal all colliding at once in a single storm.

The ground troops moved in.

Tarrin headed straight for the bedroom entry point the Varkalons had used on their way in. She knew the area well and wanted the command post retaken as quickly as possible. Marines poured out of the hole in the bedroom floor and surged through the door toward the control room. That was when things became extremely difficult. The Varkalons had established fire points on either side of the doors and were not giving ground. Frontal charges cost Tarrin marines. She pulled the force back and searched for cover from which to attack again. Nothing presented itself.

Then a door to the left opened and a Varkalon walked out eating something, finding – to its complete surprise – a corridor full of marines ready to destroy it. Blades, knives, hand weapons, and boot charges rained down on the Varkalon, which stood no chance. Its lifeless body oozed foam and foul-smelling fluid onto the floor. The significant thing was that the door was still open.

"Grab that door and check it out – now!"

The Varkalons at the fire points had heard the commotion and Tarrin's shout but failed to grasp its significance. They kept firing into the corridor, hoping to hit something.

The doorway led to a corridor running around the command centre and arriving at the bug-out door – one that opened from both sides. Tarrin moved fast, alert to the corridor being a perfect ambush point. But it was clear. She and the lead platoon reached the bug-out door without contact.

"On my count – stun flashes and thunder cones. One. Two. Three. GO."

She counted to five, then followed her marines in. They were so close on her heels she could feel them. Varkalon bodies lay slumped over consoles, screens, and the floor, riddled with shrapnel. The Varkalons outside the door tried to force their way in, but it could only be opened from within. Tarrin steadied the troops, then more flash-bangs as that door was opened and the final resistance in the room was eliminated.

Against every instinct of military training, Edessa had led the guards toward what had once been the palace gates. Climbing over stone, metal, and bodies, they fought their way metre by metre into the palace grounds. House to house, hand to hand, engaging every Varkalon they encountered. There were no Vilkyrians left in the palace to emerge and assist – all had been taken by the invaders.

Edessa called a halt at a building covered in black plastic sheeting – windows and doors completely blacked out. The guards forced the doors and rushed inside.

It was the Varkalon scientific test laboratory.

The body parts were Vilkyrian. Spread across tables, suspended in bottles, wired to electrical boards. What lay before them depicted suffering at its most extreme – a violation so profound it went beyond species. It was the reduction of life to a struggle for breath amid death, disease, and despair. None of them had seen anything like it. Grown warriors sobbed and fought for composure. But they had to continue. Every last piece of *Grask'ven* had to be removed. The Varkalons were not merely dishonourable – they had betrayed the essence of life itself, in ways reviled by every race that had ever encountered them.

Edessa and Tarrin met in the palace chamber. Troops congratulated one another on being alive. Then Edessa collapsed to the floor, sobbing, her hands at her throat. Tarrin rushed to her side, unable to understand the grief.

Edessa's *Zarn'thaal* – her deputy, bound by oath to serve her, the trusted extension of her command who had acted as her eyes, ears, and hands throughout the chaos of the assault – stepped forward and quietly explained what they had found in the laboratory.

Tarrin said nothing. She pulled Edessa close against her chest and softly kissed her hair.

Point Hope

Orvessa received a mind record from Tarrin and began to sob uncontrollably. Gough could not understand why. He was busy setting up internal weapon emplacements in case anything came through the parade square. Orvessa mumbled the phrase, *"Varnak'tel druun'khaal — Let the winds carry our wrath"* – which Gough managed to understand, roughly, as something to do with the desecration of honoured remains. He tried to comfort her, but she was inconsolable and retreated to the sanctity of her room behind the medical facility.

Gough had to carry on and complete the defences. After the Brigadier's message, time was running out.

Vorrak sent his reconnaissance troop to find the service doorway, and they returned confirming it was exactly as Harbour's mind record had described. He then set up a feint – positioning Virexion batteries facing the area where he believed the main entrance to be, deliberately visible to the scanners and screens inside. Which is exactly what was reported to Gough. He immediately sealed the medical facility to protect the wounded and Orvessa.

Meanwhile, Vorrak and his specialist forces were filing up the stairwell to the gallery. No guards, no marines, no one to prevent their passage upward. Vorrak's face took on a *Zareth'kai vel druunak* – the sick smile of a predator about to close on its prey. He deployed his forces along the gallery and gave the command:

"Krez'tal ven drakhaal — leave none to crawl. Leave no survivors."

Death stormed down onto the emplacements, the marines, and anyone near the parade square.

Gough was in the briefing room studying access points to bring reserves up to the parade area. Hearing and seeing the effect of the weapons fire focused on his forces, he scanned the map for any access to the gallery. There had to be a way up – and he needed it now. But his knowledge of the complex was nothing like Orvessa's.

Then his Pulseband glowed, and her voice came into his mind.

"Bring the marines from level four to level seven. Use scatter weapons for maximum effect. Kill them all, Gough. Please."

He launched the counterattack. Parts of the gallery were cleared, but from other positions the Varkalons continued to rain fire down on the troops below. Gough moved the marines from the entrance to the covered area that the Shadowveils had used after the first battle and briefed the Blade Leader to set up snipers with seek-and-destroy rounds. He checked the monitors for any sign of expected reinforcements.

Nothing.

Then, for no apparent reason – silence. The firing ceased. An unhurried voice drifted down from the gallery.

"Give up, Earthlings. We have no quarrel with you. Surrender and we will spare your bodies. They are of no use to me or my race – except perhaps for spare parts. Give up. Now. You are not worthy of our firepower."

A pause.

"Give me the witch Orvessa, and you can all walk free. Just one, for so many. What a deal."

Vorrak could not contain his laughter.

Gough needed time. He switched on the tannoy system within the cavern and held the microphone too close to the unit. The feedback shrieked through the space, hurting Varkalon ears as much as human or Vilkyrian ones.

"Truly sorry, old man – not used to these things. Old-fashioned equipment!" He cleared his throat. "Now, let me be clear. You are offering us our lives in exchange for Orvessa. Yes? Small problem, I'm afraid – the medical facility is sealed from the inside. No one can get in or out."

He was lying, of course.

"So, it appears we have something of a stalemate. I can come out and negotiate – but it would be me, the commander of troops here, and no one else." He kept his voice easy, unhurried.

In the back of his mind, Orvessa's words from what felt like a lifetime ago: *Over my dead body.* And her reply: *No — to be more precise, it will be over my living body if they catch me.*

He needed more time. How much could he buy?

The Cavalry Arrive

Gough looked around the room. Many of his team were shaking their heads. "Fight on, Colonel. Fight to the death. Let's rush the *Drakhaal.*"

"No. Let me see if I can get him to come down and talk."

He turned back to the microphone and let it screech again.

"Awfully sorry – did that twice. Now, I need enough time to bring my marines up to the parade area so we can arrange to leave. Once they are in your sights, so to speak, perhaps we can have a chat about resolving this tricky situation. What do you say?"

Silence filled the cavern. Gough waited. Still nothing. Vorrak was not accustomed to counter-offers or negotiation. He liked the idea of all the marines gathered in his sights. He had no desire to talk to a stupid Earthling – he would sooner shoot him. But the idea was appealing.

Gough pressed the microphone again. "We don't have all day. I need to get my men out first and foremost. We are Celestial Brigade marines – not ordinary shock troops. Let's talk this out. Man to Varkalon, on the floor of the parade square."

Still silence. He was getting the time he so desperately needed.

The screens in the briefing room showed marines and Vilkyrian guards swarming over the Virexion Lances and their Varkalon operators. Quietly. Efficiently. They no longer presented Gough with any problem.

"Get ready to fight – on my command. Open the outer doors in silent mode and bring the troops in using the red flashing lights. Slow and careful."

He opened the door and strode out into the parade square, tilting his head up toward the gallery. "There – a sign of good faith. My people will be filing in as soon as we call them. Are you afraid to talk with me?" He grinned. "What was it you said – spare my *puny* body? Good line, that." He laughed as though he meant every word of it.

The snipers had sent one man to brief the incoming forces. They filtered in quietly – some directed to use the escape route and join the Varkalons in the gallery from above. Lord Vorrak could not be faced down in front of his crack soldiers. He powered himself down from the gallery on his boots and landed on the parade square floor in front of Gough. The move drew Gough's full attention – and he did not see Number Three slip toward the medical force shield.

"Bring them in, men – into the parade area."

Marines and Vilkyrians moved from outside the cavern to inside, forming a wall of bodies behind Gough and in front of Vorrak. Vorrak's troops could no longer fire for fear of hitting their own Lord.

"On Earth, we call this a Mexican stand-off. Ever been to Mexico – you piece of camel dung?"

The marines filtered onto the gallery. The Varkalons had no choice but to throw down their weapons. Two or three tried to fire and were cut apart before the rest could follow.

Vorrak hurled a star-shaped dagger. It struck Gough's left arm – the prosthetic one. Gough looked down at the blade, then tapped it with his service-issue Tal'Vorr.

"Not a good move, old man. That one isn't real."

He shot Vorrak in the forehead with his silent flame. The snipers followed his lead without hesitation. A crumpled, half-human body lay twisted on the ground like a pile of old rubbish. Vorrak the Unyielding – and his dreams of the Seylira Bond – were no more.

As the force field came down, Orvessa stepped forward. Number Three lunged – grabbing her with one hand, his cutlass raised in the other.

"For the Lord!"

The cry died in his throat. Orvessa drove a volt discharger into his face. A brilliant light flashed from within his skull.

"Die, you piece of dung! *Kraal'ven, skarn'tul* – let the winds scatter your stench!"

The echoing gunfire faded and was replaced by a ringing silence. For one suspended moment, Orvessa and Gough simply looked at each other across the cavern – the body of Vorrak lying between them.

Then Orvessa ran to him and threw her arms around him, kissing him full on the lips.

Chapter Forty-Six

Acceptance and Rebuilding

Acceptance

The remaining Vilkyrians were in a state of despair. Orvessa and Edessa could not bring themselves to visit the ruins of the palace. The grief was like drowning in quicksand – slow, tortuous, and inescapable. The sense of loss was a palpable weight, a constant pressure on every chest that made each breath an effort. No one could process the horror and devastation that Lord Vorrak and his Varkalons had wrought in pursuit of something they could never have achieved.

Orvessa issued orders for a day of remembrance, a series of religious funerals, and for the site of the old city and the palace to be consecrated as a permanent memorial garden. None of it would happen quickly. The Vilkyrian dead had to be found, identified, and prepared for ritual burial. The Varkalon bodies would be gathered and burned together.

Reports continued to arrive from the assault on the Varkalon home world. Their cities had been decimated. The general assessment was that the planet had been rendered completely uninhabitable.

"No Varkalon will be left alive to return home," Edessa declared.

The four of them stood together outside the cavern entrance – Orvessa and Gough, Edessa and Tarrin – motionless, numb. Dust and the smell of battle and death hung in the air around them. But there was one moment of beauty: the sun setting slowly over the plains, and the gentleness of a cool breeze moving across their faces.

Tarrin spoke first. "We will rebuild and replace, protect and provide for all your people, Orvessa."

Edessa sobbed. "But it can never be the same. Never."

"The love, the care, and the friendship – those will never die, Edessa," Gough said quietly. He placed his good arm around Orvessa and drew her gently toward him. "Look at the sun. It is hope. It is a sign."

At that moment, a Phoenix appeared in the red glow of the dying light. Everyone saw it.

As one, the two couples held each other in the warmth of it, the Phoenix resting above them like a benediction.

Rebuilding

The morning brought a kind of new hope to everyone. Orvessa and Gough were drinking coffee and eating egg banjos.

"What are those things?" asked Edessa.

"Egg banjos – come and try one. They're great with ketchup."

The lightness of the banter seemed out of place. Yet it was needed. There was rebuilding to plan, and they would have to do it together. Tarrin joined them and looked at Gough with a warmth that said everything. "Only a soldier could think of egg banjos after everything we've been through. Well, done, my man. Well, done – for all of it."

Gough flexed his left hand. The synthetic skin responded with perfect fluidity – no metal, no resistance, just warmth and movement indistinguishable from the arm he had lost. The technology was Vilkyrian: elegant and organic, designed not merely to restore function but to preserve dignity. Only those who knew him well – Orvessa, Edessa, and Tarrin – could tell it was not the original.

Orvessa reached out and held his hand. Across the table, Tarrin pressed a soft kiss to Edessa's hair – and in doing so, everyone noticed. Edessa's hair was not changing colour. It had been a pale silver since the laboratory, and it had not changed back.

"What's wrong, Sis?" Orvessa asked gently.

"I don't know. It changed when we saw what they had done in that place. It hasn't come back."

Tarrin looked at her wife with quiet tenderness. "It will come back. Time is what heals these hurts. You cannot rush it. Just give it time, my angel warrior."

They all understood, without saying it aloud, that they needed to get away – from these caverns, from the smell of dust and battle, from everything that had consumed them in so short a time yet left such profound marks. But that was not going to happen soon. Healing would come at its own pace, for each of them, and it could not be forced.

The same process was unfolding across all of Nebulon 17. Battle-hardened marines sat with Vilkyrians, talking, helping with food preparation, building makeshift shelters. These men and women had known loss and grief throughout their own lives and could only begin to understand the depth of what the Vilkyrians were carrying. Yet somehow they seemed to understand the upheaval instinctively – and that mattered.

The most hopeful moment for everyone came with the release of the children from the safe zone. As they returned to their parents, the sounds that filled the air were tears and laughter together – and those sounds, more than anything else, helped people begin to come to terms with what they had all been through.

Peace had come.

But at what cost – to the humans, to the Vilkyrians, and to a nation that had been obliterated.

Chapter Forty-Seven
Medals and Rewards

The Major General arrived at area seven, which looked little more than a cluster of broken trees and a trans-pad – nothing like the grove Gough had experienced when he first arrived on Nebulon 17 all those months ago. There was no formal reception, no ceremony. Just Tarrin, Gough, and the General's adjutant.

"I am glad to see you both alive and well."

"So are we, Sir," Tarrin replied. She had hoped the human response could have waited a little longer – given the Vilkyrians more time to process everything. Yet here he was.

"How is the Commander? And your lovely wife, Brigadier?"

"As well as can be expected at this stage."

"And you, young Gough – how did things go from your end?"

"Sort of all right, Sir. I have a new arm for my troubles." He flexed the prosthetic and demonstrated its range of movement.

"Dashed good, that. Not from Earth, I imagine. Shall we get out of the open, Brigadier? Just in case."

They moved off in a Shadowveil and reached the cavern without incident. The General was somewhat put out that he could see nothing from inside the transport. Tarrin briefed him quietly. "There is not much left of the palace to see. The second city is further out – and that is destroyed. There is a great deal of rebuilding ahead, including the remembrance garden to be laid over the palace ruins."

"Yes, yes – we will assist with all of that. Cost is no object. The Celestial Alliance will lend, lease, and loan whatever is needed. Now – what happened to that Lord Vorrak fellow?"

Gough coughed. Tarrin answered. "My sharpshooter here drew him out into the open. Vorrak attacked first. Gough killed him. One clean shot to the head."

"Oh! Jolly good show, Gough. I have an appropriate medal for you – and for all the others – in the case here. The adjutant will be kept busy for a while. Will the timing work?"

"I will check with the Commander, Sir." Tarrin's reply came just a fraction slower than the General would have preferred.

Orvessa agreed, though reluctantly. A makeshift stage was erected in the parade area, with seating for combatants, families, and children. No one was left out. The Luminar Council were placed in the front row behind the award recipients as a mark of respect. The citations for both Vilkyrian and Celestial medals were displayed on a large screen above the stage.

Orvessa drew the General aside beforehand. "Quietly now – no speeches. We will list the awards and present them to the senior members present. As a nation, we are not yet ready to celebrate. This is a thank you – to you and your people for everything you did. Otherwise, this ceremony would have been months away. Understood?"

"Yes, yes – no long speeches."

"No speeches, General."

"Oh. OH. Understood – no speeches at all."

Orvessa took to the stage in her formal ceremonial dress and the Vilkyrian collar of office. The General was in his number one uniform, as were the stage party. The troops filed into their seats – Vilkyrians first, then marines, then families and children. A single gong sounded. Orvessa rose.

"Today we are gathered to honour our soldiers for their courage, steadfast actions, and skill – both Vilkyrian and Celestial marine. As a nation, we thank everyone who fought and survived the invasion that will henceforth be known as the Seylira War. All combatants will receive campaign medals from Vilkyrie and the Celestial Alliance. The following are called forward for distinguished awards, to be presented by Major General Pridou and myself."

The Major General turned to Orvessa first and presented her with the Celestial Platinum Star for bravery above and beyond the demands of senior leadership.

Deputy Commander Edessa received the Gold Star for valour and leadership. Velmaraak Absus was awarded the Silver Star for outstanding valour in the face of overwhelming odds. Orvessa then turned to her sister and presented her with the Echo of Orvessa for leadership and bravery in diplomatic service.

Orvessa faced Brigadier Tarrin. "You are one of us," she said simply. "And I award you the Vilkyrian Heart, the Sentinel's Halo, and the Echo of Orvessa for your faithful service to Vilkyrie."

Finally, she moved forward on the stage – prompting Gough to step to the front.

"It gives me the greatest pleasure to award my husband – a true Vilkyrian – the Flame-Bound Sigil for moral fortitude, sacrifice, and courage in the face of outright danger, and the Vilkyrian Heart for shielding the vulnerable and protecting so many of our people." She allowed herself the moment, and kissed him on the cheek.

The audience erupted. Every voice – Vilkyrian and human alike – joined in the same cheer. Gough was not simply Orvessa's husband any more. He was one of them.

Chapter Forty-Seven

Getting Back to Normal Perhaps.

The General's farewell included a posting order for Brigadier Tarrin – back to Earth for rest and recuperation, then to take command of the Earth training unit for combat-ready marines in the Cotswolds.

Tarrin mentioned it to Edessa and asked her to come. This time, Edessa said yes.

They went together to Orvessa and explained the situation. Orvessa had no desire to separate them – they had been apart long enough. She agreed at once, then added, "Gough will remain here, of course, Tarrin. Yes?"

"Yes, Commander. He is now base commander and resident diplomatic mission from Earth to Vilkyrie. I can't see him being posted anywhere else – unless, of course, there is another war somewhere."

Orvessa laughed loudly. "Over my dead body."

"One final point, Brigadier – can we come and visit you both in this place, the Cotswolds? Is it nice?"

"It is. We'll buy a cottage near the base. You can both visit whenever you like – perhaps come to a pass-out parade."

Gough saluted Tarrin. "I will miss your guidance, Brigadier. But I understand you are needed elsewhere." He turned to Edessa, his tone shifting entirely. "As my sister-in-law, I could not ask for better. As a military commander – thank God you are on our side. And as my friend, you will always hold a piece of my heart. Perhaps only a small piece. But it is there." He smiled. "I love you, Edessa. Brotherly love, of course."

They left the following morning. Orvessa and Gough stood together at the trans-pad and waved them off.

Building supplies and construction teams were arriving by the trans-pad load. Orvessa explained to Gough that the Vilkyrians had the ability to build cities quickly.

"How?" he asked.

"Have you ever heard of 3D printing?"

"Yes, but–"

"We do it rather larger here. Come with me, beloved, and see what is already happening."

They trans-padded to a valley beside the western mountain range, a meadow with a river running through it. A walled city was already under construction; its segments being placed as they came off a vast 3D printer.

"The materials and construction crews coming in can help cover the old palace site and build the remembrance garden. The real decision – the one I need you to look at and hopefully approve – is where the new palace should be built, and the plans for both the above and below-ground sections."

Gough stared at it all. "Orvessa – by the Creator. You don't hang around, do you?"

"Housing, apartments, stores – everyone needs somewhere to go. Time is always short. I had my team start the morning after the ceremony."

He shook his head slowly. "Something else I didn't know about Vilkyrians. Angel – do you do anything slowly?"

"Making love to you," she said. "Now and again." She stepped back toward the trans-pad, and they returned to the cavern for lunch, a few snacks, and a glass of Vilkyrian sparkling water that Gough had never tried before.

"What is this? It's wonderful – it clears the palate completely."

"I thought that was what my kisses were for. Not some fizzy liquid from a bottle."

"Your kisses are considerably better than sparkling water. How would you translate them? Your kiss transcends the physical. It bestows moments of profound connection – and the sealing of our vows. That is your kiss, angel."

A knock at the door brought the building foreman into the room – a tall man with broad shoulders and thick legs. He bowed his head.

"I apologise for the intrusion, Your Majesty. You instructed me to present the draft plans for the remembrance garden to you and the Prince upon your return."

Gough turned slowly to Orvessa and whispered, "Who in the hell is the Prince?"

"You are, my sweet. I had you promoted at the council meeting yesterday." She paused, a perfectly composed expression on her face. "Did I not mention it last night? Or were you really asleep when I got back?"

Chapter Forty-Eight

Planned or a Mistake?

Gough had grown accustomed to the constant checking and rechecking of Orvessa's health before each ceremony, so he did not think too much of it when she mentioned seeing her physician in the morning.

"Should I be worried, or is it a routine check-up?"

"Not entirely routine – but they do check me for this from time to time. I shouldn't be too long. Can you manage breakfast without me, darling?"

"I can wait for you, if you'd like?"

"No – go ahead. I'll come and find you after the examination. Where will you be?"

"I thought I'd eat al fresco tomorrow. Out by the cavern entrance. A poor lonely soul with no one to talk to." He smiled. "He he."

"I'll find you there." And with that, Orvessa was off to another meeting.

In the morning, Gough sat munching toast and sipping black coffee, his mind wandering over the plans for the remembrance garden. Orvessa returned and sat down across from him. She was quiet. Noticeably quiet. Too quiet.

"What's up, Passion?"

"Nothing really. Just–" Her voice faded. She looked up at him, directly into his eyes. "Just *Delyari.*"

"*Delyari?*" He paused. "*Delyari* – doesn't that mean twins?"

"Yes. Two lives woven from a single thread. By us. It is the deepest expression of our spiritual and emotional bond, my wonderful man."

Her face shone like the brightest sun in any sky. She looked radiant – more so than usual, and that was saying something. "Oh, Gough. You have made us complete. You wonderful, wonderful human being." Her voice broke into pure joy. "Twin girls. Oh, Gough – I knew I had something growing inside me, but two girls. That is so rare for a Vilkyrian. I have wanted this all my life, and when I felt the Seylira link with you I dared to hope. But it was only a hope – and then the war came." She reached across the table. "Oh, Gough. Kiss me, you fool. Kiss me now. That is an order."

Gough broke his stunned silence all at once.

"Put your feet up. What can I get you for breakfast? Do you need anything? You must rest – fewer meetings, fewer ceremonies, less of everything." He covered her with gentle kisses – her neck, her eyes, her lips, her forehead. Then he placed his hand softly on her stomach. "Our babies. Oh my. Our babies." He straightened up. "We need to tell the Council. And Edessa and Tarrin. My mum. Your secretary. The church. The Council–" He caught himself. "I said the Council already." He sat back down. "The new palace – we'll need two more bedrooms, with a connecting door through from our rooms. They'll have to make it work. You can tell them what's needed, but you are not to lift anything or carry anything. I know about these things – my mother told me. A long while ago, but she told me. Would you like a coffee? No – you can't have coffee. Juice. Something with vitamin C. And you'll need folic acid–"

"What on earth is all this about vitamins? And what is folic acid?"

"I told you – my mother explained that you need these things. Because you're pregnant."

Orvessa stared at him. "Excuse me – do you not think we have delivered babies on Nebulon 17 before?"

"Yes, yes, of course. But not like these babies. These are *our* babies." He stopped. Drew a long breath.

Orvessa was laughing and crying at the same time – laughing with pure happiness, and crying at the entirely unscripted, gloriously chaotic performance Gough was putting on for her, and for her alone.

"Come here," she said. "Come here and give me a cuddle, you crazy, loveable fool. My fool. And the father of our babies."

Chapter Forty-Nine

Two Steps Forward - One Step Back

Orvessa adjusted her exercise routine and, at Gough's insistence, used a carriage to travel around the countryside – reviewing the building work and talking with her people. It was not really a carriage. It was a floating sanctum: transparent yet shielded, designed to carry dignitaries, healers, or newborns through the countryside in ceremonial procession. A true *Velassaryn*. The people bowed or offered *zhayelûn* gestures as it passed.

Gough worried constantly about Orvessa overdoing things. Yet they had been together long enough now for him to know better than to tell her off too often.

It was on one of these trips – reviewing the progress of the remembrance garden – that Orvessa suddenly cried out in pain.

"Gough – get me back to the medical unit. Now."

Gough did not joke or hesitate. He told the driver to use all speed to reach the rebuilt hospital. Lights flashing, sirens wailing, the *Velassaryn* moved at breakneck pace and arrived at the emergency entrance to be met by doctors, nurses, and midwifery staff.

Gough had to stand back and let them work. He paced outside the operating theatre, bouncing between a terror he had never felt in any conflict and a desperate insistence that everything would be all right.

Please, God. Make it all right. Please.

Was it the start of early labour, or something worse? He did not know.

After what felt like hours, the senior medical officer came out and asked him to sit down.

Oh no. Gough felt the ground shift. *No. She is too healthy, too strong, too—*

He realised the doctor was speaking and had not heard a word of it.

"I'm sorry, doctor. Please – say that again."

"Our Leader is safe, Prince Gough. She will be moved shortly." The doctor paused. "The difficulty is that both babies are premature. One, I believe, will be fine. The second, however, presents what in medical terms we call Intrauterine Growth Restriction – IUGR."

"I'm a soldier, Doc. What does that mean in plain language?"

"It refers to a foetus that is smaller than expected for its gestational age, due to poor growth in the womb. It does not typically occur with Vilkyrian babies. We believe it may be a result of the human element in the pregnancy."

Gough began to shake. "Me. It's my fault. Oh Lord – no."

He waited until he could see Orvessa. "How are you feeling, my love? Are you in pain? Is there anything I can do?"

"Yes," she said. "Sit down and hold my hand. Just hold my hand."

He sat. He took her hand in both of his. "The doctor says it's my fault – about the second girl. I am so sorry, angel. I am so deeply sorry."

"Gough." Her voice was quiet and steady. "We both know it takes two to tango. I felt the Seylira first and never once thought about complications – and neither did you, nor the doctors for that matter. We have to wait and see if she can pull through." She looked at him directly. "The one thing you must stop doing – for me – is blaming yourself. It is no one's fault. No one's."

She looked up to find tears running down his face. She had never seen him cry. Not once. She tried to reach up to wipe them away but could not get to him from where she lay.

They spent a restless night. Council members and well-wishers came to the door in a steady stream but were not admitted. Gough dozed off in his chair and jolted awake the moment his head fell forward. He sat in the dim light of the hospital room, fighting to keep his eyes open, and praying – for both of them, for all three of them – that both babies would live.

They would not know for at least two days.

Chapter Fifty
God and the Phoenix

All construction work stopped. Everyone was praying for the couple and the babies.

In the afternoon of the first day, Edessa and Tarrin arrived at the hospital – flowers, chocolates, and tiny baby boots in hand. They kissed Orvessa, who managed a smile. "I am feeling better. But thank you for coming. It truly means a great deal to us both."

"What does the doctor say about the twins?" Edessa asked quietly.

"Not much." Gough cut in. "They think it might be my fault – because I'm human." He turned away.

Orvessa snapped. "I told you – it is not your fault."

Then she broke down entirely, tears coming in floods. "I'm sorry. I'm sorry, Gough. Forgive me – I didn't mean to–"

Gough moved to her side and held her while she wept.

"No, angel. None of this is your fault. Please don't cry – it tears me apart worse than anything else could. We are in this together. And together we will get through it. Like we always do."

Another troubled night came and went, though this time there were four people in the room. The staff had offered fold-up beds. All four refused.

In the early morning light, Gough looked across and saw Orvessa crying softly.

"I prayed and prayed, Gough. But no one heard me. No one. Where is God now?"

"His plan is already mapped out, my love. We have to trust him and hold on to our faith."

"But what if the baby dies?"

"We don't know that yet. We'll know soon enough." He reached for her hand. "I believe in the power of prayer, and I have faith that both of them will make it. They come from our stock – and we are fighters. So are they."

The clock ticked on. The morning unfolded like a prayer whispered into the sunlight. Tarrin stretched and quietly left the room. Edessa watched her go – and could see, through the glass, that she was sobbing silently as she walked.

Then Edessa stood up. When she spoke, her voice was loud and clear and came from somewhere none of them could have named.

"The glory of the realm is founded upon the rising and the setting of the Phoenix. Hear us, oh great Creator – save us from the flaw in the Seylira, and grant these two babies your life and your love."

No one, not even Edessa, knew where that prayer had come from. But it settled over the room like a blessing. Orvessa closed her eyes, and for the first time since the hospital, she felt something close to peace.

After only a few seconds, the doctor came in. There were tears in his eyes.

"I have lost her. I tried everything I know. I am so sorry – I have failed you both. I have failed this community."

A nurse suddenly seized his arm. "Doctor – come quickly. Now. Please."

The room fell into disarray as he was pulled back through the door. Tarrin came back in to find everyone in tears. "Oh my God – what has happened?" But no one could speak.

Minutes passed. The two couples held each other, tears falling like moonlight over sacred stone.

And then it happened.

A flash of red light filled the room – visible to everyone, inside and outside. The light took the shape of a Phoenix, aged and spent, which fell to the floor as ash. Then, as though moved by an unseen hand, it burst into flame and was reborn. It rose and flew out of the room, and in the silence that followed you could have heard a pin drop.

What they heard instead was the doctor's voice.

"It is God's miracle. She is back with us. Both of them – they are all right. I cannot explain it. She was gone, and now she is alive. Praise the Creator."

The tears that came now were of pure joy and gratitude – the answer to every prayer that had been whispered through the night. Doctors, nurses, the two couples, the specialist intensive care staff – everyone was weeping as the nurses wheeled the babies' incubators out for Orvessa and Gough to see their girls, kicking and breathing easily, alive in the light.

Chapter Fifty-One
A New Normal

Word spread through the community like blossoms opening at dawn. The churches filled with grateful Vilkyrians – followers of the Phoenix and the Creator.

The question on everyone's lips was the same: had it been magic? Had the Creator intervened? Were the old ways of the Phoenix truly real?

Orvessa was released from the hospital after one week. The babies stayed a week longer. Gough could not get over how quickly things moved on Nebulon 17 compared to Earth.

"It takes considerably longer back home, my love. Are you certain you and the babies are all right?" He had already put both girls in the same room while they slept – easier, for now, to get to them both.

"Sit down, Gough. There are a few things you need to know about Vilkyrian children."

He sat; fairly confident he was about to hear nothing he didn't already know. "I'm listening. I may even learn something."

"Vilkyrian children – all Vilkyrian children – grow faster than on Earth. It is part of the same life force the Phoenix embodies. Rapid growth, renewal, a compressed journey. One of your Earth years is three here. The children grow quickly until they reach approximately twenty-one. Then they stop."

Gough stared at her. "You what?" He did the calculation. "You mean in seven years they'll be adults?" He said it again, quietly, as if testing whether it would sound more reasonable the second time. "Three years for every one." He looked up. "They'll be smarter than me by the time they're five?"

"Almost certainly. You will need to get used to early crawling, walking, talking – and of course, puberty."

"Oh my God."

"It's entirely normal," Orvessa replied, with a casual glance at his expression.

"We need names then. Rather quickly, I'd say. Have you thought of any?"

"Yes, my love – if you agree. *Feyssa* for the firstborn, and *Jessa* for the little one. We could also give her your mother's name, as a second name. What do you think?"

Gough considered it. "That would be lovely – but I don't want to make her feel different. She has already been through enough difference for one lifetime."

"Then – Feyssa and Jessa. Agreed?"

"Agreed. Now – do Vilkyrian children have godparents?"

"Yes."

"Well, that seems straightforward enough. Edessa and Tarrin?"

"We can have Edessa, yes. But Tarrin is an Earthling – tradition doesn't allow it. What about the head of the Council, Magi Roussa?"

"Would he agree?"

"I honestly don't know. I'll ask him." She paused. "Oh – and just so you are aware, they will need to learn both Vilkyrian and English." She smiled. "Domestic bliss, my love."

Gough spent the afternoon in the new palace library, deep in thought and surrounded by volumes of Vilkyrian history and mystic writing. He wanted to understand more about the Phoenix – its origins, and what it might mean for his girls. The shelves ran from floor to ceiling, with space carved out for the electronic knowledge bases, which he had privately decided were one step above an Earth computer.

As his finger traced the words on the page, the elaborate Vilkyrian script seemed to shimmer for just a second – as if responding to his touch. He blinked. It was ink and parchment again.

He read on:

Only appears in times of crisis or joy. Only appears to select Vilkyrians, as prophesied by the ancients. It leads the rebirth by reincarnation. It never dies, and no one knows where it lodges when it is not seen. Further information can be obtained from the Arc — accessible only by authorised request from the Leader of the community at that time.

Gough touched his ring instantly. "Are you free this afternoon? We need to visit the Arc."

The response came almost immediately.

"Hi, baby. What are you doing – and why?"

"I've been reading about the Phoenix – trying to understand what it might mean for the girls. Then I found this." He read her the passage. "That's you, isn't it? The Leader?"

"Yes, that's me. Are you certain about this?"

"Never been more certain about anything – except when I fell in love with you, angel."

A brief pause. "You are opening a very deep *Zarqelûn*, my love. It will bring knowledge, yes – but also secrets, hidden intentions, things that have been buried for a long time. Are you ready for that kind of expansion in your understanding of Vilkyrian lore and mystery?"

"Yes. I am. Absolutely certain." He hesitated. "Well – mostly for the girls. And all right, maybe a little bit for me too. Are you free? Can we go? Pretty please?"

Chapter Fifty-Two
Meeting the Phoenix

Leaving the girls with the nanny, they set off after lunch to the mountain cavern that had been their home for so much of their time together. It felt strange to be walking across the parade square with no one there – through the medical facility, closed up now, and into Orvessa's back room. She pressed the button and they descended the stairs.

"Is there always this faint red glow?" Gough asked. "I don't remember it from the first time."

"No, darling. I've never seen it either. I wonder if they know we're coming."

They arrived at the entrance to the Arc and checked each other for metallic objects. None.

"Are you nervous, Orvessa? Because I am."

"That's the first time you've ever admitted that to me." She smiled. "That's sweet. But we are more protected here than anywhere else on this planet."

They sat side by side, bodies touching, hands on the handle – just as before. The flame rose before them. Orvessa had the sense that something was already present within it, but she said nothing.

"Oh, Ancients of Nebulon 17 – help us to understand the rights and nature of the Phoenix. It appeared and saved one of our children. We would respectfully wish to know more. We ask for your guidance, in unity and peace. *Thalvëa.*"

To their amazement, no voice came from the flame. Instead, the Phoenix appeared – perched in the front window of the ship's cabin, regarding them with calm, ancient eyes. When the voice came, it came not from the flame but from within their own minds.

"I know why you are here. The ancients have given me permission to speak with you both, and it is a great honour – particularly for you, Gough, as a non-native. Some of the ancients are more than pleased with you and the way you carry yourself." The Phoenix turned its gaze to Orvessa. "And you – they could not be more pleased with you, or your choices. You have done more than they ever hoped. Truly *Velmaraak*."

The bird paused and looked closely at them both. Orvessa was holding Gough's prosthetic hand as though it were his own.

"That is a lovely touch, Orvessa – holding his left hand. You are so good." The Phoenix settled. "So, Gough – you have questions. Speak them aloud, please. I hear your voice and your words even before you utter them. But you need to hear yourself speak, and so does Orvessa."

"Stupid question first – are you real?"

"What does real mean, Gough? I have shape and form, language, and the ability to reincarnate. I am also ethereal – I can speak with the ancients as easily as I am speaking with you now. Does that answer your question?" The Phoenix held his gaze. "I know what is tearing at your insides. Please – ask it."

"Oh my God." Gough's voice dropped. "You know, don't you." It was not quite a question. "Are my girls – are they less, because of me being human?"

Tears rolled down his face before he could stop them. Orvessa squeezed his hand and looked at him with quiet, steady love. The Phoenix was silent for a moment – as though choosing its words with great care.

"You are a remarkably special kind of human, Gough. The ancients saw it immediately. They allowed Orvessa the choice of her Seylira bond, and she chose you – freely, from among partners across many galaxies and worlds. It was foretold in our legends that someone would come from the planet Earth. You are that person. How could your children be anything less than the culmination of the good in Orvessa, and the good in you?"

Gough sat motionless. The Phoenix turned its head to Orvessa.

"Cherish your man, oh defender of Nebulon's faith. The Creator shines upon you and the ancients because of you, and because of your love for him. He is a good man – in the truest sense of those words. Kind, respectful, and we know he loves you more than his own life. He would die for you and your children without hesitation. We can ask no more of any soul." The Phoenix paused once more. "I will close with this: *Naevalen thir'quess ilvëa; melthira en'vethen.* Nothing so good can, or should, be changed. Cherish your love – together."

The words washed over them like a physical force.

The Phoenix fell to ash. Then, as it always had, it gathered itself, reclaimed its radiant plumage, and flew away. The light returned to the cabin. They were left sitting together, hands intertwined, faces wet with tears – and at peace.

Chapter Fifty-Three

A Visit to the Grandparents

The family were having breakfast. The girls sat in their *Lunethra* cradles – legless suspension frames of organic shell form, translucent material threaded with soft glowing veins and etched with protective runes. Gough thought they were magnificent, particularly the voice-linked guardian mode that regulated temperature and infused calming scents. Not that the girls needed calming down very often. They had also recently reached the stage where food went into their mouths rather than over everything else.

Happy days thought Gough.

Orvessa reclined in a flowing robe that covered yet still showed her legs, reading from a tablet.

"Hey, Mr Contented – we've had an invitation. They want us to visit this place, the Cotswolds. We could pop in to see Grandma on the way. What do you think?"

"By *they,* do you mean the Brigadier and Auntie Edessa? Are the girls old enough for the trans-pad? Is it safe for them?"

"No – it will turn them into uncontrollable rebels. A bit like they are now." She looked up. "Do you think your mother would like to see our offspring?"

"Would she?" Gough grinned. "She would be *Veythar en'duval.*"

"Hang on – what if it's a trap to move you somewhere else and take you away from me?"

"Easy. If it is, I resign my commission and we live off my pension."

"All right – we'll go. I'll let them know and get Syphera to make the arrangements." Orvessa set down the tablet. "We will need new clothes for the girls, Gough. We can't have them visiting Earth in these old rags."

"Excuse me – those were brand new two weeks ago."

"Yes. But the girls keep growing, lover."

Gough conceded the point. "I'll send Mum a message. Should I get dates from Syphera? Is she still working well for you?"

"Wonderfully. After seeing how well you adapted to the prosthetic arm, I arranged one for her. She has been talking about returning to the military, but I can manage the workload without her."

With Edessa not available to rule in her place, Orvessa approached the Council head, who agreed on one condition – that he and his wife be given a couple of hours with the girls before departure.

Orvessa and the girls arrived at Grandma's first. Gough followed a few moments later, wrestling the luggage. The visit was brief but wonderful. The girls kept trying to speak to Grandma in Vilkyrian, and she understood nothing whatsoever. A game broke out between Orvessa and Gough – who could translate fastest and most accurately. Orvessa won, naturally.

After the visit, it was time for the main event: the Cotswolds. Here again Orvessa and the girls arrived first. Edessa and Tarrin were waiting at the trans-pad. They waited. No Gough. No luggage.

"You can't get lost on a trans-pad, can you, Tarrin?"

"No, Orvessa. I genuinely don't know what's happened."

At that moment, a piece of paper materialised on the trans-pad. The handwriting was scrawled to the point of near illegibility. Tarrin read it aloud.

"It will cost a great deal to get him back, oh high and mighty one. A great deal — or we will send bits back to you, one at a time."

Orvessa screamed. The girls, startled, began to cry. She slammed her Pulseband. "Capture scenario. Full evac – three pods, now."

In an instant, guards surrounded her and the children and transported them to the Vilkyrian battle cruiser orbiting Earth.

Edessa turned to Tarrin, her face pale. "That's my brother-in-law." Her voice was steady, but only just. "And my sister is up there falling apart." She drew a breath, her training quietly reasserting itself. "Can you handle things down here? I have to go to her. She will need me."

"Yes, go – my *Nimel'kava.* Go."

Chapter Fifty-Four
Is He Dead?

Gough found himself lying on a dirty floor. His hands were bound with a plastic tie wrap, his shoes had been taken, and the floor was thick with dust. He sneezed.

"So – you're awake. Get him up into a chair. We're going to have a man-to-man conversation."

Two men hauled Gough into a metal chair. The stale smell of old grease and mildew filled his nostrils. A dull throb pulsed behind his eyes and the copper taste of blood tinged his mouth.

He coughed, then looked at the man in front of him. "I seem to be somewhat off from my intended destination. Are you responsible for that? Only, I'm on holiday – I should be in the Cotswolds, not in some greasy hellhole like this."

"You are Prince Gough of Nebulon 17. Married, two daughters. On your way to visit your sister-in-law and her wife. We intercepted you. Did I miss anything?"

"Yes – the offer of a coffee. Black, no sugar. Appalling manners." Gough shifted in the chair. "Also, I am not a Prince. I am a Colonel in the Celestial Marines. Not that it matters enormously. Shall we start again, my ill-informed friend?"

"My word – how does a military man become a Prince? Sounds like a fairytale to me." The man laughed. "Kiss my arse, you scumbag."

"You must be a graduate of that school down the road from where I grew up – the one for retards and idiots. This is getting us precisely nowhere."

"Sorry, old man. You're going nowhere for quite some time. So shut the hell up."

"Colonel Gough Veylan. Four five five eight zero zero." He paused. "There is something else I could tell you, but it has escaped me for the moment. It'll come back."

"Put him on the electric rack. Turn it on."

Gough tried to fight them off but was still dizzy from the beating on his arrival. As soon as he was secured to the rack, a door opened and a man with military bearing walked in.

Gough looked up. "Well, well. If it isn't my old friend Harbour." He tilted his head. "Sorry – a clone."

"What do you mean, a clone?"

"Because I killed the real one on Scar, didn't I." He met the clone's eyes. "Don't tell me you need credits and think Orvessa will trade me for them. You are well and truly out of date, you silly old sod."

The clone struck him hard across the face. His nose began to bleed.

Tarrin had called the base and activated Golden Edge. "Two full squads, two crossbow markspersons, full ammunition – transport to this location immediately. I will meet them there."

First, she had contacted the trans-pad operator at Otters Bottom, Gough's mother's home. Moving quickly back inside the house, she changed into fatigues and strapped a Bren-action phaser to her thigh, added webbing and a handful of stun grenades, then stepped back to the pad and punched in the coordinates.

Aboard the battle cruiser, Orvessa had put the girls to bed. Jessa looked up at her with wide eyes. "Will Dad come and kiss us goodnight?"

"He's a little busy tonight, angels – that's why he didn't trans-pad. Military work. You will see him in the morning. Sleep now, please."

Feyssa, confident she was being clever, said, "It's not nighttime yet."

Orvessa managed a smile. "It's dark outside. We're in space. Sleep."

She came back to the main room to find Edessa, and neither of them could hold it together. They broke into floods of tears.

"He's dead, Edessa. I know it. He's dead."

"Not our man, Sis. He is far too good for that."

Back at the location, the troops had spread out in all-round defence. The shed holding Gough was visible, and the scanners had confirmed the number of people inside.

"First platoon – surround the rear of the building. Crossbows to the two windows on the right. The rest with me. As we go in, fire. Two minutes. Hack!"

The attack was flawless. Harbour fell with a bolt in his chest. The three others were dispatched with equal efficiency.

Tarrin surveyed the scene and went completely still.

A crossbow bolt was protruding from Gough's chest.

"No. It's not possible." Her voice was barely above a whisper. The troops took him down and laid him gently on his back.

"Should we try to pull the bolt out, Brigadier?"

"No. Leave it. It's no use now." She knelt and cradled his head in her arms, tears falling onto his face. "It's no one's fault but mine. I got him killed." She could not yet think about how she would tell Orvessa.

Then – for no reason – it turned cold. Terribly cold. Every person in the room felt it at the same instant. A flame rose from the floor, producing red smoke that made several troopers cough and step back.

A deep voice resonated through the space. "He is our chosen one. He cannot fall yet."

The Phoenix emerged from the flame, wings still burning, and walked toward Gough. It jumped onto his chest, stood over the wound, and pulled the bolt free with its beak. Then it danced on his chest and burst into flame – and turned to ash. And as Tarrin had witnessed once before, the ash gathered, the Phoenix was reborn, and it flew away.

Gough coughed.

"Anyone have any water?" He blinked. "What happened to me?" He looked up. "Oh – Tarrin. How are you here?"

No one could speak. Several could not accept what they had just seen. Tarrin said nothing. She held the knowledge in her heart and helped him to his feet.

She pressed her Pulseband. "Edessa – emergency medical team and a return pod to this location, immediately. If not, he will die. He is barely alive."

The team arrived and went to work. The wound in his chest had not closed, and he was losing blood rapidly. They placed him in a medical coma and transported him back to the ship.

Chapter Fifty-Five

Family Man, Military Man, or Even the Messiah?

Tarrin gathered the troops. Around her, murmurs of shock and disbelief rippled through the group. Several soldiers made the sign of the cross. The crossbow specialist who had fired the bolt was in total distress – shaking, unable to stop the tears. Tarrin needed to bring them back to some kind of reality. But how? It had shaken her just as deeply as any of them. How could the Phoenix be here, on Earth? It was a figure of Vilkyrian folklore and religion, not something that belonged in Earth's galaxy, hundreds of light years away.

"All right – everyone sit down. Form a circle. Sit down and listen."

She had no idea what to say next. No military training manual had ever covered anything like this. Neither, for that matter, had the Bible, or any Earthly scripture. Nothing had prepared any of them for what they had just witnessed.

"That was a real shock – for all of us. Most of you have probably never seen a Phoenix before today. I suspect most of you thought it was fictional. I did, until I saw one on Nebulon 17 for the first time. It is part of their religion – it doesn't appear often, but it does appear." She paused, gathering her thoughts. "I have never seen it on Earth before today. What you need to understand is that Colonel Gough, though born on Earth, is an adopted Vilkyrian. He is married to the leader of their nation. His children are both human and Vilkyrian. He belongs to both worlds." She stopped herself. "I know what I'm saying sounds extraordinary. It is extraordinary. And I know I cannot ask you to keep this to yourselves – there are too many of you, and we speak about the things that shake us. That's human nature."

She looked around the circle.

"You will all return to barracks. I will arrange counselling for anyone who needs it – and there is no shame in that. All I can offer you in closing is this: my wife prayed for my nieces on Nebulon 17, and a Phoenix came. If you have faith – well. You never quite know what might arrive to help you." She stood. "Troops, dismiss. Blade Leaders, take them back."

The medical bay had become a completely sealed environment, the outside world gone. The steady sounds of the life-support system had become the rhythm of Orvessa's breathing as she stood at Gough's side, holding his hand. The Pulseband displayed his weak and faltering heartbeat. The Phoenix's miracle felt distant and unreal now – what was real was the man lying motionless in front of her, and her own helplessness.

She had prayed without ceasing since his arrival on the ship. The medical staff refused to share details of his condition beyond the single fact that the coma was necessary to protect him.

The senior medical practitioner approached her carefully and spoke at a measured pace.

"Madam Leader – my Queen. I request permission to speak openly."

"Yes. Tell me everything. What are his chances? Please be honest with me."

"The situation, medically speaking, is grave but clear. The ventricular damage is catastrophic. Prince Gough requires a new heart. Without a transplant, he will not survive."

Orvessa stared at him. "Doctor – this is a battle cruiser. Where would we find a sterile heart?"

"A valid concern, my Queen. However, we have the precise dimensions of his original heart, and we have a medical-grade 3D printer on board. The procedure would be lengthy and complex, but my team is the finest available – they are assigned to this vessel specifically to provide the highest level of care. The decision, however, is yours alone. We cannot wake Prince Gough to seek his consent. The risk would be far too great."

Orvessa tried to turn away, but she was still holding his hand and could not bring herself to let go.

"I need a moment to think. How much time do we have, Doctor?"

“My Queen – medically speaking, we have very little. We would need to begin the printing and prepare for surgery within the next five minutes to ensure the replacement heart is fully functional before we remove the original. Every minute of delay reduces his chances drastically. Beyond a certain point, there will be no chance at all.” He held her gaze. “There is risk in the procedure itself – I will not deceive you about that. But we have everything needed to prevent rejection, which has challenged Earth medicine for centuries. Please, my Queen. Let us help him. Let us bring him back to you whole.”

Orvessa was quiet for a long moment. Her eyes did not leave his face.

“May the Phoenix and the Creator live within him and bring him back to me.” Her voice was barely above a whisper. “My Seylira. My husband. My friend. The father of my girls. My one true love.” She drew a slow breath. “I am afraid it will not work. But I cannot lose him. I have to say yes.” She looked up. “Can I be in the surgery? I need to be there.”

“We begin immediately. You will need to scrub up, my Queen. I will show you where you can stand.”

Chapter Fifty-Six

A Miracle of Vilkyrian Modern Medicine.

Orvessa walked out of the medical room and went to find Edessa. She explained what was happening, her voice barely holding steady. Edessa sent a Pulseband message to Tarrin immediately: *Get here now. I am sending a pod. Take leave, take time off, resign if you have to — but get here now.*

Tarrin briefed her adjutant and stepped into the pod. The adjutant passed word to the officers, who briefed the troops. Many went straight to the ship's chapel and prayed.

Oh Creator — please save this man. He is a hero. He is the Vilkyrian Messiah. Help him now, and always.

Edessa and Tarrin sat together, holding each other, offering short prayers to the Creator, to the Phoenix, and to the Ancients.

Orvessa scrubbed up and was permitted to observe from a designated position near the foot of the table. She was not there to operate – she was there to bear witness, her presence a silent command to the universe to spare him. It was the greatest gamble of her life. It would also be the greatest gamble of Gough's – though he would not know that until he woke up.

If he woke up.

"All right, team." The lead surgeon addressed the room. "We are performing an orthotopic transplant. The patient is relatively young and should be able to sustain the procedure. He is a military man – fit and strong. His left arm is prosthetic and requires no blood supply, which will not affect circulation levels during surgery. We will be removing the entirety of his present heart. This is not a heterotopic procedure. Questions?" He looked around the theatre. "You all know your stations. Anaesthetist – maintain his coma and watch the machines. I want his vitals rock-solid throughout. No slip-ups, no confusion. This must be *Zenthari valkor* – an excellent endeavour. Let us begin."

Orvessa listened from the foot of the table, her hands closed around Gough's ankles. The clinical language – *orthotopic transplant, remove the entirety of his present heart* – struck her with a cold and terrible clarity. She was placing his life entirely in the hands of this team.

The 3D-printed heart had been assessed by a separate team of medical specialists and confirmed one hundred percent viable. It was delivered to the theatre in a sterile transparent case. The lead surgeon paused and examined it while his support surgeon read the test results aloud.

"Excellent. We'll use it." He looked down at the table. "Prince Gough – meet your new ticker."

Before the operation began, the lead surgeon spoke in a clear, carrying voice.

"May the Creator, the Phoenix, and the Ancients grant us the skill and ability to save this man – for our Queen and for our nation. Amen."

At that moment, from nowhere, a single Phoenix feather drifted down and settled on Gough's chest. Orvessa's breath caught. Her eyes fixed on it – this small, impossible symbol of hope. It burned away without leaving a mark, and Gough lay unharmed beneath it. It was the sign she had prayed for. And yet the fear did not leave her.

The surgeons began to open his chest.

Orvessa collapsed.

"Nurse – please remove the Queen. I anticipated this." The operation continued without pause.

It went well. The bypass machinery that had been sustaining Gough's circulation was shut down as the surgeons confirmed the new heart was functioning normally. It was.

"Good. Close up – make sure those sutures are clean. I do not want to see a hypertrophic scar." The lead surgeon stripped off his gloves. "I am going to check on the Queen. When you have finished, bring him round carefully and monitor him continuously."

He walked out of the theatre to find Orvessa sitting in a chair, pale and hollow-eyed, a bowl held in front of her.

She looked up. "Not the most dignified way for your monarch to greet you. I am sorry – I was extremely sick."

"My Queen – you held on through the opening of the chest. That is more than most could manage, and I mean that sincerely." He sat down across from her. "He is stable. We will know within a few hours whether everything has taken as it should – but it looks promising. The heart is working well and the bypass machinery has been switched off. If this holds, he will be as good as new." He studied her face carefully. "Do you have any questions, if you feel up to it?"

Chapter Fifty-Seven

The Later Years

Gough could not sit up in bed. He was awake and *Zenthara* – fully himself – but felt as though he were strapped to the mattress. He was thirsty, a little hungry, and wires seemed to be attached to him everywhere.

"Excuse me," he called out. "Excuse me – is anyone there?"

Orvessa ran into the room and stood there crying like a hungry baby.

"You are alive." Her voice broke. "Dying is not so final, my love." She moved quickly to his side, still weeping.

"Hey, angel – why all the tears? I am here. I'm not going anywhere without you. You know that. Please don't cry." Orvessa kissed his forehead – one of the few places without a wire attached to it.

A nurse appeared. "Only a few moments, my Queen. We need to check him over now that he is awake. Then you may have him all to yourself." Orvessa nodded and reluctantly released his hand. As the medical team moved efficiently around the bed, the overwhelming relief of the moment began to settle into something quieter – a new and careful anxiety for what the future held.

The moment the team left, Gough began firing questions.

"I was dead. Really? I know I was speaking with the Phoenix for quite some time, angel – but dead? What happened?"

"You were shot with a crossbow bolt. My surgeons had to replace your heart."

"So, I'm good for another few thousand kilometres, then?"

"Shut up, you fool. We were all so frightened that you would not come back to us."

"The Phoenix told me I was going to be fine. They have also asked me to write the English version of the history in the library – some sort of tasking, I suppose. I'll sort that out when I'm back on my feet."

The surgeon came in, and Orvessa made to leave.

"Please stay, my Queen." He turned to Gough. "Prince Gough – you will be up and about within a few days. Your heart needs to work, so exercise as well as rest. Chasing your daughters about might serve you well." He glanced toward the door, where two small faces were peering into the room. "Do you feel strong enough to see them? They have been very worried."

"Yes – please, let them in."

They ran to him and fell on the bed. Gough winced but used his arms to take the weight from his chest.

"Hi there, pickles. What have you both been up to?"

Jessa looked up at him with serious eyes. "You didn't come and kiss us goodnight when we came to the ship. Mummy said you would the next day, but you were in the hospital, and they wouldn't let us see you. Are you all right?"

Feyssa said nothing. She simply held his hand and did not let go. She was not going to lose sight of him again.

"Oh, you know – military stuff. I got walloped. But I am perfectly fine now, for you both and for Mummy. How about that missed goodnight kiss?" Both girls kissed him carefully and then slipped away. Orvessa kissed him again and explained that the spaceship was already en route to Nebulon 17. The journey would take some time – enough for him to recuperate along the way.

Time passed. Gough grew strong enough to walk, and eventually to run after the girls. He seemed a little more pensive than he had ever been before. Orvessa noticed but said nothing.

When the ship docked at Nebulon 17, crowds of well-wishers and dignitaries were waiting on the ground below. Cheers rose as Orvessa came down the ramp with Gough beside her.

"All hail our Guardians! The Phoenix is never wrong — Prince Gough is alive!"

Life began to return to something resembling normality. The girls went to school. Gough could be found most days in the library, reading and writing – his history of the Phoenix, and of how it had touched the lives of those who encountered it. He had served his time as a military man. He was now Prince Gough, a father, and – most importantly of all – Orvessa's husband.

Could life be any better? he wondered.

It took seven years to finish the book. It was good, and many Vilkyrians bought it as both a religious text and a prayer guide. This surprised Gough enormously, for he had never quite subscribed to the idea of himself as anyone's Messiah.

One morning he was sitting in the rose garden, drinking herbal tea and enjoying the warmth of the sun, when Orvessa came to him and asked if he was all right.

"Well, my love – I have been feeling a little tired of late." He looked at her steadily. "But you never quite know what is around the next corner." He paused. "The Phoenix visited me last night. We talk occasionally, now and then. They have a task for me – with the Ancients. I have to leave you for a while, angel." He held her gaze. "We will be together again. I know we will. I cannot refuse this request from the Creator. Do you understand?"

"No. Not really. Where are you going – and for how long? Without me?"

"I am afraid so, my love." He was quiet for a moment, gathering the words he needed. "I want you to know that you have made my life wonderful. I could never have expected such joy, such love, or such kindness as I have found in your presence, my dearest darling. You have always meant the world to me – a poor human in a world of magical charm and laughter." He looked at her one last time. "I have to go."

Gough could not reach to kiss her. The spirit left his body quietly, like a tide going out. A Phoenix feather drifted down and settled on his shoulder – and this time, it did not burn away. He had simply stopped breathing.

The Pulseband went dark. Orvessa's went dark with it.

This time, Orvessa could not cry. She simply held his right hand to her chest and kissed his lips one last time.

www.ingramcontent.com/pod-product-compliance
Lightning Source LLC
LaVergne TN
LVHW050622100826
845148LV00011B/1692

* 9 7 9 8 9 5 0 0 7 2 1 6 1 *